MASTER *of the* DELTA

THOMAS H. COOK

MASTER
of the
DELTA

Quercus

First published in Great Britain in 2008 by

Quercus
21 Bloomsbury Square
London
WC1A 2NS

Published by arrangement with Harcourt, Inc

A CIP catalogue record for this book is available
from the British Library

ISBN (HB) 978 1 84724 211 2
ISBN (TPB) 978 1 84724 212 9

Printed and bound in Great Britain by Clays Ltd, St Ives Plc

10 9 8 7 6 5 4 3 2 1

For Jim Baker and Philip Friedman, Terri and
Tim Childs, Gideon and Sandra Ehrlich, Judith Kelman
and Peter Scardino, Chris and William Martin, Nick Taylor
and Barbara Nevins-Taylor, and for Martha Warschau.

———————————

They that thrive well take counsel of their friends.
—WILLIAM SHAKESPEARE

Look you now, how ready mortals are to blame the gods.
It is from us, they say, that evils come,
But they even of themselves, through their own blind folly,
Have sorrows beyond that which is ordained.

—HOMER, *The Odyssey*

MASTER *of the* DELTA

PART I

ONE

I was badly shaped by my good fortune and so failed to see the darkness and the things that darkness hides. Until the stark moment came, evil remained distant to me, mere lecture notes on the crimes of armies, mobs, and bloodthirsty individuals whose heinous acts I could thrillingly present to my captive audience of students.

For that reason, it wasn't unusual that I was thinking of old King Herod that morning, the torment of his final days, his rotting genitals, how they'd swarmed with worms. It was a vision of guilt and punishment, of afflictions deserved by an abuser of power, and I knew that at some point during the coming semester I'd find a place for it in one of my lectures.

It was a bright April morning in 1954, a little less than one hundred years since the beginning of a conflict that had, by the time it ended, orphaned half the children of the South.

I was twenty-four years old, and for the last three years had taught at Lakeland High School. At that time, Lakeland was typically demarcated by race and class, with a splendid plantation district, where my father still lived, and a New South section where local tradesmen and shop owners congregated in modest one-story houses strung together on short, tree-lined streets. The workers who manned the town's few factories resided in an area known as Townsend, and which consisted of small houses on equally small lots, though large enough to accommodate the vague hint of a lawn. To the east of them lived that class of people for whom, as goes the ancient story, there has never been room at the inn, and which was known as the Bridges.

A Negro netherworld made up the east side of town, unknowable as Africa itself, and with nothing rising from it, at least not yet, save the fervent voices of its ministers and the singing of its choirs, both of which, during the long, languid summers of religious revival, were broadcast by loudspeakers mounted precariously in the trees gathered round their always freshly painted churches. During these humid evenings, their voices stretched as far north as the antebellum mansions where the Delta's eternal rulers sat on their verandas, sipping iced tea and chuckling at the religious revelries of the "Nigra" preachers.

As a boy I'd sat with my father on just such a veranda, evenings that despite all that has happened since still hold a storied beauty for me. There was something calm and sure about them, and it would never have occurred to me that anything might shatter the sheer stability of it all, a father much admired, a son who seemed to please him, a family name everywhere revered and to which no act of dishonor had ever been ascribed. As a son I could not have imagined a more noble father than my own, save perhaps that fabled one who'd once cut down a cherry tree, then refused to tell a lie.

And so the event my father forever after called the "incident" took me completely by surprise, though he never failed to make clear that it had sprung from a long-standing affliction he called the "bottoms," black moods that for generations had stricken the Branches, both men and women: its family disease. The "incident" itself had occurred twelve years earlier, while I was at boarding school, and though I was still quite young, it should have suggested that I lived in a world whose unsteady under-pinnings remained invisible—a walker on a pier whose rotten timbers lie hidden beneath the water.

But no such warning sounded in my mind, and so I sailed blithely on through boarding school and college, until at last I faced the decision of what to do with my life. As a fortunate son, I'd had many options, of course, including heading North, as my father suggested, and which had been his own early goal, though even this had not been as important as "writing a great novel," a hope he'd claimed to have abandoned long ago. I had no such grand ambition, however, and simply decided to mark my return to the Delta with an act of noblesse oblige.

I took a teaching job at Lakeland High School, and by that means hoped to render service to the people over whom my family, in concert with a few others equally highborn, had maintained a long dominion, and among whom it had flour-ished both before and after the Civil War. Thus I would follow in my father's footsteps, for he had taught at Lakeland for nearly twenty years before the "incident." I saw no reason why I might not do the same. After all, I was the only son of an aristocratic family whose fortune still counted among its assets that romantic vision of the world without which, as romantics hold, nothing can be changed.

Three years later, I was still at Lakeland, now quite re-accustomed to the dreamy countryside through which I drove toward school each morning, the Spanish moss and winding estuaries, the morning mists that rose sleepily from swamps and streams, the strange phantasm of the Delta, the spectral quality of its ever-changing light.

It was a spring day, the one in question. One of my students described me this way:

> Mr. Branch was already at the front of the class when I came in that morning. He said hi to us as we came in. He was smiling, like usual. He was a friendly person and it seemed like he enjoyed teaching school. In class, he liked to hear himself talk. The only strange thing about him was that he never came to the football games or basketball games like the other teachers did. Dirk said he thought he was better than us because he came from a rich family. Dirk said he looked down his nose at us. Maybe he did, but what I noticed is the way you couldn't tell who he liked and who he didn't like. At least before things changed, and he picked one to like the best. But he'd been at Lakeland three years by then.
>
> WENDELL CASEY, *Statement to Police*

True enough, but there was something Wendell left out in his assessment. I was good at teaching, and knew I was good at it, a fact that was later officially recorded in court documents:

> MR. TITUS: So you liked your occupation, Mr. Branch?
> MR. BRANCH: I believe it is a vocation, sir.
> MR. TITUS: Fine, then. But you are a teacher, are you not?
> MR. BRANCH: Yes, I am.
> MR. TITUS: And do you consider yourself a good teacher, Mr. Branch?
> MR. BRANCH: Yes, I do. Particularly for the kids at Lakeland.
> MR. TITUS: Why particularly them?

I hadn't had time to answer fully then.

Now I do.

I was a good teacher for the kids at Lakeland because I'd adapted my teaching style and course content to the kind of students they were, generally indifferent to formal learning and easily distracted, so that the real challenge was simply to engage them, keep their thoughts from drifting toward family troubles or the usual school gossip, or if not these, then into that white zone where nothing happened at all. My method was to add a shocking detail, bloody or macabre, though I'd found that tales of inconceivable stupidity also worked well, mostly by giving them a brief sense of superiority. They loved to hear about schemes they'd have seen through, blunders they wouldn't have made. But there was a painful if unspoken self-awareness in their snickering derision, because in their hearts my students suspected that they were losers, too, deficient in some quality, some ingredient left out, ineffable but potent, the alchemic mystery of their lives.

That morning they arrived at Lakeland as they always had, some on buses, some in rattling cars, one in an old brown van that would later be quite thoroughly described:

> It had a sloping front bumper and no hubcaps and all its rear windows had once been covered in black plastic torn from garbage bags and taped to the glass, and on that day it had carried a shovel and a bag of lime and had gone up an old logging road and gotten stuck in the mud and had come back down with mud all over the wheels and splattered across the sides, rocking and jolting because there'd been a bad rain and everything was glistening and slippery, and so the man behind the wheel was having trouble just keeping it on the road.

The young author of that passage no doubt walked to the building alone that morning, as he always had before, surrounded by other students, some moving singly, like himself, some pulled tightly in little knots of conversation. It was early spring, the first weeks of the last semester, the prospect of summer already crowding my students' minds. They'd shed their coats and jackets, caps and scarves, along with the gloominess that is imposed by the bleak look of a Southern winter. By then the bare trees and low, overhanging clouds had given way to budding plants and bright blue skies so as I got out of my car and made my way toward the school that morning, I found all but invisible what would appear so clearly to me later on: the world behind this world, where the string of fate spins on, and she who cuts it is stone-blind.

TWO

Though it would later prove momentous, that particular day was no different from the ones that had preceded it. As always, I stepped behind my lectern and opened the notebook that held my extensively detailed lecture notes. Today was to be the last in a series of lectures I'd entitled "Evil on the Water." I flipped to the place I'd marked and glanced at the note I'd made to myself: *Begin with the* Medusa *and end with the* Minsk.

I looked up at the class, offered a quick, no-nonsense smile.

"The *Medusa* set sail on June 17, 1816," I began in my usual somber tone. "It was bound for the port of Saint-Louis on the coast of Senegal, the lead ship in a small flotilla of three others."

It was a Friday morning, the first class of the day, so I sunk the hook in quickly and jerked them to attention.

"It was a voyage that would end in murder and even cannibalism," I added ominously.

A couple of heads lifted, along with various pairs of formerly drooping eyelids. Debbie Link's eyes glittered with anticipation, but she was a florid, dramatic girl who had already set her sights on heading west, a life's goal that, in the end, would take her no farther than east Texas. The class brain was Stacia Decker, her pen always at the ready, a stickler for detail who would later found her own accounting firm in Atlanta where, in 1983, she would be proclaimed Businesswoman of the Year. Celia Williamson, whose pale skin seemed almost transparent in the slant of light that washed over her that morning, watched me with her huge, sad eyes. She would become a Protestant missionary and die, at fifty-four, during one of the periodic plagues in the sub-Saharan desert, though not before living what the *Lakeland Telegraph*'s obituary writer called "as selfless a life as a selfish age can hope for." Toby Olson stared at me silently, but with that sympathy for all things human that would never fail to grace his life. Joe Fletcher's twitchy fingers suddenly calmed, but he was given to such extremes of spastic movement and sudden rest that it was impossible for me to know whether the opening lines of my lecture had had any effect whatsoever on his always limited attention. What later became of him, I have no idea.

But there are other fates I know too well.

Sheila Longstreet sat, as always, within the aura of her loveliness, Wendell Casey in his comic slump, and Dirk Littlefield behind the scowl of his perpetual contempt.

I'd originally planned to call the course "On Evil." To ensure that it would be approved, I'd grandly sold it to Mr. Rankin, Lakeland's quietly heroic principal, as encompassing literature, philosophy, painting, history. I'd dubbed it a "specialty class" and pledged to teach it like the college-preparatory classes I'd had at boarding school, though, given the nature of my students, with considerably fewer academic demands. I knew that I'd never be able to achieve the intellectual sweep of a course called "On Evil," but I also knew, as my father had often pointed out, that on the way to failure at something great, one often succeeds at something good. Besides, I had more than course content in mind. My true aim was to acquaint my students with acts darker than any they were ever likely to commit, which, in turn, might provide a leg up on the ladder of their always precarious self-esteem. As educational theory, it was admittedly far-fetched, but I was young, and youth without false hope might as well be age.

"Within a few days the *Medusa* had surged ahead of the other three vessels," I went on, "and thus found herself alone amid the perilous shallows of the Arguin Bank."

I liked the words "alone" and "perilous," along with the scholarly detail of the "Arguin Bank." They appeared to have worked on the class, as well. Wendell Casey wasn't glancing aimlessly toward the window and Sheila Longstreet had stopped running a comb through her long dark hair.

"On July 17, the waters off the *Medusa*'s bow turned muddy." I kept my pace measured, my tone somber, but with a slight, theatrical tautness. "At eleven thirty, a sounding confirmed the ship's dire circumstances."

My lectern was wooden, and I held its sides as my boarding-school teachers had, and like them, sometimes leaned forward for emphasis.

"The water was only eight fathoms deep," I said. "Three hours later, that depth had shrunk by a full two fathoms."

I turned toward a large map of the world. It was dotted with red pins that indicated places about which I'd already spoken or planned to speak: Elmina Castle on the Gold Coast, the famished plain of Andersonville, flattened Lisbon, Auschwitz's smoking chimneys, places on the grimly intriguing tour I'd planned for that semester.

I pointed to the pin I'd inserted just off the coast of Senegal.

"Here," I said, "at around three o'clock on that fateful afternoon, passengers and crew rushed to the gunwale and watched in utter helplessness as the bottom of the sea rose ominously toward them. Five minutes later, the *Medusa* ran aground."

"Fateful" sounded very good, and the little adverbial phrase "in utter helplessness" struck me as just right. I knew that "ominous" was overused, but it still had a solid ring.

"It was spring tide, so the water would never rise higher than it was," I added. "For that reason, there was no question but that the ship had to be abandoned."

I glanced up from my notes. There were twelve students in the room, and with one exception I'd taught all of them before. The exception was Eddie Miller, a little smaller than average, lean enough to be called skinny, with an oddly withdrawn posture I'd noticed from time to time.

"The ship was stranded four miles off the coast of Africa," I said. "And there weren't enough lifeboats for the passengers on board."

Sheila Longstreet, the universally acknowledged school beauty, lifted her delicately fashioned arm. "Why are there never enough lifeboats, Mr. Branch?" she asked.

I'd already taken the class through the tragedy of the *Titanic*, the weighty ironies of the *Central America*, the fiery end of the *General Slocum,* lectures from which Sheila had clearly drawn at least one conclusion.

"I just don't see why there are never enough lifeboats," she added.

"Because shipwreck is something we don't anticipate," I answered.

I couldn't tell if Sheila recognized my reply as purposefully philosophical, since by way of response she only smiled softly and glanced at Dirk, her boyfriend, a look that should have delighted him, though nothing ever had, or would.

"The decision was made to build a raft from the timbers of the *Medusa,*" I continued. "When it was finished it measured sixty-five feet by twenty-three feet. It had no sail or rudder, and so it simply sat in the water, filled to capacity with one hundred and fifty men. By the time it was loaded, these men were waist deep in the sea, waiting as the raft was lashed to the lifeboats, ready to be towed."

I stopped, let a beat go by, a moment of increased tension. I could see that my students were engaged now, sensing imminent disaster like cows sniffing the air of an approaching storm. Only Eddie Miller appeared uninterested in any aspect of my lecture. He sat far in the back, separated from the others, leaning forward, head down, a pencil always at the ready, but which, unlike Stacia Decker's note-taking missile, almost never moved. In that posture, his brown hair swept forward and almost touched the desk. I'd never seen him draw it back, so that on those rare occasions when he lifted his head, his dark eyes seemed to glimmer through a tangle of jungle vines.

"But the raft was too heavy," I went on. "The lifeboats could barely tug it forward. And so, after a few hours of futile effort, the ropes were cut and it was set adrift. No one expected it to float for long. But it floated for thirteen days, and from thence was born a tale that would be immortalized in a great painting."

I hoped that the sudden use of an archaic word— "thence"—along with a shift into the past tense—"was born"— might serve to good effect, but I also knew that it was time for a picture.

"It's called *The Raft of the Medusa*."

I hit the switch on the overhead projector upon which, before class, I'd placed a photograph of Géricault's famed rendering of the raft of the *Medusa*. The painting immediately flashed onto the white wall to my right. I had no doubt that its dramatic nature, the dark sea and sky, a rescue ship in the distance, the raft with its gruesome cargo of dead and cannibalized bodies, along with the few ravaged creatures who'd survived the ordeal, would hold the class's attention just long enough for me to add a hasty smattering of facts.

"Only fifteen people were left alive on the raft," I said. "And within a few days, five of that fifteen also died."

I quickly gave a few details about the painting: its stupendous size (sixteen by twenty-three feet), the amount of time it had taken Géricault to paint it (two years), the fact that he'd died, of a fall from a horse, at thirty-three, five years after its completion, the painting so much a celebrity by then that a French consortium had attempted to buy it with the intent of chopping it up and selling the individual pieces.

"That'd be like cutting up a Cadillac," Wendell Casey said.

The class laughed, and as I let their laughter run its course I glanced toward the back of the room where Eddie Miller always took his seat. He'd straightened himself and was staring fixedly at *The Raft of the Medusa* as if he recognized some aspect of it, a face in its anguished crowd.

I turned toward the map, grabbed my wooden pointer and placed it on a red pin that rested far to the north, the icy reaches of Stalinist Siberia. "The *Minsk*," I said, "was a prison ship."

By the time the bell brought the class to an end, I'd fully detailed the *Minsk*'s Dantesque horrors, the cold and hunger, the unspeakable filth, and finally its infamously long "streetcar," the word used to describe the line of men that had snaked through the creaking belly of the ship, each man awaiting his turn at the latest unfortunate woman to have been spread out, naked, at the front of the line.

"Lying on her back," I concluded in a slow, dramatic tone, "starved and freezing, she provided her desolate service until she died or became unconscious. At which time she would be yanked from her place, hauled up the stairs to the deck, and tossed overboard."

I noted the silence in the room, the stillness, exactly what I'd hoped for, so that I knew the moment had arrived to bring my lecture to its somber conclusion.

"No one knows what happened to the *Minsk*," I said. "Perhaps it still sits, rusting away in some ghostly Siberian port. We know only what happened—day after day—as it made its way to the frigid camps of Kolyma. The cries that once echoed through its metal chambers, the splash of the women's bodies as they were slung into the sea, the line of men already forming for the ones who'd replace them, everyone awaiting the director's crude command." I hardened my voice. "Mount up."

I held them briefly in a steady gaze, my eyes moving from one face to the next until I settled them on Eddie's, and using the exact words and grave intonation with which my father had often ended his own classes at Lakeland, I said, "Remember the course of these lost things," paused briefly, then added, "Class dismissed."

Perfect, I thought, right on the beat.

I briefly remained behind the lectern as my students gathered up their things, then stepped over to the door as they filed out. Eddie Miller was the last to leave, moving so slowly at first that he seemed to hold back, then think better of it and pass quickly by.

The hall was full of students rushing to their classes, but I was free for the next hour, and went to the library, perused the stacks, noticed *Billy Budd* and drew it from the shelf.

Outside, I strolled to the small grove of trees that spread out in front of the school, took a seat at one of the wooden benches there, opened the book and read: "In the time before steamships . . ."

And I was there, on that long-ago day, watching as the "handsome sailor" strolled with his mates, cheerful and carefree down the wooden planks, toward where his fate crouched, waiting for him like a jungle cat.

I'd read nearly fifteen pages, marveling at the sheer number of Melville's classical allusions, when I saw Sheila Longstreet drift down the walkway to where Eddie Miller slumped against one of the two short brick columns at the entrance to the school grounds. Sheila said something, tossed her hair in that flirtatious way of hers, and to my surprise, reached out and touched Eddie's arm, a gesture so bold and explicit I knew it must have sent a current through him, such a beautiful girl, and so close: desire's electric charge.

Normally I would have gone back to my book, but something held my attention on Eddie and Sheila as they stood together. They seemed less like sweethearts, or even fellow students, than representatives of two subtly different species, Sheila leaning sultrily against the short brick colonnade while Eddie stood before her like a soldier at attention. Sheila laughed, brushed at her hair, lifted her right foot and toed the ground, moves that were, to my eyes, transparently coquettish.

Eddie, however, appeared entirely taken aback by this display, so that when Sheila finally stepped away, turned, and swept airily up the walk, he seemed both stunned by her attention and unable to explain it. From his place below, he watched Sheila float from him until she reached the bottom of the stairs, where in a movement obviously calculated and infinitely slow, she circled back toward him, a dancer on a music box, lifted her hand to wave to him, but abruptly stopped, as if called, and spun around to where Dirk stood at the school entrance.

Dirk shouted something like "Where you been?" though I couldn't make out his exact words. He gave a quick motion, like someone slashing the air with an invisible knife, and in response Sheila quickly sprang up the stairs toward where he stood looming over her.

Looming, yes, though now when I think of Dirk, he stands with his hands bound behind him, like a figure in a tumbrel, bumped and jostled through the town streets, shunned, despised, with straw from the dungeon floor still clinging to his hair, myself the sole companion of his ride.

THREE

Nowadays it is an old postman who limps up the long road to Great Oaks at the close of each day, bringing learned journals of history and literature, along with the local paper and an occasional package from New York. The townspeople think him fuzzy because in his recitation of town events, he often confuses one person with another, assigns unclear identities, fails to grasp a telling detail. "Mr. Drummond's home visiting his son," he told me on one occasion. But Harry Drummond had only one son, and that son is dead, so it was only a grave he visited.

My father once wrote a "character sketch" of Harry Drummond, a description that for all its literary mannerisms, remains unexpectedly evocative of the man it portrays:

> **Sheriff Drummond was never still. Not his eyes. Not his hands. No part of him knew rest, nor even brief repose. His bones clawed at his skin like cats within a sack. He never sat back without simultaneously inching forward. A drawn breath incrementally expanded his tightened frame, as if**

by one stretched cell at a time, slowly, painfully, like a drum being hammered from inside. The fingers of his right hand incessantly rolled an invisible coin. His head dodged invisible blows. Asleep he rocked in angry waves or hung from rocky crags till dawn. He never strolled, he lurched. His eyes jabbed and his tongue whipped and even when he was absolutely silent, one detected a manic inner buzz, like a wasp inside a jar.

And yet not one word of this description was physically accurate. It was all interior, what my father saw, Drummond's futile strivings.

I saw him last a full fourteen years before he died. I'd heard that he'd retired and gone farther south, perhaps to Florida, which turned out to be true. But through the years he'd periodically returned to Lakeland, and it was here, while strolling in our town burial ground, that I suddenly came upon him sitting alone on a concrete bench, a wooden cane slanting from his left hand, trembling slightly with his great age. For a moment, we seemed mutually confined within the prison of an old dead world.

"Drummond," was the only greeting I could summon from the great smoldering mound of what I still felt for our shared history.

He seemed unsure that the voice he'd heard was real. He turned with the arthritic slowness of one who lived with great pain.

"Mr. Branch," he said.

Countless times I'd imagined him on his deathbed, lying on his back, hands folded together, ready for the coffin, a great agitation calmed at last.

But here he was, Harry Drummond, beneath the bare limbs of a wintry pecan tree, wrapped in a wool overcoat, a tie knotted at his throat, shoes polished, wearing a snap-brim hat, everything present that had been of old, save the white meerschaum pipe.

He closed his eyes and for a moment I couldn't tell whether he'd begun to doze or was lost in thought. But as I eased down on the bench beside him, his eyes opened in a spasm, then instantly narrowed.

"Somebody said you finally left town," he said.

I could not imagine who this "somebody" might have been since, for most of the people of Lakeland, I was known only as the old man who lived in the decrepit mansion outside town, rarely left its declining splendor, spoke only to the postman who brought the daily mail.

"I took a brief vacation," I told him.

Only eight days, as a matter of fact, during which I'd driven somewhat aimlessly about the Delta before turning eastward into the bloodier regions of our old Lost Cause. I'd visited the battlefields of Fredericksburg, Petersburg, Antietam, stood in the evening shade and contemplated the quiet fields over which the long-silent cannon seemed still to hold sway. But every time, in the final moment, as I'd turned from the scene and headed back to my car, my mind had brought me back here to the Delta, where tragedies were less numerous but no less terribly enduring.

Drummond looked up at the line of somber gray clouds

that was steadily advancing from the far horizon. "Storm coming in," he said.

Of all the subjects I'd ever expected to discuss with Harry Drummond, weather had surely been the least likely.

He peered toward the horizon, where clouds massed darkly like some fierce, invading army whose victory, despite its cause, was heavenly ordained. "Too bad you left it," he said.

I knew he meant teaching.

"I wasn't fit for it," I told him.

His withered eyes moved down from the clouds. "What was that word you used in court?"

I instantly recalled both the word and the moment I'd said it, Mr. Titus staring at me from the defense table, the odd grin on his lips, knowing how easily he could use my "fancy" word to discredit whatever else I'd said, show the jury I was just a "fancy-pants young man," as he'd later put it, "from a fancy-pants family."

"Vocation," I answered softly, and with that word I felt the leaden foot of unforgiving time, how the lake of consequence shimmers deep and still.

Drummond lifted his cane and thumped the ground softly, his gaze now directed toward the nearby stone upon which his son's name had been chiseled. "You sure liked it," he said. "Teaching."

"It was my heart's desire," I said.

I instantly recalled the spare provisions of my old classroom, a map of the world, four rows of desks, the wooden lectern behind which I'd held forth, confident, self-assured, speaking of doomed ships, the *Medusa* and the *Minsk*.

Drummond drew in a slow breath. "Seems like forever, that business with Eddie."

I shook my head. "It was yesterday."

His body listed to the left like a storm-ravaged ship struggling into harbor, fatally damaged, barely afloat. But he righted himself quickly, as if in preparation for a final, fruitless go at wind and weather. "Probably never would have happened if you hadn't gone to dinner with your father that night."

His mention of my father suddenly returned me to April 16, a Friday evening, and so, like all Friday nights, one I'd scheduled for dinner with my father.

"You wouldn't have been riding around like you were," Drummond said. "Wouldn't have seen anything. Or talked to anybody."

I remembered the twin beams of oncoming lights, the quick glimpse of a dark-haired girl. "That much is true, but still . . ."

"Wouldn't have felt obligated to help him," Drummond added. "Which you did, I guess, Mr. Branch. Felt obligated, I mean."

He meant to Eddie Miller.

"And after that," he added.

I felt like a book already read and closed.

"After that . . . ," he repeated, letting the words trail off into the wintry air.

"After that . . ." I looked over our field of stones. "The rest."

The night "the rest" began I'd made tuna sandwiches and coleslaw and deviled eggs sprinkled with paprika, the sandwiches neatly wrapped in aluminum foil, the slaw and eggs packed in individual Tupperware containers. Since getting a place of my own, I'd scheduled Friday evening dinners with my father as a way of keeping watch on his mood, always concerned the "incident" might be repeated. I'd come up with the idea of various dinner themes. This was the third Friday of the month, thus "picnic night," when I brought the simple fare the two of us had once enjoyed in his back garden, always sandwiches and fixings that were easily made and even more easily transported.

My father never locked his door, or at least I'd never found it locked. As usual, I glanced up at the family motto, inscribed on a modest plaque beside the door. It read VENERATIO SILEO VERA, which translated as "Honor rests in truth." After this quick act of deference, I gave my customary two gentle raps of the old lion's head brass knocker, then opened the door just enough for my voice to echo through the foyer.

"Father?" I called.

"In the library, Jack."

His students had thought him fussy and joked about his careful dress, the three-piece suits always buttoned, the burgundy bow tie, along with the fact that he was a stickler for grammar, forever insisting that "unique" could not take an adjective, or that "fun" should not be used as one. He was not yet a truly elderly man, but he seemed older than his years because during the time since the "incident" he'd descended into a kind of hermit life, never going out or inviting anyone to Great Oaks despite its splendid rooms and glorious history, walls decked with portraits of august men and dazzling women. Even so, the house remained his great pride, and he took care to maintain its splendor. "Great Oaks is a monument," he once declared. As it still is, I suppose, though now to fallen things.

On that particular night I found him seated in a large brocade chair that like everything else in the house seemed larger than human life could adequately sustain. It had a high back and rounded arms, and he'd placed faded doilies on the arms, yellowed by time and badly frayed, but priceless to him because they'd been crocheted by his long-dead mother. There was a matching sofa and a lovely old mahogany desk with brass-handled drawers, both of which rested on an expanse of carpet that would have been perfectly at home in the drawing rooms of Versailles.

"You know, Jack," he said, "this old library is still my favorite room."

Which was not an easy thing, given what he'd done inside it.

"Of course," he added, "it's changed a little."

A little, yes.

For example, he'd replaced the old original artworks that had once hung around the room with prints of famous paintings he admired, Monet's *Water Lilies,* which he called "visible poetry," and *Houses of Parliament,* which, though painted in 1900, as he was careful to point out, he'd found useful in conveying the "shrouded density of Dickensian London." These two hung on opposite ends of the room, while van Gogh's self-portrait retained its place in the rear corner, the stains he'd never quite succeeded in cleaning from its surface still disturbingly visible, a faint pattern of ghastly rust-red dots sprayed across van Gogh's tormented face.

"But the room still has a meditative air, don't you think, Jack?" he asked.

"Very," I said.

Which was true, for the room's real extravagance resided in the books, classics all, most in English, but many in Latin and even more in French. They were bound in leather, with titles etched in gold, and like all things beautiful and rare, they seemed destined to render lonely anyone who loved them.

"Tuna and coleslaw," I said. I lifted the plastic bag that contained our dinners. "Deviled eggs."

My father smiled, but since the "incident," there had been little twinkle in his eyes. "Let's dine here, rather than in the garden," he said. "There's a chill in the air."

There was no such thing, of course. In fact, it was unseasonably warm for April, but if he preferred the library to our customary picnic in the garden, that was fine with me.

"Life is a tragedy of unpreparedness, Jack," he added with a slight flourish, so that I knew that this was the topic he'd chosen for the evening.

I retrieved a silver tray from a nearby breakfront and placed it on his lap.

"E. M. Forster makes a different point, of course," he continued thoughtfully.

I peeled the foil from his sandwich. "Which point is that?" I asked.

"The tragedy of being well prepared," he answered, "but for a call that never comes." He glanced down at his hands. "Did you know, Jack, that in the *Song of Roland,* the Knights of the Round Table sometimes died of lost honor?" Even slightly in his cups, he seemed himself a product of that lost age of courtiers, knights devoted heart and hand to a single passion. "They had it right, Jack," he added. "A man should die when his honor dies."

"That would certainly thin the population," I said lightly.

Polite as always, he waited until I'd unwrapped my sandwich and opened the two Tupperware containers. When all was prepared I gave him my best smile and lifted a fork in salute.

"Bon appétit," he said.

We ate almost in silence, and when we'd finished I returned the foil and the containers to the plastic bag and placed it on the table that rested between us. "Okay, another fine dinner put to rest," I said.

My father leaned back in his chair and suddenly seemed mysteriously burdened. "It's only food," he said softly. "Only sustenance. We should live on pine straw, like the sparrows."

His stricken body appeared knit together at the end of time, fraying slightly with each breath. It was as if he'd offended his own life in trying to take it, and that life had retaliated by making itself more labored in the physical living of it, but not a whit more precious to him or in the least bit pleasurable.

After a moment, he released a long breath. "Books," he said. "Let's talk about books. What are you reading, Jack?"

"True tales of horror for my specialty class," I answered. "The one on evil. At the moment, I'm reading about Tiberius. He was a terrible man, especially when it came to children."

"Yes, I know," my father said. "But as to the class, how is it going?"

"The students seem engaged."

I related the day's lecture, though not all the details.

"So dark," he said. His gaze drifted over to the old wooden lectern that stood in the rear corner of the room, and above which hung van Gogh's self-portrait in its spattered ruin. "Such dark things."

I decided to draw him back to a more congenial topic.

"How goes the biography?" I asked.

He had been writing a biography of Lincoln in the long years since the "incident," his progress agonizingly slow, but "ever onward," as he'd once said, "into the poetry of our most tragic life."

"I received a copy of his autopsy only yesterday," he told me. "From the Library of Congress. It seems that when they weighed Lincoln's brain, they found it of ordinary weight."

"But did they weigh his heart?" I asked.

My father smiled. "Very good, Jack. A beautiful response."

"Will you put it in *The Book of Days*?" I asked, now referring to a second work my father had long been writing, and which, by the chronological arrangement of the volumes, I took to be some kind of journal, though he remained entirely secretive as to its contents, an attitude that further suggested the intimacies of a personal diary.

"Many things find their way into *The Book of Days*," he said by way of answering my question. "Not one of which will ever be revealed to your prying eyes, Jack."

"Racy stuff?" I asked lightly.

He offered an oddly disheartened shrug. "A poor thing," he said, paraphrasing Shakespeare, "but mine own."

We talked on awhile, but shortly he grew yet more tired, though I sensed that he was weary less of the subject than of human company, mine or anyone else's.

I left him at eight thirty, still early, so I decided to drop by Jake's, a little diner on the outskirts of town.

The usual assortment of local people sat at small tables and booths, some of whom I recognized, but none of whom felt sufficiently at ease to do anything but nod to me. I was, after all, a Branch, and therefore one who summoned other people but who was never summoned by them.

When the waitress came over I ordered a coffee and drank it slowly, continuing with *Billy Budd,* noting certain phrases from the book, the "mysteries of iniquity," Melville's telling description of the villainous Claggart as having "rabies of the heart," the gentle terms of endearment used by Billy's mates, the way they called him "Beauty" and "Baby Lad," how odd the appreciation of his innocence seemed in men whose own lives had been so relentlessly hard. It was something I might mention in a later lecture for my specialty class, I decided, a needed anecdote to my many tales of inhumanity, a little taste of honey to soothe life's bitter draught.

Nearly half an hour had passed before my cup was empty. I could have had a refill, of course, but the caffeine would have kept me up all night. I glanced at my watch. It was still relatively early, but I didn't want to linger, so I paid the check and headed for my car.

Dirk Littlefield was parked two spaces from my car. He was sitting behind the wheel of a battered old pickup, Wendell Casey in the passenger seat. They were talking in a very animated way until Dirk caught sight of me, nodded abruptly to Wendell, who wheeled around and stared at me with his usual comic grin, part clever clown, part half-wit.

"Hi, Mr. Branch," Wendell said.

"Hi." I was now at my car, reaching for the door handle.

"I've never seen you at Jake's."

The fact that Wendell saw me at Jake's now clearly struck him as a curiosity, though by no means an unpleasant one.

Dirk's manner, however, was abrupt. "How long you been here?" he asked sharply.

His disrespectful tone put me off, so I answered crisply. "Half an hour."

"Didn't see Sheila, did you?"

Before I could answer, he got out of the truck and came around to the back of it, the collar of his jacket turned up, as if against a cold wind. There was something hard-edged and metallic in his every move, as if bolts and pistons were continually shifting beneath his skin.

"I've been waiting for her," he added. He slumped against the back of the truck, his body now in profile, the sharpness of his features made more so by the diner's lighted window. In that misty light, his skin seemed to shine dully, like smudged chrome.

Wendell got out of the car. "I think Sheila stood old Dirk up," he said as he sauntered toward Dirk. "What do you think, Mr. Branch?"

I couldn't tell whether this was a serious question, or meant as one of Wendell's amiable barbs.

"Perhaps," I answered, with a slight smile.

THOMAS H. COOK

Wendell now stood next to Dirk, slouched in typical side-
kick mode, less a force to be reckoned with than a presence to
be noted, the foam lightly boiling from the beaker's mouth
rather than the poison at its bottom.

"Dirk don't like it when Sheila's late," he said with a comic
wink. "He gets a notion she's cheating on him."

"I'm sure she'll turn up," I said.

"How would you know?" Dirk said grimly.

This was not a question and certainly not an attitude I
wished to address. I opened my car door. "See you Monday," I
said curtly.

Wendell nodded, but Dirk remained motionless, his hands
sunk in the pockets of his jeans, both of them clearly balled
into tight fists.

I got into my car, turned the ignition, and backed out of
Jake's. By then Dirk and Wendell were making their way toward the restaurant, Dirk tall, with broad shoulders, Wendell
small and wiry, a Mutt 'n' Jeff team yoked together by a harness
no one had ever understood.

On the way home, I noticed the dimly lighted entrance to
Glenford State Park, and for a reason I could never explain, I
turned off Route 4 and headed out to Breaker Landing. It was
little more than a square of rough pavement that fronted Glenford Lake, but it was the place I'd occasionally gone when I had
a problem, intellectual or otherwise, I wanted to think through.
I parked there for a time and stared out at the water, so lost in
some nameless wave of thought that I didn't notice whether
the moon was full or half full or in a crescent, the surface of the
lake calm or agitated, and thus was unable to answer even the

most routine questions that were later posed to me about my whereabouts that night.

But there was something else I did remember, a pair of headlights coming toward me as I pulled out of the park a few minutes later. Route 4 was more or less deserted by then, so it was never a question of seeing several cars, perhaps none of them clearly. There was only one car, an old brown van, and as it swept by, I saw a young woman in the passenger seat. She had long dark hair, and I immediately had the impression that it was Sheila Longstreet though the van had rushed past much too quickly for me to be sure. The strange thing was that as I continued toward home, I kept thinking about the girl I'd so briefly glimpsed as I'd pulled onto Route 4. There was something in her posture that disturbed me, the way her right shoulder seemed folded in, along with the fact that her head was clearly bowed, her long dark hair falling forward, covering her face. I'd gotten only a glimpse of her, and yet the image that lingered in my mind produced a tangible disturbance, so that suddenly—and very oddly—I imagined the naked, shivering women of the *Minsk*, herded together and awaiting their awful turn at the streetcar, bereft of all their female power, heads lowered in desolate submission, staring down at their tied hands.

FOUR

It was this unexpected sighting that Sheriff Drummond would note decades later as we sat together in the town cemetery. *After that,* he mutters in my memory, the last words I would ever hear him say, *After that . . .*

After that, nothing really, so that the following morning I was much more concerned with a dream I'd had in my sleep than anything real I'd seen while awake. It was a dream so vivid that it had intruded upon me all weekend, and on Monday morning, when I found myself standing next to Nora Ellis, I still felt oddly troubled by it. We were at the wall of mail slots just outside Mr. Rankin's office, and she'd simply said, "How are you, Mr. Branch?"—a polite enough greeting to which I would normally have responded with, "Fine. How are you?"

But her question took me off guard, and before I could stop myself, I said, "I had a bad dream. Do you ever have bad dreams?"

"Everyone does."

"Of course, but this one keeps hanging on."

She looked at me quizzically.

"It was about torture," I explained. "The old tortures. From the Spanish Inquisition. A man in a spiked chair and a woman on the rack."

But the disturbing element was not just that it was made up of scenes of torture but that in these scenes I'd not been the victim, nor even some nameless, half-imagined observer.

Cautiously I said, "The thing is, I'm the torturer. In the dream I hook the straps and turn the lever and squeeze the pincers. I'm wearing a brown robe with a pointed hood, like a monk."

"A cowl," she said.

"Yes," I said, surprised that she knew such a precise yet arcane word. She'd hardly ever spoken in faculty meetings, and for that reason I'd come to think of her as unsure of herself, certainly nothing like the loudly ringing Southern belles I'd known at Vanderbilt.

"Are you a Catholic?" I asked.

A burst of laughter broke from her. "Oh, no," she said. "We're all Baptists. My people, I mean."

"My people" was a common expression of that time, meaning one's kin, at least as far as distant cousins.

"We were Presbyterians," I said. "My people."

She smiled softly. "So you have bad dreams," she said thoughtfully, then looked as if the cause of my bad dream had suddenly occurred to her. "Maybe it's that course you're teaching."

Until then I'd been unaware that anyone other than Mr. Rankin was sufficiently informed of my specialty class to have any notion of its actual content.

"Have you been reading about torture?" she asked.

"From time to time," I answered. "For the lecture I'd planned for the end of the course."

"That could be it, then, don't you think? Why you had that dream?"

I wasn't sure. "Maybe, but why am I the one torturing people?"

"That's just your imagination," she said with what struck me as great confidence. "I'm sure it'll pass." She nodded and stepped away, leaving me with at least some hope that she was right.

But as it turned out, she wasn't, so that when the bell rang and I headed for my classroom, I continued to feel a lingering uneasiness that must have been visible in my expression, some aspect of my manner that later prompted Wendell Casey to describe me as "looking weird."

Once behind my lectern, I decided to face the subject head-on, flipped ahead in my notes, found the photograph I'd put there and placed it on the glass plate of the overhead projector.

"It is known as the Spanish horse," I said. I switched on the light and the image I'd selected flashed onto the screen. "It is fashioned of the finest wood, polished to a shine."

I paused and let them take in the cruel details of the instrument, how demonically perfect it was for slowly sawing, crotch to skull, through a human body. Then I elaborated on its diabolical mechanics, how it used weight alone to produce the agony, required not a single gear, nor any human hand to so much as turn a screw, yank a rope, or pull a lever.

"Ouch," Wendell whispered, though in a voice oddly drained of its usual comic tone, and to which the other students reacted either silently or with a mild sense of the remark's inappropriateness, an attitude at odds with the casual laughter that generally followed one of Wendell's witless asides.

I glanced about. Dirk Littlefield sat just behind Wendell, his face stark and unsmiling. Stacia Decker and Celia Williamson looked the same. Jed McPherson had the glimmer of a smile, but it was very faint. Sheila Longstreet's desk was empty, and the instant I noticed it, I felt myself drawn back to the last glimpse I'd had of her, head bowed as she'd flashed briefly into view, then vanished.

It was precisely at that point that Eddie Miller came into the room, moving not exactly in a slump, but, like always, with a certain guardedness, as if, at any moment, he expected some invisible force to strike at him.

"Sorry, Mr. Branch," he said. "My van stalled."

Over the years I'd noticed that despite their humble circumstances, some of Lakeland's students gave off a sense of imminent success. Luck would be on their side. Fortune would smile on them. They would by chance acquire a piece of property that would later have some unexpected value, or hit upon some enterprise that would prosper to their complete surprise. Success would come to them because the time for it had come. They had waited for it through unnumbered fruitless generations, and so it was their moment to be crowned with a coronet of luck. Eddie, on the other hand, seemed to slouch beneath the burden of his own unluckiness, shoulders slightly hunched, head crunched down, as if he were walking beneath a swinging sword. There was nothing in him that suggested there was any relief in sight, a ship at the horizon that would pluck him from *Medusa*'s raft.

"Just take your seat, please," I said to him.

He immediately did as he was told, but the way he did it, the wary turning away, the backward glance over his shoulder as he headed down the aisle, and finally the defensive curl of his body over the desk, suggested a state of mind I couldn't describe save to say that it heightened the anxiety I was already feeling, added to my sense of something heavy in the air.

When I brought my attention back to the class, I noticed that the other students were watching me with an unusual degree of concentration, a silent gaze Dirk Littlefield later described as "acting jolted."

I glanced at my notes. "The Spanish horse was carefully constructed with a spine of razor sharpness," I said. "Straddling it, with feet weighted by bags of sand tied to the ankles, a human being would be quickly torn, but slowly severed. Its purpose was to—"

The door of my class abruptly swung open and Mr. Rankin stepped into the room, two sheriff's deputies behind him. His face was very troubled, like a man who'd just received a dreadful diagnosis.

"Excuse me, Mr. Branch," he said, then turned and addressed the class as a whole. "I know you've all heard the news by now. I'm going from room to room hoping that someone will have something to say that can help these gentlemen."

The two deputies stood stiffly, their faces quite grave and still, save for the shorter one's eyes, which drifted briefly to the photograph of the Spanish horse, then to me with an indecipherable glint.

"I want each of you to think very carefully," Mr. Rankin continued. "Try to recall anything Sheila might have said or done, anyone she might have mentioned. Anything at all." He stared solemnly at the class. "If you do think of anything, please call the sheriff's office. We've posted the number on the bulletin board outside the office. Don't wait. Time is very important. Please, don't wait." With that, he stepped back, an officer at each side, and in that formation left the room.

"What's this all about?" I asked.

Wendell and Dirk exchanged astonished glances, while the rest of my students only stared at me in disbelief.

Finally Stacia Decker spoke up.

"Sheila's missing, Mr. Branch," she said. "She's been missing since Friday."

I instantly saw her in a grainy black-and-white photo, blurry, indistinct, her hair splayed across her face, so that I could make out little more than a body in a ditch, clothed in a white blouse with a badly ripped collar, her scotch-plaid skirt soiled with mud and scattered with dry leaves.

Involuntarily I glanced toward Eddie Miller, and as if programmed for dramatic effect, the overheard projector suddenly went out. Not with a slow fade, or a series of flickers, but abruptly, so that the entire room was instantly fixed in a dull, gray light.

In literature, as I thought later, such a moment comes as a thunderclap or a jagged strip of lightning across a stormy sky. It comes as a dead bird hanging upside down from a bare limb, a cow that suddenly drops dead in the pasture, the erratic movement of wild herds, the backward flow of water. But in every case, it is not so much the nature of the omen as how one responds to it that decides one's fate, whether one does, or does not, beware the Ides of March.

My response was almost comic. I merely fumbled with the switch, though unsuccessfully, so that I finally gave up and simply resumed my lecture without benefit of visual effects.

"Well," I said, trying to calm a sudden inner turmoil, "I suppose we have to go on, so . . ." I glanced down at my notes, which seemed a safer place for my eyes to go, took a quick breath, and looked up.

"Torturers have also quite often relied upon nature itself to carry out their cruelties," I said. "A rising tide that slowly drowns a man staked on the beach, for example, or the ferocity of starving dogs and rats, even swarms of angry bees."

From there I returned to the course's ongoing discussion of why people did such things to other people: religious fervor, political ideology, and the like. I made the usual references to the Spanish inquisitors and the Turkish impalers, the Roman crosses that lined the Appian Way and the standing cells of Dachau.

As the class neared its end, I gave them their project assignment, the one that would be due at the end of the term. "I want you to pick someone evil and write an essay about that person. It can be a person from history or a character from a book or a play, or a figure from religion or mythology."

Other than the unceasing whisper of Stacia Decker's pen there was absolute silence as I continued, dutifully giving the length of the paper, the number of references required, when it was due, what part of the overall course grade it would represent.

"Any questions?" I asked.

There weren't any.

"All right," I said. "Class dismissed."

They rose, gathered their things, and left the room in tight knots of conversation, Eddie Miller the last to leave, as if this were the position ascribed to him by life, that he was doomed to be a straggler.

I walked out behind him, closed the door of the classroom, and since I had a break before my next class, headed down the corridor toward the faculty lounge.

The hall was buzzing with movement as usual, a little flowing stream of bobbing heads in which, I noticed, Eddie's appeared to float on a different current, dodging left or right in response not to the common jostle of the group but to rocking waves no one else could feel. About halfway down the corridor, he stopped, made a slow turn, clutching his books to his chest as if expecting them to be knocked rudely from his grasp, and backed against the wall, where he stood silently waiting for the corridor to clear. I passed him without comment, and by the time I reached the lounge he'd vanished completely from my mind.

I hadn't watched the local news over the weekend, nor bought the local paper, and so it wasn't until I joined other teachers in the lounge that I found out more about Sheila Longstreet's disappearance.

"Evidently Dirk got worried when Sheila didn't show up for a date," Mrs. Cavanaugh said. She was a round coconut cake of a woman with tight curls of snow-white hair, and whom I never saw play any but a deeply maternal role. She would end her days caring for an addled father and an invalid husband, fearful that she would not outlast them, but because death came suddenly in her sleep, would rest forever unaware that she had not.

"He started calling around, asking if anyone had seen her," she added.

Instantly, it passed through my mind: the distant head-lights, the brown van, the girl with bowed head.

"I thought I saw her Friday night," I said.

All eyes turned toward me.

"Where?" Mrs. Barton asked, in her forties then, but near-ing a hundred now, and said to be living with her daughter somewhere in Minnesota.

"Route 4," I answered. "She was riding with someone. I couldn't see who was driving."

"What was the car?"

"It wasn't a car," I said. "It was a van. Brown, I think."

Mr. Crombie's features turned very grave. He looked at the other teachers as if the same thought had to have entered their minds at the instant it had entered his. "Eddie Miller drives a brown van," he said.

I knew that in his social studies class, Mr. Crombie dis-cussed the Kallikaks and the Jukes, lineages that infused the human stream with a toxic spore of criminality, producing end-less waves of drug addicts and prostitutes and pedophiles, a poison whose only antidote, according to the thinking of the time, had been mass incarcerations and compulsory sterilization.

He looked at me intently. "Have you told anyone about this?"

Before I could answer, Mrs. Cavanaugh leaned forward, and with her usual motherly manner, touched my arm. "Jack, you know about Eddie, don't you? About Linda Gracie? The girl who was murdered in Glenford Park?"

It had happened twelve years ago, Mrs. Barton interjected, Linda Gracie, seventeen, a Lakeland senior bound for college, and so misnamed a "coed" by the Jackson paper.

"I wasn't living in Lakeland twelve years ago," I said, though careful not to add what they probably already knew, that at the time of Linda Gracie's death, I had been sequestered in an expensive boarding school outside Richmond.

"They arrested a local guy," Mr. Crombie said. "A handyman. The paper called him the Coed Killer."

Mrs. Cavanaugh again dartingly touched my hand. "Luther Miller," she said quietly, as if no one else was to know the details of this shameful incident.

Mr. Crombie looked at me pointedly. "He owned a brown van," he said. "His boy still has it."

And so Eddie Miller, as I realized suddenly, so alone, so awkward and isolated, so prone to silence, a slumped figure at the back of my class on evil, was the Coed Killer's son.

"When you saw this van, what direction was it going?" Mr. Crombie asked.

"East," I answered.

Mr. Crombie released a sigh that suggested he now considered the case essentially closed. "East." He looked knowingly at the others. "That's toward Glenford Park."

"You have to tell the sheriff this, Jack," Mrs. Barton said urgently.

I felt a tremor pass through me, and in that instant imagined the horrible interrogation rooms I'd talked about in my lecture, the inquisitorial chambers of Torquemada, the gray cells of the Stalinist purge, confessions gained by Spanish horses and spoons applied to eye sockets. I tried to block these visions, but the rooms kept trundling forward on the grim conveyor belt of my imagination: the dank police basements of Warsaw and the humid ones of Buenos Aires, rooms with drainage and blood-spattered fans.

"But I don't really know anything," I said.

"Of course you do, Jack," Mr. Crombie said. "You saw a girl who might have been Sheila Longstreet in a van that might have been Eddie Miller's."

"Such a pretty girl," Mrs. Cavanaugh added quietly, "with her whole life ahead of her."

"We don't know that Sheila's dead," I reminded her.

"I didn't mean Sheila," Mrs. Cavanaugh said. "I meant the one Eddie's father killed."

Mr. Crombie's eyes narrowed. "You need to tell the sheriff about this, Jack."

The air abruptly grew heavier and I thought of Joseph K. in Kafka's novel, an object of unspecified suspicion, hauled into a great chamber filled with jeering spectators.

Mr. Crombie plucked his wallet from his trousers and handed me a small slip of paper. "I keep all the emergency numbers," he explained. He stood. "Come on, Jack, you can call from the office."

We walked out of the lounge, down the corridor, and into the main office.

"Jack needs to use the phone," Mr. Crombie said briskly.

Mrs. Garraty, a large woman with wiry red hair, looked as if she'd suddenly been struck by a charge of electricity. "Of course," she said, reaching for the phone. "Here you are, Mr. Branch."

I took the phone and waited.

"Number, please?" the operator asked.

I read the number Mr. Crombie had neatly written, along with those of the local hospital and—oddly—the National Guard.

"Just a moment, please," the operator said.

The usual clicks followed, then . . .

"Shenoba County sheriff's office," a voice answered.

"Hello," I said. "This is Jack Branch. I understand that Sheila Longstreet is—"

"Just a moment," the voice interrupted. There was a click, after which another voice came on the line.

"Sheriff Drummond."

"This is Jack Branch," I began again.

"Yes, Mr. Branch," Drummond said. His tone was deferential, so that I knew he'd immediately recognized my name. "How is your father?"

"Well," I said.

"I'm glad to hear it," Drummond said. "He taught my son, you know."

"Actually, I didn't."

"Noel," Drummond said. "Noel Drummond."

He seemed to think that I should recognize the name, but I'd never heard it, knew nothing of his son.

"He died in the war," Drummond added quietly.

"Oh . . . I'm sorry."

"Yes," Drummond said. "A brave boy." He drew in a quick, oddly reviving breath. "So, how may I be of help? I understand you have some information?"

"I'm not sure it's information," I said. "Just something I saw. A girl who looked like Sheila Longstreet. She was riding in a van. An old brown van. I don't know the make. But old. On Route 4. She was sitting on the passenger side."

"Did you see the driver, Mr. Branch?"

"No, I didn't . . . but evidently another student from Lakeland has a brown van like the one I saw."

"What is this student's name?"

I held back, but only briefly, then released the dark arrow and watched it fly into an even darker sky.

"Eddie Miller," I said.

In response to the series of polite questions that followed, I reported the time I'd seen the van and the direction in which it was going.

"How did Sheila appear when you saw her?" Drummond asked. "Was she smiling? Did she look like she was having a good time?"

"Her head was down."

"Did she look frightened?"

"I couldn't tell," I answered. "It's just that she was looking down. At her hands." The women of the *Minsk* returned to me just as they had the very moment Sheila had flashed into view. "Like she was tied."

Drummond's voice tightened. "Tied," he repeated. Suddenly he sounded very busy. "All right, Mr. Branch. Thank you. I appreciate your help."

"Thank you."

"Please give my regards to your father."

I hung up and turned to Mr. Crombie.

"Well, I guess I've done my civic duty for the day," I said.

He looked pleased. "Yes, you have," he said. He gave me a brotherly pat on the back and I felt relieved by what I'd done, a burden lifted, a dilemma resolved, the whole room suffused with light, as dark beginnings almost always are.

FIVE

For the rest of that day I followed my routine, taught my classes in American literature before lunch, then taught a class in composition after it. I finished off with a class in European literature and a period of study hall during which I returned to the section on Tiberius that I'd been reading in Suetonius's *Lives of the Caesars,* one of my true tales of horror source books.

Old Tiberius, perverted to the end, had wiled away the hours by arranging children in pornographic poses in the gardens of Capri and watching slaves hurled from the rocky cliff that bore his name. Demented, paranoid, screaming false accusations, he'd reveled in the very excesses that were draining from him the last drops of his always limited humanity and which would, in the end, leave him, in Suetonius's merciless rendering, surely among the most nefarious of emperors and least admirable of men.

Study hall was the last class of the day. When it ended, I walked directly out of the building and headed toward my car. I'd just made it to the edge of the walkway when I saw it coming toward me, an old brown van with a sagging rusty bumper.

Eddie Miller, I thought, and stopped dead to watch as the van closed in upon me, then, in a riveting instant, swept by.

There was a girl in the passenger seat. She had long dark hair, but she had pushed it back so that her face was fully revealed. It was not a pretty face, and certainly not a beautiful one. Her name was Carol Pride, and she was riding with her boyfriend, a Lakeland junior named Lonnie McCabe who'd already had more than one run-in with local law enforcement, sometimes in company with Carol, so that their fellow students had dubbed them "Lonnie and Pride."

I stood in place and watched the van continue on toward the end of the parking lot, where it turned and headed off into what suddenly seemed an infinite and indefinable space. Students were moving all around me and other cars were drifting by. But for me the world abruptly stopped, so that I felt myself held in the ineffable stillness of a still-life painting or the motionless body of a stillborn child.

And I thought, *What have I done?*

The nature of what I'd done was quite clear of course. There was no way to discount the urgency I'd heard in Sheriff Drummond's voice when I'd told him about Eddie Miller, Sheila Longstreet, the brown van, how quickly he must have felt compelled to act, and against whom. With one phone call, I'd made Eddie a prime suspect in Sheila's disappearance.

And so, at home a few minutes later, I made another call.

"Sheriff's office."

"My name is Jack Branch," I said. "I'd like to speak with Sheriff Drummond."

He was instantly on the line. "Mr. Branch, how are you, sir?"

"Sheriff, I wanted to let you know that Eddie Miller, the boy whose van I saw, well, it may not have been Eddie's at all."

From here I related my second spotting, the girl I'd seen on the passenger side who clearly was not Sheila Longstreet.

"So, you see, I could have been entirely wrong in everything I told you," I said.

"Well, I've spoken to the boy," Drummond said. He gave a short laugh. "Grilled him a little, just to see how he'd react." He laughed again. "In this job, you have to do a little acting, you know."

"I see," I said dryly.

"I hope you're not troubling yourself over any of this, Mr. Branch," Sheriff Drummond said. "There's no harm done, believe me."

"Thank you."

"And I'll certainly keep what you've just told me in consideration," Drummond added.

"I'd appreciate that, Sheriff."

"Anything else I can do for you, Mr. Branch?"

There wasn't, and so after hanging up the phone, I tried to distract myself by reading, but my concentration continually flagged, so that I walked into my living room and turned on the television, hoping to see that whatever suspicions had been directed toward Eddie were now proved unfounded. But instead, through the black-and-white "snow" of the six o'clock news I saw a reporter on the steps of Lakeland High, bulky microphone in hand, speaking earnestly into the camera, "The disappearance of Lakeland High School junior Sheila Longstreet continues to baffle local police." A school photo of Sheila flashed onto the screen. She was smiling softly, her hair falling in rich waves to her shoulders. "Miss Longstreet attended classes here at Lakeland on Friday, but did not return home, and has not been seen for the last two days." The reporter reappeared, her expression now incontestably grim. "Local police are asking the public for any information regarding Miss Longstreet's whereabouts." The phone number of the Shenoba County sheriff's office appeared on the screen, the very one I'd called earlier in the day.

The phone rang just as the news turned to other matters. I switched off the television and answered it.

"Mr. Branch?"

It was a soft, hesitant voice. I could scarcely tell if it was male or female.

"Yes."

"I'm sorry to bother you, Mr. Branch." The volume was little above a whisper, and the words themselves seemed reluctantly offered. "It's Eddie Miller."

I said only, "Oh."

"I need a ride home, Mr. Branch," Eddie said. "They just said I could go. I'm at the sheriff's office."

I pretended that this was all a surprise to me, though I had little doubt that it was my call to the police that had first landed him in trouble, and my second call that had now secured his release.

"It's about Sheila," Eddie added. "They think I know where she is. They're keeping my van. I guess they're going to search it."

"How long have you been there?" I asked.

"They were at my house when I got home from school," Eddie answered. "They think I hurt Sheila, but I didn't. I just took her home."

I felt a glimmer of hope that I had at least not been wrong in what I'd seen on Route 4. "When did you take her home?"

He seemed surprised, and perhaps even a little wary of the question. "After school on Friday." His tone changed, his words now coming in small explosions, like spurts of pressured water. "I told them about it. I'm not hiding anything, Mr. Branch."

I imagined him standing at some desk, the phone squeezed tightly, random movement all around him, disorienting in itself, but to which was added a set of eyes, perhaps two sets, observing him closely or from a carefully chosen distance, all of this done within a silence that didn't actually exist amid the police station's noise and hustle but which seemed like silence nonetheless.

"I'm really sorry to bother you, Mr. Branch," Eddie said.

He was clearly trying to keep a grip on his own deepening dread, something I'd seen before, my father fighting back the "bottoms."

"I'd call my mother, but she . . . she . . ." He seemed to lose energy suddenly, or whatever hope he'd had in calling me— how crazy he'd been to do it, a teacher he barely knew. "Anyway, I just thought maybe, what with your course, you might . . . understand."

Understand what? I wondered. Then the answer came: evil.

"Should I come now?" I asked.

I heard a very quiet release of breath, like a small animal miraculously eased from the jaws of a metal trap. "Yes, sir," he said. "I mean, I can wait if you're busy with something."

"No, I can come now," I told him. I glanced at my watch, calculated the time needed to reach the sheriff's office. "I'll be there in five minutes."

The Shenoba County sheriff's office was in a squat brick building with a short flight of concrete stairs that led to a wide glass door. The words SHERIFF HARRY DRUMMOND were written in large black letters above the door. The windows of the building were small and square. The grounds were as modest as the building, a flat swath of grass adorned by nothing more than a flagpole rooted in a stubby rectangular column of gray granite. Some words had been etched into the granite, IN HONOR OF THE FALLEN, followed by a single list of names. One of them, as I noticed, was Noel Drummond.

The parking area lay just beyond the flagpole, so that as I got out of my car the entire face of the building was visible. It was an ordinary structure in every way, not the least imposing, and yet my mental conveyor belt jerked to life and I saw other places of detention as if in overhead transparencies: London's gray-walled Tower; the stately yellow façade of Lubyanka, from whose windows, the inmates joked, one could clearly see Siberia; even Bentham's famed Panopticon, all glass and light, a see-through prison of "invisible omniscience," as the old philosopher described it, the wardenship of God.

The Shenoba County sheriff's office was neither infamous nor imaginary of course, and I had little doubt that whatever excesses had been committed within its walls had probably been exceptions to the general routine rather than the product of policies decided in well-lighted rooms and carried out in dark ones.

I headed across the parking lot, then up the stairs and into the building. The interior was as modest as the exterior, and yet I felt a very real unease, as if I suddenly expected to be taken into custody. I even recalled the little signals of imminent arrest I'd read about in various memoirs, an idling car motor at an early hour, unrecognized footsteps on the stairs, a neighbor's wary glance.

"Hi, Mr. Branch."

The voice belonged to a young man sitting behind the glass-enclosed front desk of the station.

"Hi," I said.

He looked at me quizzically. "You don't remember me, do you?" he asked. Without waiting for an answer, he added, "Junior Collins. I was a senior when you first came to Lakeland."

I vaguely recalled his face, but I'd never taught him. "Oh, Junior," I said. "Of course. I've come to pick up Eddie Miller."

His smile faded and he appeared suddenly to see me in a different light. "Okay," he said. "Just a minute."

There was a slot in the window, which he closed, then opened again when I remained in place. "Just have a seat, Mr. Branch." He nodded to the right. "The waiting room is over there."

———

It was not a room at all, but three rows of wooden benches evenly arranged before a squad of vending machines for coffee, soda, candies, chips, the bleak fodder of the station house. People were scattered about on the benches, usually at a distance, as if to keep their troubles to themselves.

I sat down at the far end of the second bench. I'd brought nothing to read, and because of that my eyes wandered from one fellow bench-sitter to the next. They were varied in age and gender, and to some extent in means, though at that moment they seemed to share a sense of reduced standing, as if some part of what they'd previously considered inalienable had been taken from them. It hadn't been done with a slap or a sneer, as might have happened in some third-world dictatorship, but by suddenly finding themselves in the grip of authority, subject to its processes. They had rights, these people, ways to navigate a system that was, after all, far from arbitrary, and yet they now appeared somewhat less than full citizens, hung low to the ground, like flags at half-staff.

A few minutes later Officer Collins called my name. I walked to the booth and took the paper he held toward me. "It says you're taking responsibility," he told me.

I glanced at the form. Though the legalese was daunting, I could make out that the "responsibility" I was taking was very limited, merely a matter of declaring that I was, indeed, who I said I was, an adult without criminal record or intent, and that Eddie Miller, a minor, was being released to me at his own request. I signed the form and handed it back to Officer Collins.

"He'll be right out," he said.

"Thank you," I said. I offered a smile he awkwardly returned as he snapped his attention back to the stack of forms that rested on the desk in front of him.

I returned to my place on the bench and waited with the others, looking at their blank faces and recalling the last time I'd seen people gathered in this way. It was shortly after I'd gotten word of the "incident." I'd rushed home by train and bus, a journey of several hours during which I'd been unable to get any word of my father's condition. I'd been horribly anxious at first, but as the hours passed, I'd felt myself sink into an enervation I'd subsequently noticed in pictures of displaced persons, famine victims, refugees, or people fixed in the aimless grip of underdevelopment, inert and unmotivated, as if stirring accomplished nothing but collapse.

I was lost in all this, trying to fit something of it into my course on evil, when Eddie Miller was escorted through the double doors at the rear of the waiting room. The man at his side didn't have him by the arm, but Eddie looked cuffed and shackled anyway, his arms glued to his sides, his gait consciously measured, walking at the exact pace of the officer until they reached me.

"I'm Deputy White." We shook hands. "Okay, he's all yours." He looked at Eddie. "You remember what I told you, right?"

Eddie nodded. "Yes, sir."

White glanced at me, then turned and seemed almost instantly to vanish.

I offered Eddie a smile. "How are you?"

"Good, I guess."

"Well," I corrected.

Eddie looked at me quizzically.

I felt utterly foolish in having corrected Eddie's grammar at such a moment, no less "fussy" than my father. But I'd made the leap, so now I had to get to the other side.

"You only use 'good' when you're not talking about action," I explained. "Cake is good. But when you describe action or what they call 'state of being,' you use 'well.'" None of this could have been more inappropriate to the moment, as I well knew, so I brought this particular grammar lesson to a speedy end. "So, when someone asks how you're doing, you're doing . . . well."

Eddie nodded. "Yes, sir." He glanced about the room, as if still trying to understand the place. I thought of Jonah afloat in the whale's cavernous belly, without light and surrounded by unknown sounds and smells, a tiny morsel within a vast digestive machine. "I tried to call my mother. She works at the truck stop on Highway 9. But she was out delivering something. Nobody knew when she'd be back, so I—"

"Don't worry," I interrupted. "It's no trouble taking you home."

"You sure?"

His voice was weak, but his gaze was very intense so that I felt oddly on the brink of some great choice, Lord Jim balanced on the storm-tossed deck of the *Patna*, the final decision not yet made, whether to hold firm to a crewman's duty, or abandon it and leap into the waiting lifeboat. It was just an instant of suspension, one of those unforeseeable folds in time that opens to or closes upon a wholly different life.

"Yes," I said. "I'm sure."

SIX

I remember seeing the last orphan to have lived in the Confederate Orphanage that once stood on the main street of town. He had returned to commemorate the building as a historic oddity, though the forward-thinking members of the Lakeland Town Council have recently voted to tear it down. He was an old man, this last lonesome exile of the old Confederate Orphanage, bent and gray, walking with two canes, and even with these he still required considerable assistance as he mounted the stairs of the platform that had been erected for the occasion. There on the platform, he took his place behind a table, his small, wiry body framed by the welcoming sign that hung from the wall behind him: Welcome Back Ethan Greer, October 12, 1914. The old man took no notice of this sign, but just stood there, staring silently into the crowd for what seemed a very long time. Still, though impatient, I waited. I was glad I did, too, for I will always remember what he said: "When you cut away a father, you cut away a leg."

JEFFERSON BRANCH, *Lakeland Telegraph*

My father had told me this story long before I stumbled upon it among the cartons of papers he left behind, dusty reams of old lectures and lecture notes, occasional articles and essays written for the *Telegraph,* various sketches and portraits. He'd added a little inspirational flourish at the end of the story: "To replace a father, that's the most a man can do for a boy, Jack." I was twelve years old when he told me about the old orphan, and that night, before I dropped off to sleep, I imagined myself helping some lost boy find, and in some way reattach, that lost limb. In this vision I saw myself nobly surveying the halls of the Confederate Orphanage, a tall man, with black hair flecked with gray, elegantly dressed in a perfectly tailored light blue summer suit. I would see a boy sitting alone on a wooden bench at the end of the corridor. He always had golden hair, and his cheeks were always flushed. I would walk over to him and stare down. He would look up at me with large blue eyes.

And who are you, young man? I would pose the question gravely, as if I were inquiring into the core of this child's being.

The boy would tell me his name in the voice of some Southern version of a Dickens workhouse urchin.

I would introduce myself, Thomas Jackson Branch, and offer my hand.

He would put his small white fingers in my open palm. *Pleased to meet you, sir.*

I'd peer at him with mock severity. *All right, young fellow,* I'd say with a soft paternal smile, *come with me.*

Then I'd turn and lead him down the gloomily lighted corridor, out of the Confederate Orphanage, and into a life of vast good fortune.

Later I would realize that the actual living out of this imagined act of benevolence had quietly become my romantic ambition at Lakeland High School, to find a fatherless boy and place myself in the role of that boy's father, a goal so obvious that it was subsequently pointed out to me in the blunt manner of a skilled defense attorney:

MR. TITUS: So, Mr. Branch, in regard to your duties at Lakeland, you wanted to be more than was strictly called for, isn't that right?

MR. BRANCH: More than what?

MR. TITUS: Be more than a teacher.

MR. BRANCH: I don't know what you mean, sir.

MR. TITUS: You don't? Well others at Lakeland, colleagues as well as students, have suggested that you had a special relationship with Eddie Miller.

MR. BRANCH: I did have a special relationship with him.

MR. TITUS: And you sought that special relationship, didn't you? You sought a wayward boy?

MR. BRANCH: A wayward boy?

MR. TITUS: A wayward boy whose life you could change.

MR. BRANCH: Whose life I could change?

MR. TITUS: Mr. Branch, may I ask that you answer my questions rather than repeat them.

MR. BRANCH: Was I looking for a wayward boy whose life I could change, that's your question?

MR. TITUS: It is. Please answer it.

MR. BRANCH: Yes.

But as we walked together out of the Shenoba County sheriff's office that night, I had no idea that it was Eddie Miller's wayward life I wished to change.

"My car's at the very back of the lot," I told him, trying to keep my tone light, as if we were mere acquaintances leaving a movie theater. "Where do you live?"

"Right at the edge of Glenford Park."

"Through town then."

Eddie nodded, and I suddenly thought, quite surprisingly, of Genghis Khan and how, for all the mighty structures that lay within his realm, he had never once slept within four walls. He'd valued only those things he could take with him, the treasures of the saddlebag, portable abodes, a life lived not only rootlessly but in distrust of roots. Eddie, it seemed to me, had that same distrust, along with the sense of some impending and inevitable doom. I had seen this in other students before him, and after the "incident" had even felt it in my father, that nothing could change his downward direction, provide, or even make possible, a less determined end.

Because of that, it didn't surprise me when Eddie stopped suddenly and said, "Everybody thinks I did it, Mr. Branch."

"I wouldn't say that," I told him.

"Everybody knows they took me here."

"That doesn't mean you did anything."

I could see that Eddie didn't believe a word of this, but chose not to dispute it.

We reached my car and got in. Eddie sat quietly but his mind seemed lit by a thousand small fires. I could only imagine what he was thinking, how unsettling it must have been to be snatched from the usual surroundings, taken to the sheriff's office, questioned, then released into the custody of a man he barely knew.

I decided to stay upbeat.

"White seemed nice enough," I said casually.

"He was okay," Eddie murmured. "But he's not the one who talked to me about Sheila."

I inserted the key into the ignition and turned it. The motor jumped to life. "Who did?"

"Sheriff Drummond." Eddie glanced toward the police station as we drifted by it. "He was like the cop in that book you assigned. The one about the guy who kills this other guy on the beach. You know, when the light flashed in his eyes."

"*The Stranger*," I said. "The killer's name was Meursault." I immediately regretted my pedantic tone. "Anyway, go ahead."

"Drummond was like the guy who talks to Meursault," Eddie said. "Like he'd already made up his mind."

We were now edging slowly toward the wide road that fronted the sheriff's office, other cars backing out of other spaces, joining the line.

"I told him Sheila needed a ride after school," Eddie said. "She had a fight with Dirk." With this much in the open, he offered a bit more, like a small crack in a vast dam, his words trickling out in a small, narrow stream. "I was okay with giving her a ride, but she was afraid Dirk would see us, so she wanted to meet away from school."

We wheeled onto the main road in the direction of the town square. As we crossed it, Eddie glanced toward the imposing façade of the county courthouse. "I let her out at Clear-water. That's her street."

"Why didn't you take her all the way home?" I asked.

"She didn't want me to," Eddie answered. "I figured she thought it might worry her mother. Her being with me."

Because Eddie Miller was the Coed Killer's son.

"Or maybe she was afraid Dirk would be there." He peered out the side window, into the passing scene, watching the streets with familiarity but without pleasure, nervously, like a scout in Indian territory. "The sheriff told me that someone saw my van going toward Glenford Park. I said, okay, that's possible. After I dropped Sheila off, I went to Breaker Landing. To read."

Cautiously, I said, "But that would have been after dark, wouldn't it, seven thirty, around there?"

"Yes, sir," Eddie said. "But I have a flashlight for after dark." He appeared to see the beam of a flashlight on the words he read. "That book you assigned, it's pretty good. The other one, I mean. About . . . Winston."

He meant *1984*, a book I'd hoped the students in my class on evil would find somewhat more brisk and up-to-date than the classics they confronted in their other English classes.

"So, you like to read," I said encouragingly, then realized how banal my remark was, mere teacher-talk, which was the last thing Eddie needed at the moment, though exactly what he needed, particularly from me, remained unclear.

We drove on in silence for a time, past the entrance to Glen-ford State Park. A quarter mile onward, Eddie pointed to a dirt road. "You can turn there," he said.

It was barely more than a break in the surrounding woods,

without a sign or anything else to distinguish it, but as I made the turn I thought of another place I'd read about for my lecture, how at first glance it had appeared so unspectacular, the rocky beach of Naqaevo Bay where thousands had disembarked into the Siberian gloom, a few immediately struck by just how unremarkable the place was, that hell, for all its vast and fiery spectacle, could be entered through a simple cellar door.

SEVEN

Eddie would later describe his house this way:

> It was not a shack like the newspaper called it, but a real
> house with sheetrock on the walls and a real ceiling, not a tar
> roof. From the outside it might have looked like a shack, but
> my father had built it strong, so that when the wind blew it
> didn't lean or creak, and on that day, in the rain, it didn't leak
> because he'd sealed cracks and caulked seams and hung gut-
> ters and done a good job with the flashing, and all this care-
> ful work made it seem to me like he had wanted it to stand
> after he was gone, and I thought that I could learn maybe
> just that much from him, to do things good (which I would
> have said before you taught me, Mr. Branch) . . . well.

It was the only house on Chambers Road. The road itself
ran for nearly two miles along the eastern border of Glenford
State Park. There were no streetlamps, and so the darkness grad-
ually thickened into a kind of black syrup until Eddie's house
suddenly flamed out of a forest break.

"People don't like to come out this way," Eddie said when we came to a stop in front of the house. He seemed reluctant to get out, as if the world outside my car were more perilous, a jungle he knew well but still dreaded. "People think my father picked it because it was isolated and he could do anything, and nobody would see him."

I glanced toward the house, noted that it was close to the road, with nothing but a bare lawn between the two. A blue Chevy sat heavily in the reddish clay, slumped and dusty, like a creature struggling for breath. There were no shrubs, and only one tree, and that a relatively small one, so that it seemed burdened even by the unpainted wooden swing that hung by two gray ropes from its sagging limb.

"It doesn't seem very secluded to me," I said.

"There's a shed behind the house, way back in the woods," Eddie told me. "The sheriff thought I maybe took Sheila there." He shrugged. "I guess he thinks we're two of a kind, my father and me." The stain of that blood connection flickered painfully in Eddie's eyes, a darkness that seemed to fall over him, deepening as it fell. "But I didn't hurt Sheila."

I glanced at the house cheerfully, as if it were a bright suburban ranch, complete with father and son together on a big sofa, eating popcorn and watching a ball game. "So, how long have you lived here?"

"Always," Eddie said in a tone that revealed a sense of forever, that he would never leave this place, that it wasn't a house at all but a destiny.

I started to address the issue directly, mention graduation, ask what he planned to do after that, but the hard slap of a screen door abruptly stopped me.

"Mom," Eddie said.

I turned toward the house and saw a woman with ragged brown hair that fell to her shoulders. She wore a housedress that had some kind of pattern on it. A cigarette dangled loosely from the fingers of her right hand.

"Somebody must have told her," Eddie said.

She stood on the dimly lighted porch, staring at the car, her left fist pressed into her side. She took a draw on the cigarette, then plucked it from her lips and blasted a column of smoke into the air. "What are you waiting for?" she called.

In response, Eddie reached for the door handle. "Thanks for the ride, Mr. Branch."

"No problem," I told him.

He gave a quick nod, then got out of the car.

His mother had come down the stairs by then, and was moving toward me. They met and exchanged a few words, after which Eddie headed into the house, though reluctantly, as if obeying orders he didn't like.

I would have pulled away by then, but something in the whole scene held my attention, a bedraggled mother and a boy in trouble, both of them orphaned, as it were, by a murderous man. Still, it surprised me that I didn't leave but instead waited as Eddie's mother came forward, a trail of cigarette smoke flowing behind her like a ghost's ragged veil.

I rolled down the window as she drew near, got a whiff of smoke.

"So you're Eddie's teacher?" she said.

"One of them," I told her. "He's in my specialty class."

"Any good?"

"I try to make it interesting."

Her laugh was a cackle. "I mean Eddie. Is he doing good in your class?"

"He does all right," I said. "He reads the material."

She cocked her head to the side and took a long draw on the cigarette. "You think he's like his daddy?" She saw that the question shocked me, and that I had no answer for it. My awkwardness clearly thrilled her, almost physically, a trembling delight that ended in a sharp laugh. "You know who he was, don't you, Eddie's daddy?"

"Yes. I do."

She released the cigarette like a bug she'd crushed. "Now Eddie's in trouble," she said with a resignation that hardened into a strange, vocalized bruise.

"Maybe not," I said.

Her eyes sparkled with something that could only be described as the opposite of light. "Maybe not?" She laughed mockingly. "What would you know about trouble?"

I saw the man she thought I was, an effete schoolteacher whose experience of life had come more or less from books, a creature of secure salary and vested pension, a bloodless little twit of a man who knew nothing of the cruel arbitrariness of things, life's gruesome pits, how deep they are and how suddenly we may find ourselves at the bottom of them.

"Eddie's in trouble, all right," she said firmly. "Unless that girl turns up." She stepped back and looked at me closely, like someone trying to bring a blurry photograph into focus. "What's your name?"

"Branch," I told her. "Jack."

"Branch," she said, as if turning the name over in her mind. She started to say more, then stopped and stared at me silently.

"Well, good night, Mrs. Miller," I said.

She gave no reply, not so much as a nod or a wave, but simply stood, watching silently as I eased the gear into reverse and drifted back into the concealing blackness of the unlighted road.

Back at home I turned on the television to check if there'd been any developments. On the small screen, a man in a bow tie gave the forecast. There was to be rain and thunder. We were to take care.

I switched off the television, retrieved Suetonius's *Lives of the Caesars* from the table where I'd left it, and sat down to read. Normally I had no trouble concentrating on whatever I was reading, but I found myself distracted, my gaze continually drawn to the mantel above the fireplace. There were only two pictures there. One was of my father and me on the day of my college graduation, I in cap and gown, he in a neat black suit. The other picture was of myself as a little boy, standing some-where on the vast grounds of Great Oaks. I'd lived there in lux-ury, but also in seclusion, and in that solitude, made imaginary villains of kudzu vines and stalks of pokeweed against whom I'd defended the nobility of Great Oaks. In the evening, my father read to me from the Bible in order, he explained, to acquaint me with the language of King James, how august and gravely beautiful it was. He had not meant me to receive any of it as a sacred text, and yet the New Testament's tender call to the wayward and unmoored, the lonely and by all else abandoned, might have wooed me to its faith had not he also introduced me to a wholly secular field of interest, beginning with, of all things, Chesterton's letters to his son, then on to a host of similarly paternal figures—Cicero, Aurelius, Montaigne—the bounty of which was actually playing in my mind when the knock came at the door.

When I opened it I found a small bantam rooster of a man, with florid cheeks and tufts of red hair peeking from beneath his snap-brim hat. A field of scars, very faint but still visible, ran along the sides of his face, the mark of the rabid acne that had no doubt once afflicted him. He wore a dark suit, with white shirt and tie, and he'd pulled his hat down low, so that his eyes, small and round with somewhat yellowed whites, glimmered just beneath the brim. He smoked a white meerschaum pipe, the bowl yellowed with time and use, so that when he took it from his mouth I was surprised at how pristine he'd kept the stem.

"Mr. Branch?" he asked.

"Yes," I said.

In a clear display of his professionalism, he took out his identification. "I'm Sheriff Drummond. We spoke earlier."

I recalled that in literature men in Drummond's position were always smoking. Perhaps it went back to Faust, whose demonic inquisitor had been all but made of smoke. Compared to so imposing a figure, Drummond appeared quite innocuous, a little man with a deferential manner, who seemed determined to ape the careful dress of the class above him, and to which he'd added the "intellectual" touch of a white-bowled pipe.

"I don't mean to intrude," he added.

"You're not," I assured him politely.

"I understand you picked up Eddie Miller this evening," he said as he returned the identification to his jacket pocket.

"Yes, I did."

He glanced just over my shoulder, to the open book I'd left on my chair.

"Like your father." He took a long puff on his pipe. "A scholar."

"You were asking about Eddie Miller?"

He looked like a man suddenly called to account. "Yes," he said. "Eddie Miller. I was wondering if he might have said anything to you on the way home."

"Just what he'd already told you," I said.

"Did he say anything about Sheila Longstreet?"

"That he let her out at Clearwater. The corner there. On Route 4."

"He didn't strike me as a bad boy," Drummond said. "You're his teacher?"

"He's in my specialty class."

"Is that a class for problem kids?"

"No, it isn't."

"Slow?"

"Eddie's not slow," I said.

He took another puff on his pipe. Blue smoke twined up from its bowl. "Special in what way then?" he asked.

"It's not part of the general curriculum," I answered. "The teacher picks the subject."

"What's the subject of your class?" Drummond asked.

"Evil," I answered.

"I'll bet it's very interesting," Drummond said. "I'm sure you read wonderful books. I have very little time for reading, I'm afraid. My son was a great reader. I still have his books, but I rarely . . . well . . . I'm sure you understand, Mr. Branch. A workingman's life has little leisure."

It struck me that although Drummond was no doubt in the midst of performing a professional duty, he was also a man who sought information along other lines, an autodidact who garnered shreds of learning from conversation, then filed them away in precious nuggets.

"What do you have them read in your class?" Drummond asked.

He saw that I found the question odd, and suddenly looked as if I'd come to feel him rather odd, as well, and so returned immediately to Eddie.

"Of course, you probably have no time for idle conversation," he said. "So, well, I do have a few matters I'd like to be clear about." He drew a small notebook from his jacket pocket. "Where were you again when you saw Eddie's van?" He smiled. "If it was Eddie's van, of course."

"On Route 4. I was coming home from dinner with my father. Around eight. I went to Jake's and had a cup of coffee. After that, I drove to Glenford Park."

"That's a nice place, Glenford Park," Drummond said amiably. "Nice night, too. Friday night. Clear. Nearly a full moon. You probably had a good view of the lake."

"I don't remember," I said. "I wasn't there very long. I didn't even get out of my car."

Drummond said nothing, but his silence worked on me like a heavy instrument, a pry rod he used to open my mouth, keep me talking.

"I stopped at Breaker Landing," I told him without being asked. "No one else was there. I stayed a few minutes, then went home." I waited for a question, but it never came. "Which is where I stayed until Monday morning," I added.

"Was Sheila Longstreet in your class?" Drummond asked.

"Was? She still is, as far as I know."

Drummond started to respond but stopped because, in one of those unpredictable swerves that renders life a maddening uncertainty, a metallic voice suddenly came from the police radio in Drummond's car.

"A call," Drummond said. "Excuse me." He walked to his car, got in, and remained there awhile, listening. Then he got out again and came back to my door.

"They found Sheila Longstreet," he said with what seemed truly good cheer.

I thought of the dark reaches of Glenford Park, then the countless deserted places of the Delta where over the years other murdered females had been found, ditches and ravines, weedy fields, culverts, marshes, their bodies disposed of like rusty car engines or old metal filing cabinets, stuff the dump won't take.

"In Jackson," he added happily.

It was the basements and cellars of our capital city that now circled through my mind, made soundproof with thick sheets of fiberboard, windows covered with black plastic sheeting secured with packing tape, wooden rafters hung with ropes, equipped with pulleys, gouged with meat hooks.

"She's alive."

Now I imagined Sheila carried out on a stretcher, breathing faintly through bruised lips and cracked teeth, her arms and legs covered with scratches and cigarette burns, barely able to see through her swollen eyes.

"Alive and well," Drummond said with a broad smile. "At her cousin's house in Jackson." He shook his head, as if at the whimsy of life. "She took the bus there late Friday afternoon."

On those words, I saw Luther Ray Miller's old brown van draw up to an electrical pole at the corner of Clearwater Drive and Route 4, the rectangular blue bus-stop sign winking in its rearview mirror, the short list of towns the bus route served, Bryerton, Milburg, Jackson.

"It seems she had a fight with her boyfriend," Drummond went on. "She just wanted to make him miss her."

"She put a lot of people to a lot of trouble," I said.

Drummond released a short, affable chuckle. "Well, kids. What can you do?" He touched the brim of his hat in farewell. "Well, good night, Mr. Branch. Sorry for the trouble."

With that, he returned to his car and drove away. I watched him until the car turned off Maple and abruptly disappeared, then went back to the sofa, read awhile, and went to bed.

Normally I would have dropped off very quickly, but the vision of Eddie unjustly accused continued to unsettle me.

For a time, I waited it out. But after a while, I gave up, walked back to the living room, and turned on the television.

She was there almost instantly, Sheila Longstreet ushered down the steps of Jackson police headquarters and into a waiting police car that immediately pulled away, lights flashing brightly until it vanished around the corner.

Then it was the same woman, microphone in hand, who'd last reported from the steps of Lakeland High. Earlier she'd stared grimly into the camera, but now she was clearly relieved that things had turned out as they had. "So there we have it," she said happily. "A rare thing indeed in cases like this. A happy ending." She smiled and seemed to think the whole world smiled with her, all the trees and streams. But I felt something entirely different, the lingering power of a dark legacy, how Sheila's brief disappearance had, in a sense, disinterred Eddie Miller's father, Eddie now more stigmatized than ever, a victim of town memory with a sign hung round his neck: COED KILLER'S SON.

No one should have to live like that, I thought. It was the very opposite of how I lived. Eddie's family name made him infamous while mine bestowed upon me all manner of deference and respect. In addition, there was his poverty, his public-school education, both of which made him a do-gooder's dream, the little boy I'd imagined crouched in a shadowy corridor of the Confederate Orphanage and upon whom I wished to bestow my own noble beneficence.

This, too, Mr. Titus saw:

MR. TITUS: So, you felt sorry for Eddie Miller, sorry for his background, for the way he'd been treated?

Mr. Branch: Yes.

Mr. Titus: You'd had so much and he'd had so little, and so you wanted to help him, isn't that right?

Mr. Branch: I made myself available to him, yes.

Mr. Titus: He became your, what . . . project?

Mr. Branch: I would make myself available, if he asked.

Mr. Titus: And what did you expect him to ask you for, Mr. Branch?

Mr. Branch: I don't know. Help with his studies.

Mr. Titus: That's all?

Mr. Branch: At the beginning, yes.

Mr. Titus: With no idea where it would lead?

Mr. Branch: Does anyone ever know where anything will lead?

Mr. Titus never answered that question.

But I answer it every day, and my answer is always, *No.*

PART II

EIGHT

A short walk through the town cemetery reveals how many lives are destroyed not by someone else's enmity or their own poor choices or bad behavior, but simply by misfortune: women who died in childbirth, men killed by some accident of farm or factory labor, children taken by whooping cough or diphtheria. Most of the people who lie in Lakeland's well-shaded memorial garden are as innocent as the leaves that hang above them. They lived as blamelessly as it is possible to live, infected with the usual prejudices and given comfort by the usual illusions. A few, a very few, rose beyond what could have been expected of them. And one, against all odds, did a mighty thing.

Most of the stones are gray, but the one over my father's grave is black marble. It is larger than the ones around it, though not at all imposing, and I find it entirely appropriate that only one word is chiseled beneath his name: TEACHER. The word has faded with the years, and now seems pale and sickly, as if to suggest a profession that no longer thrives. Which is true enough, I think. After all, what would my father have thought about the fate of his vocation had he been sitting with me at a local restaurant some weeks ago, listening to the four people who occupied the table directly to the right of mine? They were all English teachers at Lakeland's spanking-new, state-of-the-art high school, but there was no discussion of books, nor ideas, nor any mention of the deeper things of life. As I listened, it became obvious that they team-teach to avoid work, and assign the same books year after year because they've already read them. Worst of all, as their conversation so clearly betrayed, they show the movie versions of the books they assign, then give test questions their students can answer by having watched the movie alone. One of these teachers produced a student paper and with great hilarity read its opening sentence: "*The Great Gatsby* is about how Robert Redford has this huge jones for Mia Farrow and takes the blame when she runs over this other actress that I don't know." I could hardly imagine my father in the company of such people, or part of a profession that had sunk so low.

But teaching can grow heady, as well, take on a certain arrogance, a truth Mr. Titus was determined to explore:

MR. TITUS: Clay. Isn't that how you saw your students, Mr. Branch? As young people you could mold?

MR. BRANCH: Shouldn't every teacher try to mold his students?

MR. TITUS: But there were certain students you rebuked, isn't that so?

MR. BRANCH: I never rebuked anyone.

MR. TITUS: Oh, really, sir? What about the witches?

Right there, seated in the witness box, I saw it all again. It was the morning after I'd taken Eddie home. I'd planned to follow the set course I'd outlined weeks ago, give my lecture on the evil of captivity, a broad-ranging lecture that would begin with one of history's oddest kidnappings, move through the general history of slavery, then circle back again to end with the kidnapping and murder of the Lindbergh baby. But the sight of Sheila, Dirk, and Wendell strolling to their seats brought a quite different lecture to mind. Here they were, Sheila, whose "self-capture" had landed Eddie Miller in police custody, along with Dirk and Wendell, both of whom were evidently oblivious to the fact that their descriptions of me as "looking weird" and "acting jolted" had that very morning gotten back to me through the agency of George Frobish, the school's indefatigable tattler.

I waited until the rest of the students had settled in, Eddie once again in back, then flipped a few pages forward in my lecture series, gripped the sides of my lectern, and began a talk that struck me as far more immediately relevant than the one I'd originally scheduled for that day.

"The Puritans called it 'crying out,'" I said. "And in 1692, in the little village of Salem, Massachusetts, it ended in the execution of twenty totally innocent people."

A few still-restless bodies shifted into place. Stacia Decker dutifully flipped open her notebook and grabbed her ever-present ballpoint.

"Still others, perhaps as many as thirteen, died in prison," I continued.

I paused for the usual number of coughs and cleared throats before I went on.

"The youngest person arrested was Dorcas Good," I said. "She was five years old."

By now Stacia was scribbling away, every detail recorded in her famously neat script.

"The oldest victim was Rebecca Nurse. She was seventy-one." I stopped, let a beat go by, then dropped the hook. "The crime of which they were accused was witchcraft."

I settled my gaze on Dirk Littlefield.

"To 'cry out' means to accuse," I added. "And in Salem the ones who made the accusations were very young. Susanna Sheldon, for example, was eighteen." I pointedly directed my gaze at Wendell Casey. "How old are you, Wendell?" I asked.

He stiffened suddenly, clearly taken aback both by my singling him out and by the look in my eyes when I did it.

"Sixteen," he answered in a tone that resembled wary confession.

I looked at Dirk. "And you?"

Dirk glared at me like one who'd been left back twice, older than his classmates, caged with kids when he should long ago have been released into a world of men. "Eighteen," he said.

I drew my attention back to the class as a whole once again. "These girls of Salem were young and they were reckless." I looked at Sheila. "And by their acts of recklessness they caused a great deal of uproar and finally a great deal of harm to their communities."

From there I went on to enumerate that harm in considerable detail, the hysterical behavior of the crying-out girls, the helplessness of the accused before their crazed accusers, the deluded magistrates who'd conducted the trial and handed down the sentences, and finally the executions themselves, the bump and jostle of the open wagons that carried the guiltless doomed to Gallows Hill, their slow ascent to the hangman's noose, the final words they'd addressed to God or the grim-faced crowd, and at last the drop, nineteen bodies swaying in the autumn wind.

Stacia Decker, a true monster of exactitude, raised her hand, her eyes on her fastidious notes. "I thought you said there were twenty people executed."

"There were," I said. "But one of them, a man named George Cory, was pressed to death." Stacia took this down, clearly pleased to have gotten to the bottom of an obvious discrepancy.

"When they demanded that he confess to witchcraft, he refused," I told the class. "Instead, he said, 'More weight.'" I waited for this to sink in before I added, "George Cory also refused to accuse others of crimes he knew they hadn't committed." Finally, quoting my family's august motto, I pointedly added, "Veneratio Sileo Vera."

The class watched me quizzically.

"Honor rests in truth."

A hand went up in back, and to my surprise, it was Eddie Miller's.

"Yes?"

He seemed hesitant and unsure of his place, as if he didn't feel entitled to speak. "So the whole town went against them?" he asked. "Just because of what those girls said?"

Dirk released a bored groan, and in response a ripple of laughter swept the room.

In its wake, Eddie shrank back slightly.

"The whole town, yes," I answered.

I hoped he might engage me in further discussion, but Dirk's groan and the accompanying laughter had done their job and it was obvious that Eddie now regretted having spoken.

But I wanted him to know that he didn't have to be cowed by the likes of Dirk Littlefield, nor the low response he inevitably called forth in others.

"History provides a great many examples of people being falsely accused," I declared forcefully, then chose the first one that came to me. "It is called the butcher's tale."

In the teacher's lounge an hour later, the talk was all about Sheila Longstreet. Mrs. Cavanaugh defended her actions as those of a "troubled" teenage girl.

"She comes from the Bridges," she said. "You know what that's like."

The Bridges was a singularly blighted neighborhood of twenty or so square blocks that ran along the tracks at the south end of town, so called because the tracks themselves spanned a series of shallow culverts littered with an unsightly debris of empty crates, rusty bedsprings, and sodden mattresses. The houses of the Bridges were mostly dilapidated railroad flats, wood-framed, with tin roofs and cement porches that looked out over weedy lawns dotted with car parts and old household appliances, discarded iceboxes that dated back to the Depression and washing machines that were little more than huge aluminum buckets mounted with hand-cranked rollers for wringing out the wash. It was universally regarded as the seedbed of local crime, mostly petty, as well as the prime recruiting ground of a newly rising Ku Klux Klan. The men were semiliterate and the women, either bone-thin or grotesquely fat, were often rabidly religious. In their lowly midst, Sheila, in her radiance and in the opportunity afforded by her beauty, must have shone like a diamond in a field of muck.

"The Bridges," Mr. Crombie snorted. "Who'd expect anything but trash coming from there?"

A steely voice sounded in our midst.

"I'm from the Bridges."

It was Nora Ellis, a presence I'd hardly noticed at the table before she spoke.

Mr. Crombie suddenly looked taken aback. "I just meant that being from the Bridges is no excuse for doing what Sheila did." He pressed a finger against the bridge of his glasses and pushed them back. The finger trembled very slightly as he drew it away, which gave me the impression that he was perhaps embarrassed by what he'd said, though in fact, it was only the first sign of the Parkinson's disease that would steadily debilitate him from then on.

"There are good people from the Bridges," Nora added in a voice that was not strident though she was clearly determined to make her stand. "Like anywhere else."

She was a small woman with reddish brown hair that hung

pine-board straight to her shoulders. Her skin was darker than usual for the region, and a scattering of freckles dotted her nose. Her voice was soft, but I detected something very solid just below it, like smooth stone beneath gently running water. Though I had no inkling of it then, she was the noblest human being I would ever know.

"Then you'd agree that being poor is no excuse for bad behavior," Mr. Crombie added. He had clearly decided that he would not retreat from his earlier statement, and so had returned to his usual, vaguely bullying tone. "And that the day it is, this country is finished."

Nora nodded, though I couldn't tell how much this signaled any actual agreement with what Mr. Crombie had just said. Certainly she hadn't wanted to provoke a fight. After all, she'd been recently hired at Lakeland, and even then only because Mrs. Potts had suddenly keeled over in class, been rushed to the county hospital, and was now recuperating from what Mr. Rankin called "a case of nerves."

"If this whole thing had only involved Sheila, it would have been different," Mr. Crombie continued, "but other people were drawn into it." He cast about for an example and immediately found one. "Take Branch, here. An innocent bystander if there ever was one, and yet he got dragged into this thing."

"Dragged?" I asked. "How so?"

"Well, didn't you pick Eddie up at the sheriff's office last night?" Mr. Crombie asked.

That this piece of information had already flown to Mr. Crombie made me wonder if perhaps he was a member of some secret law enforcement underground.

"Yes," I said. "Eddie called me from the station. He couldn't get in touch with his mother, so——"

"That woman covered up for him," Mr. Crombie blurted.

"Eddie didn't do anything she needed to cover up," I said.

"I don't mean Eddie," Mr. Crombie said. "That woman covered up for her husband. She knew what he did. She had to have known. She's just as guilty as Eddie's father."

I had no answer for this since I knew nothing of the case. So I said only, "Well, the bottom line is that Eddie was completely innocent."

"It must have been a strange feeling though," Mrs. Cavanaugh said pointedly. "Having Eddie in the car with you. Considering what he might have done."

"I never thought he'd done anything," I said.

"Despite his father?" Mr. Crombie barked. "Or the fact that the police clearly thought he was a suspect? That didn't generate any suspicion in you, Branch?"

It had generated some, I told him, but the suspicion had remained unspecific, like seeing someone through wisps of cloud, still the same person, but for a time oddly shaded, a suspicion that had turned out to be unwarranted, I emphasized again, and because of that now made Eddie seem not only innocent but wronged.

And so, despite the fact that I'd later called Drummond and tried to remove whatever suspicion I'd cast on Eddie Miller, I suddenly saw myself in the guise of a shrieking girl, Abigail Williams before her Puritan inquisitors, detailing hideous visitations, describing old Rebecca Nurse in dreadful witchery, pointing her finger, naming names, filling Salem up with demons.

"Actually, I should apologize to Eddie for the part I played in bringing him under suspicion," I added.

Nora smiled at me approvingly, and bathed in her favorable regard, I suddenly felt like a knight of old, bravely determined to win a gentlewoman's hand.

"And so," I manfully declared, "I will."

NINE

I came upon him later that same afternoon.

I was headed for my car at the end of the day. Eddie was sitting alone in the little grove where I'd watched as he talked with Sheila Longstreet on Friday. He was reading a book and didn't look up as I approached. He probably expected me to pass through the grove and head on down the path to the parking area. He continued to read until I stopped just in front of him, at which point he looked up, his expression slightly puzzled.

"I want to apologize to you, Eddie," I told him. "I told the police that I'd seen you with Sheila the night she disappeared. But, obviously, it wasn't you."

He stared at me silently, so that I wasn't sure he'd understood my confession.

"I saw a brown van going past Glenford Park," I added. "There was a girl in the passenger seat. I told the police that it looked like Sheila, and that she was staring down at her hands, like they were tied."

It was clear Eddie deserved an explanation for such a statement, so I added, "Because her head was bowed. And I'd been thinking about the *Minsk*. Remember? The boat with the 'streetcar,' those poor women, how helpless they must have been, like slaves." I shrugged. "It was all in my imagination. And so I shouldn't have said it. I'm sorry the police picked you up. It was probably my fault."

When Eddie remained silent, I gave up on any further discussion of this particular matter, glanced at the book in his hands and saw that it was *The Trial,* the third in what I thought of as an interrogation trilogy. Students had been required to read only one of them, so it was clear that Eddie was actually reading more than had been strictly assigned, a rarity indeed at Lakeland.

"What do you think about the book?" I asked.

That I'd asked him such a question appeared both to surprise him and to put him at a loss.

"It's good," he said hesitantly.

"But you liked *The Stranger* more?"

He thought a moment, then said, "He's not mad at the town. Meursault, I mean."

It was a small insight, but given the source, I considered it, as the Bible says, "sufficient unto the day."

"And that's strange, isn't it?" I said. "After all, wouldn't you be mad if you were falsely arrested and the whole town did nothing about it?"

"I guess," Eddie said. "But Meursault's not. At the end he wants everybody to hate him. I looked up the word he used, 'execration.'"

"You're building your vocabulary, I see," I said with a light, congratulatory smile.

I saw that he'd heard the condescension in my voice, rec-ognized the empty teacher-praise in the words I'd said to him. I knew that he expected me to leave now that I'd done my little task of encouragement. And so, rather than leave, I sat down on the bench across from him.

"Which book do you like the best?" I asked. "Of the three I assigned, I mean."

"The one about Big Brother," Eddie answered immediately.

"Why that one?" I asked.

"It sort of shows a whole world," Eddie said.

"A nightmare world," I told him. "Where the people in charge make things up."

Eddie nodded, and from there I thought we might have a brief discussion of *1984,* but instead he said, "Thanks for giving me that other example. You know, about the boy cut up in pieces."

I thought of young Ernst Winter's dismembered body, a man accused of that crime by a butcher's lying tale, and thus the scapegoat of my example, Jewish, alien, bearing the blood libel of his father, as in some sense, it seemed to me, Eddie did as well.

"I'm afraid there are lots of examples of this kind of thing," I said, returning to the safe ground of my erudition. "The blood libel goes back to the eleventh century."

I thought Eddie might ask a question, show some spark of interest in medieval history, but he didn't.

In the distance, the buses began to pull out, their engines churning loudly, a sound I took as a signal that I, too, should be on my way.

"Well, I better be getting home," I said.

I rose and to my surprise Eddie also got to his feet and accompanied me out of the grove, the two of us walking shoulder to shoulder toward the parking area.

"They let me have my van back," he said.

I glanced out into the parking lot where the van sat forlornly in a far corner, a relic of his father's crime. When I looked back at Eddie, he was staring at it with a strange intensity.

"It was your father's," I said.

He was clearly surprised that I'd mentioned this.

"Do you think about him a lot?" I asked.

"Yes, sir," he admitted shyly. "Sort of like that bad angel you talked about once."

"Mephistopheles," I said, and instantly recalled a line from Emerson about the "monstrous corpse" of the past we drag behind us as we go. I wondered if perhaps the best therapy might be for Eddie to dig up the corpse of his father, the one he'd been forced to drag behind him all his life, and thoroughly examine it.

"Have you ever thought of writing about your father?" I asked.

Eddie looked puzzled by the question.

"You could make him the subject of your paper," I said. "The one for my class."

"But I really didn't know him, Mr. Branch," Eddie said. "I was just five when he . . ." He stopped, quite obviously unable even to speak of what his father had done. "I mean, I wouldn't know how."

"Well, you could start by making a list of people who knew

him," I said. "Then you could talk to them. They would be the basis of your research."

We had now reached a fork in the sidewalk, one of which led to the student parking area, one to the area reserved for teachers.

"It's an option for your paper, that's all," I told him. "Let me know if you decide to do it."

"Okay," Eddie said, and with no further word, turned and headed toward the parking lot.

I watched him weave among the cars until my attention was drawn to a nearly motionless tableau, three figures, Dirk, Wendell, and Sheila in a tight knot at the entrance to the student parking lot. Dirk was the only one facing me, but when he noticed Eddie, he nodded to the others and they turned and watched as he made his solitary way to the far end of the lot, three heads rotating smoothly, and which I saw not as they actually were but in a way that was shockingly macabre, not as living faces, young and vibrant, but as shriveled, blackened heads, mounted on the battlements of Tyburn Bridge, revolving slowly on their separate, blood-smeared poles.

"He seems like a nice boy."

Nora had come up beside me. Her astonishingly light blue eyes shone in the afternoon light.

"Yes, I think he is," I said.

Suddenly I thought of my father's long solitude, the wife whose death he'd never quite gotten over, the loneliness in which he was now encased, writing about Lincoln or adding pages to *The Book of Days*. It was not a fate I wished for myself.

"Nora," I said, "would you like to go to dinner sometime?"

She was clearly surprised by the abruptness of the question. "Well, I don't know if that would be . . . appropriate."

"Why wouldn't it be?" I asked.

"Both of us working here at Lakeland, I mean," Nora said. "It might not be allowed."

"Allowed?" I laughed. "We're both adults, aren't we?"

Her smile was of the type called bashful, a term that now seems so ancient, so descriptive of a vanished reticence, that I half expect to see it only carved in stone.

"Aren't we?" I repeated.

She nodded firmly, a woman who could make up her mind. "Yes," she said. "We are."

"Good."

For a moment we only stared at each other. Then, as if turning from some invisible heat, she peered out over Lakeland High's small landscape where Eddie could be seen weaving among the cars toward his old brown van. "So, Sheila's back and Eddie's not in trouble anymore." She glanced over to where Sheila slouched under Dirk's arm. "The end of the mystery," she added softly. "And everyone got away unharmed."

I nodded. "Yes," I said, and safely housed within the grace of my experience, believed it to be so.

TEN

I read somewhere that the Haitian dictator known as Papa Doc watched children being tortured and children at play with exactly the same dead gaze, his eyes as lightless and unmoving as small brown stones. My father's eyes, when I last saw them, had shone with a liquid melancholy gleam, as if the flesh they were made of was half dissolved in tears. The gleam in Harry Drummond's eyes at our last encounter was neither cheerful nor sinister nor full of sorrow, but merely the neutral light that living flesh emits until it lives no more. Wendell Casey's eyes became deeply thoughtful in the weeks before he died, his clownishness long dissipated by misfortune. Dirk Littlefield's gaze never lost the sullen anger that held his life in thrall. Luther Miller's eyes, at least in photographs, appear deeply creased for so young a man, and I often imagine them as curtains behind which sprawls the body of a murdered girl. Sheila Longstreet's eyes never lost their beauty, and on that final, sad occasion, they'd offered what I knew to be the last warmth I would feel on earth.

As for my own eyes, they are dark brown, and now, in my old age, seem on the verge of assuming their permanent position, either open and staring blindly into nothingness or forever closed in that same oblivion.

But of all the eyes I've known on earth, it's Nora's that most often float into my consciousness, sometimes glittering in bright sunlight, sometimes deeply shaded, but always incontestably piercing.

She'd given me her address but no further directions so that I'd gotten the idea that she thought me at least vaguely familiar with the Bridges. But the fact is, I'd never gone to that part of town and knew it only by reputation. The actual feel of the place was new to me, particularly the way the eyes on the street followed my car as I drove through the neighborhood looking for Nora's house. From driveways and front porches, they followed me as if I were a prowler, or if not that, some outlander sent to assess houses from which they would soon as renters be evicted or as owners be forced to sell to some government or private concern, either of which would immediately tear them down.

Nora's house, as it turned out, was located almost dead center within the Bridges, a factory house, as they were called, because they'd first been used to house the workers of the Truman Mills, a textile-producing complex whose enormous brick façade still towered over them.

To my surprise, Nora was sitting on the steps when I pulled up.

"So, you found me," she said as she walked over to the open window on the passenger side of the car.

"Not without a few wrong turns," I said.

She got in and pressed a wrinkle from her skirt. "Really? I figured you'd been here before."

"No, never."

"You never visited Wanda Ruth's place?" She pointed to a tumbledown flat across the street. "She used to run boys in and out all night. The 'fine-family boys' she called them. Boys like you. From the plantation district."

Then I knew. "I take it Wanda Ruth ran a house of ill repute?"

Nora nodded. "But like I said, it wasn't just some old whorehouse. It was strictly the white-glove treatment."

"White-glove treatment? In the Bridges?"

"Where else could even a fancy whorehouse have been, Jack? We're not in New Orleans." She laughed. "It couldn't have been more than a few minutes after Wanda Ruth died when the cops showed up. Three cars. They went through the whole place to make sure she didn't keep . . . well . . . attendance, you might say."

"Power does show its hand from time to time," I said.

Nora glanced about. "So, where are we going to eat?" she asked.

"Milford," I said. It was a small town, but larger than Lake-land, and one that permitted a private club, to which my father had always belonged, to serve alcohol though state law still firmly prohibited it, one of those oddities of Mississippi gover-nance that strangers no doubt found as inscrutable as the Ori-ent. "A place called Regis. It's not a restaurant, but it has a dining room."

"Sounds fancy."

Which it was, at least in the sense that it had a wine list.

Once there, I ordered a red and the way Nora cautiously took the first sip from her glass made it clear to me that this was her first taste of wine, though I had little doubt that a girl from the Bridges had known beer and hard liquor practically from birth.

"Um," she said softly as she lowered the glass to the table. "Good." She seemed surprised that the taste appealed to her. "Nice."

She wore a plain blue dress that was wildly out-of-date, perhaps a hand-me-down from an older sister, or even from her mother. It had white piping and padded shoulders, a look so clearly associated with an earlier decade that she actually seemed still of that time herself, tender and forthright as the women in old war movies, writing their soldier husbands and boyfriends each and every day, letters that ended with "Yours forever faithful," and which they sealed—at least in movies—with a soft but audible sigh.

"So, how did the week go?" I asked by way of getting the conversation started. "Anything interesting happen?"

"Not really," she answered, then added, as if it were a bit of spice to an otherwise lackluster week, "On Friday I had a talk with Sheila Longstreet."

"What about?"

She took another sip from the glass and seemed briefly to conceal herself behind it. When she came into view again, she said, "Dirk, mostly. She doesn't know if he's Mr. Right."

"He's not," I said. "For anyone."

Nora laughed. "You know, I think she's a little interested in Eddie Miller."

This completely surprised me, since I'd never seen any sign

of such an interest in my class, and I'd quickly dismissed the incident I'd witnessed from the grove some days earlier as a mere coquettish turn.

"She probably picked me to talk to because we're both from the Bridges," Nora added. "You know, white trash."

I took this as an opening to inquire into her background.

"Where did you go to college?" I asked.

"Bradford."

Bradford was a "normal school," as they were called at that time, designed to educate teachers in the art of teaching, but with little emphasis on a truly rounded education, and so ranked very low in the academic hierarchy. It had no graduate program and there were no professional schools, law, medicine, and the like, attached to it.

"Where'd you go?" she asked.

"Vanderbilt," I said.

"I mean high school."

"Danville Academy," I said. "It was a boarding school out-side Richmond."

She said nothing, but I knew what she was thinking.

"Rich kids. Except for me."

"You're not rich?" Nora said with a small laugh. "Everyone says you are."

"My father has a big house," I said. "But he hasn't worked in a long time, and when he did, it was as a teacher, and you know what they make."

She set the glass down very carefully, as if in fear of spilling. "He taught at Lakeland, didn't he?"

"For twenty years."

She started to speak, then stopped, but not before I got the idea of what had crossed her mind, the grim pall that had suddenly fallen across my father's life.

"It's not some dark family secret that he shot himself," I told her.

Her gaze drifted down to her now half-empty glass.

"He calls it the 'incident,'" I added.

For an instant, I saw the whole dreadful spectacle reflected in her eyes, the room hung with prints where romanticized Delta landscapes had once held sway, the towering shelves of books, gold leaf winking in the light of a chandelier, and last, the man himself standing rigidly against the wall, drawing the pistol upward, squeezing the trigger as it rose, but too hard, so that it fired before he'd intended and at a saving slant.

"It was a family heirloom, the gun," I told her in a voice that was not very different from the one I used in my lectures. "He wasn't accustomed to it. He wasn't really accustomed to guns of any kind, but especially that one." I made no effort to avoid the grimly comic aspect of this. "And so he missed the mark and dug a trench right up the side of his head." I sat back slightly, like a man committed to full disclosure. "As for my mother, she died on what my father still calls 'the crossing,' of a fever while at sea." I lifted my glass as if toasting myself. "Which makes me quite the tragic figure, don't you think?"

Rather than answer such a frivolously posed question, Nora asked one of her own. "Why did you stay here in Lakeland?"

"It's my home."

She looked at me doubtfully.

"Why do you think I stayed here?"

To my surprise she said, "Probably because you were afraid to go anywhere else."

The frankness of her answer inspired me to give a similarly frank response. "You may be right. I wouldn't be anything special in someplace like New York. People wouldn't think I was rich, for example."

She shrugged. "Money's nice, but when you're born with it, you can't ever know what you'd have made of yourself without it."

This was true, of course. I had come from sufficient money and standing that I could never know what I might have been, or failed to be, without them. I could survive all manner of bad judgment and miscalculation, be a rogue, a fool, a dilettante, almost anything but a class-A felon, and yet sail on and on, my little boat eternally lifted by a wave I had done nothing to create.

"Do you think you can like me anyway?" I asked.

She smiled. "I already do."

We left Regis just after ten, then drove back to Lakeland under the sort of cloudless sky poets call "star-sprinkled."

On the outskirts of town, she said, "Do you still live in that big house you mentioned?"

"You mean, with my father?" I asked. "No, no. I'm renting a little house just off Route 4. Nothing much at all. The big house is in the plantation district."

"I wonder if I've ever been to it."

"Why would you have been?"

"Because my mother and I used to work in those houses," Nora said. "When I was a little girl. You know, cleaning. We worked for lots of those families. The Rankins and the Brantleys."

"What did your father do?"

"Mostly yard work," Nora answered.

"Like Eddie's father," I said. "Do you know much about all that, Eddie's father, what he did?"

Nora shook her head. "I was just a girl when it happened, but I heard it was a crime of passion." Her expression darkened. "He beat her up, you know. Before he killed her."

"Actually, I don't know anything about any of it," I said. "I wasn't living in Lakeland when it happened."

"Oh, it was big news," Nora said. "Linda was pretty. I remember seeing her picture in the paper. And she was on the rise, too, people said."

"On the rise?"

"Heading off to college, climbing up the ladder." She glanced out into the night-bound reaches of the Delta. "A girl from the Bridges can get in trouble doing that. Especially with a man who's stuck on the bottom rung."

I thought of Luther Miller's lowly work, raking lawns, cleaning flower beds.

"Why would Linda have been seeing a man like Luther Miller?" I asked. "A man who was, as you said, 'stuck on the bottom rung.'"

Nora turned to me, a playful glint in her eye. "People on the rise sometimes come back for a little taste of the Bridges." Her smile was impish but knowing, a clever, clever smile. "Even plantation boys go slumming there," she said. "Like you."

———

The porch light was on when we got back to Nora's house, and a large man in his early thirties, dressed in bib overalls, was sitting in a wooden swing.

"That's my brother, Morrell," Nora said.

The man rose and took a step forward. "You said not late," he called to her. "You said not late, Norie." There was a hint of both fear and irritation in his voice, like a child left too long alone.

"He's retarded," Nora told me. She rolled down the window. "It's not that late, Morrell," she called back to him.

Morrell was now at the edge of the porch. "You said not late, Norie."

"Stop it, now," Nora scolded him gently. "I'm coming right in." She faced me. "I had a good time," she said.

"Me, too."

I started to get out, accompany her to the door.

"No, don't," she said. "Morrell's afraid of strangers. Especially at night."

"Okay," I said.

She looked back at me very forthrightly. "It would never be because of money, Jack," she said. "I'm not that kind of Bridges girl."

No one had ever spoken to me more frankly, nor more readily admitted to the suspicions and misapprehensions of class.

"And I'm not slumming," I told her.

She swept forward and kissed me firmly on the mouth. "Okay, everything's clear," she said as she drew away.

ELEVEN

Such were the lingering effects of my evening out with Nora that I dawdled beside the mail slots in the office the following Monday morning hoping to run into her. She didn't appear, however, and so after a time, I stepped out into the adjoining corridor. Students were streaming into the building and clogging the hall. Among them, I glimpsed Eddie Miller making his hunched way toward my class.

I glanced at my watch. There were still a few minutes before the class began, and seeing Eddie, remembering our last conversation, I decided to take a quick look at his file.

Student files were kept in a small room that adjoined the office. They were completely available to faculty but closed to everyone else. I opened the drawer marked "M," flipped through folders, Matheson, Matthews, McCain, until I found "Miller, Edward Luther." It was predictably slender, easy to draw out, light to the touch. A cover sheet with an accompanying photograph detailed the spare facts of Eddie's life: date and place of birth, his parents listed as Luther Ray and Annabelle Miller. There was a notation next to his father's

name, handwritten in the neat script that I recognized as Mrs.
Garraty's: Deceased.

The photograph was black-and-white, and as I looked at
it, I recalled the conversation I'd had with Eddie in the little
grove last week, how he'd mentioned the fact that he sometimes
thought of his father. Luther Ray Miller, deceased? *Not quite,* I
thought.

I turned the page and perused Eddie's academic record.
He'd taken the basic courses in history, science, English, and
math. He'd stopped math at the level of algebra, science at basic
chemistry, and history with the rudimentary requirements in
American and European. He'd taken no advanced classes, and
across the board his grades were average, with a bump up here
and there in English and a bump down in math. It was a
mediocre record that promised more of the same. There were
no citations for misbehavior, and his teachers' comments in-
variably mentioned that he was quiet and well behaved, the
standard positive remark for students who were otherwise completely lackluster when it came to either personal or intellectual attributes. Clearly Eddie had never done or said or written
anything that any of his many teachers had found worth including in the emaciated little folder that contained his history
at Lakeland High.

I closed the folder and again noted the school photograph
that had been clipped to the front, which showed Eddie as a
freshman, his hair somewhat unruly, dressed in a checkered
shirt, a smile on his lips that seemed out of sync with the
slightly troubled aspect I noticed in his eyes, not exactly puzzle-
ment, and certainly not pain, but a sense of being lost in a

perpetual incompleteness, so that I recalled one of the stories in Lewis Carroll, a lock that runs frantically about, searching, searching, as it says, "for the key to me."

"May I help you, Mr. Branch?"

I turned to find Mrs. Garraty standing beside me, and for some reason, the odd look in her eyes brought me up short, as if she'd caught me in the midst of some unwholesome act. Her attention drifted down to the photograph I'd been staring at as she approached.

"Are you looking for anything specific?" she asked.

"No." I closed the folder as if Eddie's freshman photograph were a pornographic picture she'd caught me with. "Nothing specific."

She smiled, but it was a wary smile, not the sort of cheerful one she generally offered. Then she turned, walked to her desk, and appeared to look busy, though it seemed to me that her gaze followed me as I returned the folder to the files, closed the drawer, and left the room.

In the hall, the usual morning bustle was in full swing. From a great height, it would have appeared chaotic, a mad rush in all directions. Only each student's purpose, whether headed to this room or that one, gave direction to an otherwise indecipherable randomness.

My students were already in their seats when I entered the room. They looked surprised that I'd come in last, and when I glanced at the clock, I realized that I'd barely made the bell, which, in turn, meant that I'd spent more time than I thought with Eddie's folder, which was probably what had caused Mrs. Garraty to look at me so strangely, a man lost in suspension, standing motionless, peering at the photograph of a teenage boy as if captured in his spell.

"Good morning," I said, as I stepped behind my lectern.

They shifted about, as always. Stacia Decker flipped open her notebook and reached for her pen. Dirk and Wendell sat in their usual places, but Sheila had moved over one seat, so that she no longer sat directly beside Dirk, a distance he made every effort to ignore, talking to Wendell instead, or sometimes to Doris Blackburn, who, though no beauty, was rumored to please in other ways, and who during the coming years would drift from man to man, having children with them all, until, at forty-three, she at last found love, as the song says, in the arms of a preacher man.

I opened my notes to the appropriate date and looked at the name I'd written beside it, along with the opening line of my lecture: *Edgardo Mortara was twelve years old and living quietly with his family in Bologna, Italy, when, on an otherwise perfectly normal evening, he was kidnapped by the Catholic Church.*

I knew it was an opener that would get their attention, the bizarre notion that a church might seize a child.

"The Mortaras were Jews, and a Christian maid in their household claimed that she had converted and baptized young Edgardo in her faith," I continued. "And by the laws of Italy at that time, converted children could be seized."

But just as I was about to continue through the later course of Edgardo's life and his family's long battle to get him back, I glanced up from my notes and found myself looking squarely at Eddie. He'd been in the same seat since the first day of class, but I'd never gathered the symbolic nature of his choice, how separate and isolated he was. Nor could I tell whether this isolation had actually been a choice or a distance imposed upon him. I knew only that I wanted to narrow the space that separated him from the rest of us, and thought I might be able to do so by simply opening up the subject of murder in a way I hadn't yet come to in my specialty class, the killing of one individual by another, though in the case at hand, there'd been more than one murder, and each had been carried out in very grisly fashion.

"The story of Edgardo Mortara will continue tomorrow," I said, trying to act as if it were merely a preview I'd presented to them. "But for now, I have another story."

I flipped forward through my notes until I reached a later lecture to which I'd clipped the pictures that went with it. I took the celebrated crime-scene photograph most often used in books about the case, placed it on the glass panel of the overhead projector, and turned on the projector. Immediately the disemboweled body of an adult female flashed onto the screen.

"Her name was Catherine Eddowes," I said. "No one knows who did this to her."

I glanced back toward Eddie, who stared transfixed at the photograph.

"Though infamous, her killer is unknown." I allowed the pause called for in my notes. "We have no name from him, save the one he called himself." Another pause. "And that name was 'Jack.'"

———

For the next forty minutes, I detailed the ebony streets of London's infamous Whitechapel, the grim, unlighted neighborhood in which Jack the Ripper's female victims had been murdered and hideously mutilated. It was one of my bloodier lectures, complete with yet more overhead projections of the horribly mutilated corpses of Jack's hapless victims. Through it all, my students reacted like kids at a first-rate horror movie, gasping and shifting in their seats. At one point Wendell Casey had made a great show of wiping his brow with his shirtsleeve. "Wow," he'd breathed. "That's sick." And everybody laughed, though some, like Sheila, only slightly and nervously, unsure as to what her reaction should be to the gruesome aspects of my lecture.

Only Eddie had remained still and silent. He'd appeared to listen with ever-deepening interest as I'd related the chilling facts of the serial murders and mutilations that had terrorized London for several months in 1888, a level of attention that suggested I'd succeeded in moving him closer to writing a paper on his father. For good measure, however, I decided to make a brief detour for Eddie's benefit, introduce the notion that in crimes like those of Jack the Ripper it is inevitable that innocent people are brought under suspicion.

"There were many suspects in the Whitechapel murders," I said. "Some of them were lowly people, tradesmen, day workers. Some were from the professions. One was a doctor. Another was a painter. There was even one suspect from the royal family." I glanced at Eddie. "To be suspect is not the same as to be guilty."

With that, I returned to my original lecture.

"But despite the range of suspects, the true identity of Jack the Ripper was never discovered."

I took the pause my notes instructed. "And so Jack received the fame he sought, but never the penalty he deserved. He got what he wanted, his name in history, and avoided what he didn't, punishment for his crime. In that sense, I suppose, you'd have to conclude that Jack the Ripper won."

It was a shocking little conclusion, and I knew it would send a shallow quiver through the class. As a final note, it was melodramatic to say the least, and shamelessly manipulative in the way it turned the moral order and certainty of judgment they were taught in Sunday school directly on its head. But I hoped it would get them thinking for a moment, linger with them for at least a few seconds, and I'd long ago decided that if I had to use a crude tool to crack open their provincial, religion-encrusted minds a little, so be it.

I asked if there were questions, glanced toward the back of the room, hoping to see Eddie's right hand lift into the air, but it remained in place on the top of his desk.

Stacia Decker asked her usual round of technical questions. Did fingerprinting exist at the time? Could a weapon be traced?

A little time remained before the bell when I answered the last of them. I used it to ask if anyone had decided on the subject for his or her paper. Predictably, Stacia Decker's hand once again flew into the air.

"Adolf Hitler," she said. "He seems more evil than anybody."

Hitler was an obvious and uninspired choice, of course, but I nodded my approval.

"Anyone else?"

Celia Williamson was next. "I would like to write about Judas Iscariot."

I approved Judas, too.

Then Eddie lifted his hand.

"Yes, Eddie?"

"I'd like to write my paper on my father," he said quietly. "His name was Luther Ray Miller."

A charge went through the class, silent but powerful, and in its aftermath everything went briefly still save for Sheila, who shifted around to look at Eddie.

I acted as if I hadn't already suggested that Eddie write about his father. "That's an interesting choice, Eddie," I said. "Very interesting."

I could feel everyone's growing anticipation, the tension with which they waited for my decision. "Approved," I said with a slight smile.

The bell rang and they began to gather up their books and file out of the room. They did this at their usual pace, Stacia and Debbie in the lead. Dirk walked to the door, hung back, and waited for Sheila. It was one of those "let's make up" gestures I'd seen many times before, and so it didn't surprise me when Sheila walked over to Dirk. She said something I couldn't hear, and with that, they turned and walked through the door, though I noticed that as they did, Sheila glanced over her shoulder and stole a quick glance at Eddie.

He was still at his desk, though he'd gotten to his feet and was at that moment tucking a black notebook beneath his arm. He came down the aisle slowly, still a straggler, but with a slightly less hunched posture, as if his public announcement had lifted a tiny weight from his shoulders.

He stopped when he reached me. "I just want to thank you, Mr. Branch, for giving me the idea, you know, to write about my dad."

"I'm sure you'll do a good job," I told him. "Let me know if I can help you."

He nodded. "What happened to that little Jewish boy?" he asked. "Edgardo."

"The church never returned him to his parents," I answered. "He became a priest."

Eddie started to move away, but stopped and turned back to me. "Do you want to see where it happened?" he asked tentatively.

He saw that I didn't know what he meant.

"The shed where my father did it," he explained. "I think I should go. You know, for my paper."

It was obvious that he was not looking forward to visiting so grim a place, least of all alone.

"Sure," I said. "If you want company."

"We could go today," Eddie said. He seemed to fear that I'd back out of going to the shed with him if we didn't do it right away.

"All right," I said quickly and lightly, with no sense of dread, since the steps we take are small, even when they lead us to the gravest things.

And so I wasn't thinking of Eddie or his paper at all later that afternoon when I wandered down to the athletic field and took a seat in the empty bleachers. It was a nice place to read and at the same time take a bit of sun. I was in the midst of doing both when I glanced up from my book and noticed Sheila Longstreet ambling across the field.

She saw me in the bleachers, waved softly, then surprised me by walking over. In the bright sun of that afternoon, her long black hair gleamed almost as mysteriously as her equally dark eyes. Her skin was milk white and seemed to radiate a glow all its own.

"Hi," she said quietly.

I looked up from my book. "Hi."

"I like your class."

"Thank you."

"Usually, I don't think about things like that."

"Like what?"

"You know, bad things. Torture, things like that. Cutting people up. That was horrible, what that guy did."

"Yes, it was horrible."

"People don't like to think about things like that," Sheila said. "They're like my mother."

"What does your mother think about?"

"Jesus, mostly."

"Well, that's as good a thought as any, I suppose."

She knew that I didn't mean it, and the fact that I'd spoken to her in a way that was both glib and false seemed not so much to offend as wound her.

"Well, you probably want to get back to the book," she said softly.

In response to this, I only shrugged, but in that casual, inoffensive movement, she saw that I had no interest in her other than what any man would have in the presence of a beautiful girl. She sensed that I would not mention what I was reading to her, or ask if she had read it or wanted to.

"Sorry to bother you, Mr. Branch," she said.

As she turned, she lowered her head, and her hair fell across the side of her face, and once again I thought of the women of the *Minsk*, only this time as victims of a very different form of low regard.

I saw all this, but I knew it was too late to feign an estimation higher than the low one I'd already shown, so I simply returned to my book, expecting her to amble back to the school, link arms with Dirk, and spend the rest of the day dully going through the usual motions of her life. But she stopped instead, held a moment, then turned back to face me.

"I think it's good you're letting Eddie write that paper," she said.

Now was my chance to make up for the slight I'd unwittingly offered her. I closed my book firmly, a gesture meant to suggest that I preferred conversing with her than continuing to read it. "I'm glad you think so," I said. "I wasn't sure at first."

"No, you did the right thing," Sheila said. "He needs to write that paper. It's like he's this kid in a house, you know? And there's this room in the house and everybody says, 'Don't go in that room. There's bad stuff in that room.' So he has to go into it."

I decided to draw her out on this point if for no other reason than to continue the ruse I had begun. "Why do think he has to go into it?" I asked.

"Because if he doesn't, he'll always be afraid of what's there." She shook her head. "Nobody should live like that."

I smiled. "No, nobody," I said.

She returned my smile. "He'll be okay," she assured me.

"I'm sure he will," I said.

And I saw no reason why he wouldn't.

TWELVE

It was around five in the afternoon when I pulled into Eddie's driveway. His van was parked in front, but the old blue Chevy I'd seen the night I'd dropped him off was gone.

He came out of the house immediately, holding a plain black notebook I'd seen earlier in class. A yellow pencil peeped from his shirt pocket.

"You look like a reporter," I told him.

The puzzled look on Eddie's face made it clear just how inconsequential he'd been made to feel during his years at Lakeland. Obviously no one had ever suggested, even by some casual reference to his appearance, that his fate was anything but sealed. Throughout his years at Lakeland, he'd existed as a presence barely noticed by either his teachers or his classmates. In fact, I surmised that had his father not murdered a hapless young woman, Eddie would have been more or less invisible, and so left simply to sink, as Willa Cather once wrote, "into the immense design of things."

"So," I said. "Where's the shed?"

He nodded softly and pointed toward the woods behind

his house. "It's up an old logging road. There was a time when you could drive up it, but not anymore."

We walked toward the break in the woods Eddie indicated and which now looked like an actual road with parallel ruts through otherwise impenetrable undergrowth.

"My father drove partway up the road that day," he said.

The day of the murder, he meant, and to which he seemed to be returning with each step he took.

"But it had been raining, and the road got muddy, and he was afraid to go all the way up," he continued. "So he got her out and made her walk the rest of the way to the shed."

"How do you know that?" I asked.

"My mother told me," Eddie answered. "She knows a lot about it, so I put her at the top of my list."

"List?"

"Of people who knew my father."

"Oh, yes," I said, pleased that he'd taken my first little suggestion. "Of course you could also read the trial transcript," I added. "My father knows people at the courthouse, so I could help you get that."

"But my dad never had a trial," Eddie told me. "He got killed by another prisoner." He handed me the black notebook. "I started it already." His intention was clear. "Just to see if I'm on the right track."

I opened the notebook and read the first lines of his paper:

She may have heard little animals in the bushes that were all around her. She may have seen a bird, too, in a tree or flying overhead. Or maybe she was too afraid and it was all a blur and so she didn't notice anything around her but my father walking behind her. Her head is bowed when I imagine her, and her hands are tied, which they were, so at least I know I get that right. Her hair hangs across the side of her face like I once heard described the women on the Minsk. Her hair is always trembling when I see her, because she is always crying, soft, like a little kitten does, but human, and with this little question at the end, like she's asking herself: Is this really happening to me?

The writing was very simple, with the usual tendency toward run-on sentences to be expected from so untutored a young writer. I was flattered that he'd made reference, however awkwardly, to something he'd learned in my lectures, of course. But apart from all that, I found myself somewhat surprised and even slightly impressed by Eddie's plainspoken portrayal of Linda Gracie's last moments on earth, not only her terror and her suffering, how dark and deep it had surely been, but her consternation, the sheer unreality of suddenly finding herself in a world abruptly changed from the one she'd lived in moments before, and which she would scarcely have been able to imagine before it overwhelmed her.

"Is it okay?" Eddie asked.

"It's better than okay," I told him.

"But too many 'hers,'" he said. "Ten 'hers.' I counted them." He took the notebook from my hand. "Look, right there. A 'her' at the end of a sentence. Then another 'her' at the beginning of the next one." He looked up. "Too many 'hers.' It doesn't sound right."

I knew what he meant. "Just take out the first one there," I instructed, "so that the sentence ends with 'behind.'"

He thought a moment. "That's right," he said. He crossed out the first "her." "That makes it better."

"Things like that are easy to fix," I told him. "But what you've written has a feel to it. That's hard to do, but you've done it."

A smile broke over him, along with a visible wave of relief, so that he looked like a long-thirsty boy who'd just been given an unexpected drink of water.

"Then you think I should keep going with it?" he asked.

Fatefully, I said, "I do."

Eddie made no notes as we walked up the road, though I noticed that his gaze was continually shifting, sometimes directed into the trees, sometimes into the surrounding undergrowth. But though his attention changed, it remained concentrated. As if equipped with tiny antennae, his eyes seemed not just to see objects but to absorb their waves.

"How do you know where it is?" I asked after we'd been walking for about ten minutes.

"My father took me there a few times," Eddie answered. "We'd go on walks in the woods. He carried me on his shoulders."

We continued down the road, brushing away the encroaching growth as we moved forward. The ruts narrowed slightly the farther we went into the woods, but the way never became difficult. It was easy to talk as we continued on, and Eddie, for that matter, seemed driven to do just that.

"My mother kept some clippings," he told me. "They're in this old scrapbook."

"That's a good place to start," I said. "The written record." It seemed an opportunity to give a little added instruction. "There are two kinds of sources, you know. Primary, which are things like letters and journals, diaries and government documents. And secondary, which are history books and newspaper accounts. The clippings your mother has in that scrapbook would be called secondary."

He stopped and turned toward me. "Do you want to read them, Mr. Branch?"

In light of the pledge I'd made only minutes before, I told him that I did.

"Okay," Eddie said. "I'll get them for you when we get back."

We continued down the road and didn't stop or speak again until we reached the shed, a structure Eddie, in one of his later drafts, described not only physically but as a reflection of his father's way of thinking:

The shed my father used was built from wood he'd stolen from the sawmill outside town. He would go there at night and steal wood or whatever else he could find laying around because he didn't see the border between what was his and what was someone else's, so if it was there, and no one was watching, it became his just because it would be his if he took it. He felt this way about everything, that whatever he wanted ought to be his just because he wanted it and it didn't matter if it belonged to someone else before he took it for himself. The chicken wire he put around the garden was stolen, and the rope he used to make me a swing in the front yard, which was the same he used to tie Linda Gracie's hands.

Only then did he move on to a physical description of the shed itself:

It was just scrap wood and the planks had never been painted or weather-treated and so they cracked and bowed out and got moldy almost as soon as he nailed them in place. Because of that the wood turned gray, and looked sick, like it had flu or TB or pneumonia. The shed always looked like it needed to spit. There was a tin roof that wasn't very high and trails of rust ran from the top of the roof to where gutters should have been, but there weren't any, and so when it rained, the water came pouring off the roof in little yellow streams that looked (maybe I shouldn't write this and I can take it out, Mr. Branch, if you think I should) like pee.

Eddie went into the shed first, though he hesitated just an instant before he pressed against its already slightly open door. There was a cry of rusty hinges followed by the sound of something skittering across the interior floor, a field mouse, perhaps, or a small squirrel.

"I guess something lives in here," he said. He pushed the door with more force and it swung fully open, so that I saw how dirty the interior space was, the floor covered with dried mud and shriveled leaves, along with scores of cigarette butts and charred match stems.

"My father smoked all the time," Eddie told me. He walked farther into the shed and stood almost at the center of its cramped space.

I remained at the door because it seemed to me that this was more Eddie's place than mine. The crime his father had committed here had ended Linda Gracie's life, but it had ended some aspects of Eddie's, too, made of him at least half an orphan, as well as a local curiosity: the Coed Killer's son.

He glanced out the window, where the surrounding woods pressed in close upon the shed, a wall of tangled green. For a moment he seemed to be attempting to unravel some element of its entanglement, a vine here, a leaf there.

"In the paper, they had a picture," he said. "It was made right here, inside the shed. There was a shovel and a bag of lime." He looked back into the shed as if trying to place these phantom items, the shed's grim inventory, in the exact place where he'd seen them in the photograph.

"Did you see your father that day?" I asked.

The question clearly drew him back to that very instant.

"He was supposed to come home early because we didn't have any groceries," he said. "He told my mother he knew where he could get some money and I guess that's where he went." He shook his head slowly. "But when he came back home, he still didn't have any money, she said, so we didn't have supper that night."

I saw him suddenly as that hungry little boy, as needful as the one I'd imagined at the Confederate Orphanage, sitting in a shadowy corner, forever doomed to wait for a bounty that, without miraculous intervention, would surely never come.

He bowed his head briefly, silent, thoughtful, then lifted it again. "We should head back now, Mr. Branch," he said. "It'll be dark soon."

In fact, the air had already taken on a hint of evening shade by the time we got back to Eddie's house. He asked me to wait on the porch while he retrieved the newspaper clippings from his mother's room. Through the screen door, I could see the sparse furnishings of the living room, an old sofa and a few chairs, a frayed rug spread over unvarnished pine flooring. The kitchen was in the back. I could make out a stove and a squat little refrigerator, but nothing else. It was all very spare, and I felt oddly ill at ease in the presence of such lowliness, as if it were an embarrassment, something a stranger shouldn't see. And so I walked down the stairs and stood in the yard, forcing myself to face away from the house, until something drew me back to it, the unlighted windows, the creaking wooden stairs, the ragged swing in which I imagined Eddie as a child of five, waiting hungrily—and this in the most literal sense—for his father to come home.

Seconds later the Eddie of present time came back out of the house. There was an old scrapbook in his hands that looked like a tattered family album.

"Your paper's going to be very good," I assured him, and at that moment felt the scrapbook quiver slightly, something stirring within it, not in a sinister way, but as an awakening hope, as if within the dark things they recorded, Eddie might find a guiding light and follow it to a better life.

THIRTEEN

I got home a few minutes later, and had just started to open the scrapbook Eddie had given me when the phone rang. The voice on the other end came in quick gasps. "Jack, could you come over."

The problem was obvious and familiar. I'd dealt with it before. "I'll be right there," I said.

My father was sitting in the library when I arrived. He was smoking a cigarette, as he always did after these episodes, and which he claimed had a "calming influence." In fact, he did now appear somewhat calmer than when he'd called minutes ago.

"Everything settled down now?" I asked.

He took a quick draw on the cigarette. "Yes," he said. He carefully lowered the tip of the cigarette to the rim of the crystal ashtray on the table beside his chair. "I shouldn't have bothered you."

The waves came upon him suddenly and without warning. They'd started three weeks after the "incident," and his doctor had told him that they were the product of some unspecified damage to his nervous system. Each attack began with a sense of growing terror, followed by a fierce wave of it, like a car hurtling toward him, too fast to outrun or avoid, and yet suspended in its furious velocity while he stood frozen in its lethal path, wave after wave of panic sweeping over him, each stronger than the last, drawing energy as it passed, so that at the end of it he collapsed like a deflated balloon and merely sat, silent and inert, until slowly the energy returned.

He looked entirely drained at the moment, and so I knew this latest attack had been a particularly severe one.

"Is there anything you need?" I asked. "Water?"

He glanced at the liquor cabinet. "I think I'd rather have a glass of port."

"I'll get it for you."

"No," he said, almost sharply. "No, let me."

He rose and walked to the nearby cabinet, his movements weak but also edgy, like a man on a ledge or a tightrope, a fearful space beneath him. "Care to join me?" he asked.

"It's a bit early for me."

"What a correct young man you are, Jack," he said somewhat mirthlessly, as if such correctness were a disappointment to him. "So very . . . correct."

"Perhaps only too little tempted," I joked.

"Speaking of which," my father said, "how are you faring with this new girl of yours?"

I'd told him about Nora at our last dinner, how spirited and appealing she was, how I suspected undiscovered depths.

"Very well, I think," I answered.

"Am I to be introduced at some point?"

"At the right moment."

"And that will be?"

"Yet to be determined," I said.

My father lifted his glass. "My curiosity stands rebuked." He returned to his chair and took another sip of port. "Love," he said quietly, almost privately, as if only to himself, "can come from the strangest place."

"You mean the Bridges?" I asked.

"No," my father answered. "But desire can be a guttersnipe, don't you think?"

"A guttersnipe? In what way?"

He waved his hand, now dismissing what he'd just said. "I was probably thinking of that French phrase: *La nostalgie de la boue.*" He glanced toward the self-portrait of van Gogh. "The allure of the gutter."

For a moment he seemed lost in thought, then, just as quickly, he returned to the present.

"So you were reading," he said, though without his usual degree of interest so that I knew he was only making conversation, and even doing that out of mere courtesy, since he'd summoned me and I'd come to him, and so he now felt obligated to speak with me awhile before he showed me the door. "Suetonius?"

"No," I said. "I was just about to read some old newspaper clippings when you called."

He rested his faintly trembling hands in his lap. "Does that mean you've lost interest in Tiberius?"

"No," I answered. "It's just that this evening he wasn't the particular evil person I was reading about."

He drew the glass toward his lips. "Who was?"

"The Coed Killer," I answered.

The glass stopped its ascent. "You're reading newspaper clippings about Luke Miller?"

"Luke?"

"That's what he was called at Lakeland."

"You taught him?"

"Yes," my father answered. "Along with every other child in town. Or should I say, every Bridges child."

"Does that mean you taught Linda Gracie, too?"

"Of course I did, Jack," my father said. "Lakeland is a small town. Its poor go to the same school." He took a sip from his glass. "How did you happen to come by these clippings?"

"His son is a student in my class on evil," I said. "Eddie."

My father's light blue eyes watched me silently but he said nothing.

"Do you think I ever saw Linda Gracie?" I asked.

"Why would you have?"

"Well, you sometimes brought students here, didn't you?"

"Only certain students," my father answered. "To see the art. The architecture. To feel the history. Linda would not have been favored."

"So you never got caught up in the investigation?" I asked.

My father looked at me as if I were one of the interrogators in the books I had assigned, a figure in wire glasses, with a twitchy rodent face and eyes that gnawed like little yellow teeth. "Of her murder? Why would I have been involved in that?"

"Sometimes you can just get pulled into something," I told him. "I did."

"You?"

"When Sheila Longstreet went missing last week," I explained. "The girl from Lakeland High. The one who turned up later. I got embroiled in the investigation." I smiled, remembering the little figure in the half-light, a smooth dark hand on the pale bowl of a meerschaum pipe. "Sheriff Drummond actually came to my house."

"Poor Drummond," my father said. "With that meerschaum pipe." He laughed. "Such clownish airs." He raised the port to his mouth, took a slow sip, then set the glass down on the table beside his chair, his thoughts now turned toward the past, as I could see. "But at least he escaped the Bridges, which is very hard to do."

I thought I might reap some benefit from his experience, and so I said, "Can you predict the ones who will? Among students, I mean."

"Not really," my father answered. "I was many times surprised."

"But suppose you had a particular student," I said. "One you thought might have some potential. What would be your . . . strategy?"

"I'd start by offering him a vision," my father said. "A feeling that it's not impossible." He made the correct surmise. "Who is this student?"

"Eddie Miller," I answered. "I don't think it's ever occurred to anyone at Lakeland that he might achieve something."

"Why has it occurred to you?"

"Well, this afternoon he showed me the shed where Linda

Gracie was killed. He read me a few lines he'd written about it. The writing was very simple, but it also had something."

I thought of what Eddie had written, his description of a Linda Gracie force-marched through the woods toward the shed in which she was to die, her hair trembling softly as she cried.

"It seemed heartfelt," I added.

My father rose, walked to the liquor cabinet, poured himself another port, and with his glass firmly in hand, returned to his chair. "Heartfelt," he said softly, on a weary breath. "That's the most important thing, I suppose."

"Which is why I wanted to help him with the assignment."

My father plucked a cigarette from the silver case that lay open on the table next to him and shot me an inquiring glance. "Assignment?"

"To pick an evil person and write about him."

"Or her," my father reminded me. "Women can be evil, too, you know. In revenge and love, more barbarous than man. So Nietzsche said." He perused the shelves of books for a moment, clearly gathering his thoughts. "Tell me then, if you've become an expert on evil, which do you consider the most tempting of the seven deadly sins?"

"Pride," I answered. "It hurled an angel out of paradise." I smiled, happy that we were now engaged in just the sort of intellectual banter my father seemed to prefer in his conversations with me. "And you?"

"Desire," my father answered immediately.

"Why that one?"

"Because it isn't a thing of the mind," my father said. "It is purely of the body, and because of that, beyond our control."

"Yes, but . . ."

My father waved his hand. "Enough," he said. "I'm sorry to be rude, Jack. But I'm quite tired."

He rose, and proper in his manners as always, politely escorted me to the door.

"My apologies for this abrupt end to the evening," he said. He placed his hand on my shoulder and gave a weak squeeze, his usual gesture of farewell, and beyond which he never went, so that I'd long ago learned to expect only this fleeting physical contact, my father not a man of hugs.

"I do appreciate your devotion, Jack," he added.

"I'll always come to your aid," I promised him with a gallant flourish.

He smiled. "May hosts of angels see thee to thy rest," he said.

FOURTEEN

Once at home, I took the scrapbook Eddie had given me to the small breakfast table in the kitchen and opened it, fully expecting to see a picture of Luther Ray Miller already in custody, but saw Linda Gracie instead, her high school photo on the front page of the *Lakeland Telegraph*. The headline read simply: MISSING COED LEAVES FEW CLUES.

In the photograph, Linda Gracie is smiling brightly, her hair pulled back in a ponytail, her large, somewhat oval eyes peering languidly into the camera. She is incontestably attractive, though hers was not the icy beauty of classical sculpture but the sultriness of a vamp, her face composed of oddly disparate parts, a cracked and rearranged beauty without the precise balance and proportion that usually create it.

Or was that merely an affect, I wondered, the impression of something beneath her features that gave them a sense of being discordant?

I drew my attention away from the photograph and read the article that detailed her disappearance.

She'd simply vanished, according to the story, leaving her car in a deserted spot deep inside Glenford Park. The car had been spotted by a park ranger who'd reported it to the state police. They'd traced it to Linda, gone to her house in the Bridges, and searched her room. They'd also questioned her mother and a few neighbors, though the paper gave no hint of anything they'd learned, and certainly nothing of the romantic attachment about which Nora had spoken.

I turned to the next clipping, dated two days later. There was another picture of Linda Gracie, along with an update on the current state of the investigation. The police had found no sign of a struggle inside her car. Nor had they found anything in the surrounding woods to suggest that Linda had ever gone into them.

A thorough search of the forest and trails has disclosed nothing of Miss Gracie's whereabouts to police, and there is some doubt that she ever entered the wooded areas of the park at all, though authorities are quick to point out that this is purely speculation.

The story detailed another speculation, as well, that Linda had come to Glenford Park as a "point of rendezvous" with a person she already knew, though the nature of that relationship remained unstated.

The uncertainty continued throughout the following day. The headline told the story: CASE OF MISSING COED STILL BAFFLES POLICE.

There was a second picture of Linda Gracie, this one taken

with books clutched to her chest, smiling. It was far more casual than the other photograph, and in it Linda stands with her back pressed against a brick column. She has thrown back her head, and lifted one leg, bent at the knee and turned inward like a prancing majorette. It is a coquettish pose, and yet I couldn't help but wonder if there had been more to her than that, though I failed to pose the question Eddie later asked and tried to answer in a draft of his paper:

> I know that she fought very hard to live. Maybe everyone does in a situation like that, with someone about to kill you. Or maybe it's just that Linda Gracie had come up hard, and had taken a lot, but still had big hopes, anyway, like for college in the fall. So maybe she fought really hard for her life because she'd really wanted to change it.

During the next two days, the investigation moved forward predictably. The area around Breaker Landing was thoroughly searched a second time, but with no better results. As far as anyone could tell, Linda Gracie had gone there, gotten out of her car without locking it, and vanished into thin air. One story, this one from the *Lakeland Telegraph,* reached a grim conclusion:

> With no clues to Miss Gracie's current whereabouts, nor the circumstances relating to her disappearance, authorities now must depend on the public for some break in the case.

The break came two days later in the form of a park ranger's report. On a rainy day nearly a week earlier, the officer had been at his post on a watchtower in Glenford Park. From that height, he'd seen a wisp of smoke at the far western edge of the park where it bordered Chambers Road. The smoke had quickly dissipated, and the park ranger had thought nothing more of it. But later he took out his incident book and noticed that he'd spotted this unexpected smoke on the day Linda Gracie disappeared, a very rainy day, unlikely to have campfires. No body had been found. A young woman had vanished without a trace. Could it be, he'd wondered . . . could it be?

Within hours of his call, the authorities were moving down the old logging road toward the shed.

The next day's headline told it all: LOCAL MAN QUESTIONED IN COED DISAPPEARANCE.

The "local man," of course, was Luther Ray Miller, identified by name and labeled, for the first time, as the "suspected killer of coed Linda Gracie," a married man, the Jackson paper reported, with a five-year-old son.

Before that night, I'd seen no photograph of Luther Ray Miller, and he was far more handsome than I'd imagined. He was twenty-five years old, but although he was both a husband and a father, there was nothing about him that looked domesticated. Just the opposite, in fact. There was a feral quality in his eyes, like an animal on the prowl. I could almost imagine him pouncing, pantherlike, from an overhanging limb. To be within his power, held within his clutches, as Linda Gracie had been briefly, seemed terrible beyond words.

The final clipping added little more to this picture. There was another photograph of Luther Ray Miller, this one a mug shot, complete with a number plastered across his chest. It was no doubt the picture that had been taken immediately after his arrest. He was dressed in work clothes, a flannel open-collar shirt that appeared badly wrinkled and with a frayed collar, a poor man's clothes.

Then suddenly, he was dead.

The relevant details were few and spare. After giving a complete confession, Luther Miller had been returned to his cell, where within a few hours he'd been killed by his cellmate.

Two days later Luther Ray Miller was buried in that part of the old town cemetery that is reserved for the indigent among us, a little field of small gray stones.

A final photograph recorded the burial. It was a very modest affair, with few mourners. Mrs. Miller stands beside the grave, and next to her, with his arms held rigidly to his sides, dressed in a jacket at least a size too big for him, a little five-year-old boy with long dark hair.

So there Eddie stood, a child watching his father lowered into the ground, a man he could hardly have known and of whose dark propensities he could not have known at all. How powerfully it must have appealed to him, I thought, my suggestion that he should write a paper on his father. What an opportunity it must surely have provided for him to reopen that long-closed grave, discover what was still discoverable about the man whose name and grim legacy he bore.

All of that was clear.

What remained unclear to me as I turned the last page of the scrapbook was that others might react differently to his paper.

By a week later, however, that was clear, as well.

FIFTEEN

On the following Monday morning I learned that news of Eddie's paper had spread through Lakeland High School like wildfire.

Eddie Miller is writing about his murderous father. This, as it turned out, was big news.

Over the last week, and quite predictably, the content of Eddie's classroom declaration had gone through the usual rumor mill and emerged in various guises. According to one "eyewitness account," Eddie had told the class that he'd actually seen the murdered girl's body. A second version claimed that he'd helped his father cut it up and bury it. Yet a third spread the equally groundless but far graver notion that Eddie had actually been made to participate in the killing.

Eddie had not said any of these things of course, but that didn't matter. He was the talk of Lakeland High, and so was the class in which he'd allegedly made such disturbing and revelatory statements. Suddenly my little specialty class was propelled from the featureless mound of instruction that made up the school's general curriculum and sent soaring into celebrity, a

genuine, if macabre and grossly exaggerated agitation of the waters that had even penetrated the walled precincts of Lakeland
High School's administrative offices.

"Mr. Rankin would like to see you," Mrs. Garraty told me
when she spotted me just outside the office door.

She indicated the principal's office. "He's waiting."

Douglas Rankin had once been an attorney, but he'd left
his practice years ago and had taken up school administration.
He'd been the head of Lakeland High for more than thirty
years, and he had about him the air of a man who'd seen much
of life's varied troubles and to whom nothing human was truly
alien. At seventy-six he was said to be the oldest public-school
principal in the state. He carried himself with a physical grace
and sense of command he'd probably gained in the blood and
thunder of the Ardennes, where he'd won a medal for valor he'd
never spoken of and which no one had ever seen. His voice was
soft and gentlemanly, and I'd never heard him raise it. In the
years of his tenure he had dealt with all manner of afflictions:
alcoholic teachers and depressed ones, teachers who fell in love
and out of it, teachers stricken with terrible diseases in the face
of which they either stood firm or crumbled. He'd confronted
the personal problems and idiosyncrasies of hundreds upon
hundreds of students, all the contortions of character a human
world could produce. And yet, for all that, he seemed to sense
that what faced him now was new.

"Good morning, Jack," he said as I came into the office.
He nodded toward one of the two chairs that sat in front of his
desk. "Please."

I sat down and waited, the notes for my lecture solidly in

my lap, where I placed my hands, as if I expected him to snatch them from me and toss them into the large metal wastebasket beside his desk.

"How's your father?"

"Fine."

"Please give him my best."

"I shall."

With these niceties now completed, Mr. Rankin lowered himself into the old wooden swivel chair behind his desk and ceremoniously unhooked the bottom button of his vest. "It's come to my attention that Eddie Miller's writing a paper," he said.

"Yes, he is," I said.

Mr. Rankin gazed at me silently, and I saw that I was in the presence of a master interrogator, not the physically intimidating sort who populated the books I'd assigned, but a man who questioned you by asking—with a peculiarly Southern politeness—that you kindly question yourself.

"It's for my specialty class," I explained. "The assignment is to write about an evil person. Eddie chose his father."

Mr. Rankin closed his eyes and began to rock softly back and forth in his chair. "He's writing about his father. Hmm." When his eyes opened again, they seemed oddly prescient, as if he were able to take any presently forming human situation and project its volatile course through time, knew well before the experiment was done that this chemical when combined with that one always resulted in explosion.

"When I made the assignment I didn't say that it had to be

a famous person," I told him. "So when Eddie asked if he could write about his father, I didn't see how I could disapprove of it."

Mr. Rankin looked somewhat baffled by my reasoning, as if it indicated an abandonment of responsibility, perhaps even some level of adulthood.

"A teacher can disapprove of anything that isn't of benefit to the student," he said. He leaned forward very slightly, and yet in so large a man the forward shift seemed mountainous. "That is, in fact, part of the job, isn't it?"

"Yes, of course," I said.

"So clear judgment is everything," Mr. Rankin added. "Sometimes at a moment's notice." Now he resumed his former position, pressing his enormous back against the wooden curve of his chair. What he said next, despite the years, still echoes through my mind. "So fast, the choices we must make, both good and bad."

But at the time, this statement seemed no more than a platitude. I didn't even bother to nod my head in agreement or question, either him or myself, as to what it had to do with Eddie's paper.

"I think Eddie's paper will help him," I said.

"In what way?" Mr. Rankin asked.

I answered him with the full confidence of my bottomless inexperience. "Mr. Rankin," I said, "Eddie Miller has always been set apart by what his father did. It's hardly ever mentioned, of course, but that doesn't change the fact that everybody knows it. I think it would do him good to have it all out in the open." I paused, waited, then went for broke. "As a matter of fact, I think it would be of benefit to the whole school, probably the whole town."

"And all the vaulted heavens, no doubt," Mr. Rankin said with a smile whose meaning I couldn't read. He removed the gold wire-rimmed glasses from his eyes and began to rub the lenses with a Kleenex plucked from the box on his desk and which alerted me to the fact that he must have seen many tears shed in this office, students, teachers, parents, and that of all the people I'd thus far come to know, he was the most deeply schooled in breakdown and recovery.

"I'll look out for Eddie," I assured him.

Mr. Rankin regarded me silently for a moment, still rubbing the lenses of his glasses, a movement I suddenly interpreted as no less calculated for effect than my own stage gestures. Then he said, "A difficult circumstance once taught me that it's not altogether a good thing for a teacher to become overinvolved in a student's life." He returned the glasses to his eyes, and looked at me as I thought he must have looked at the young soldiers of the First World War, replacements fresh from training, who'd come under his command, anxious but unseasoned, eager to spill blood until they saw it spilled.

"All right, Jack," he said, his tone tentative, guarded, unsure of the decision he was at that very instant making. "I'll trust your judgment in this matter."

He rose and shook my hand, a firm grasp that had held pistol grips and raised rifles in steady aim, then escorted me out of the office and all the way to a corridor now crowded with students on their way to class. He said nothing else, but simply watched as the students of Lakeland High flowed by, his gaze oddly melancholy, as if he could see the battle they faced, hand-icapped by poor equipment and clothed too lightly for the cold.

At the end of the hall, I glanced back toward the office to see if he were still there, but by then he'd turned and vanished into its inner precincts to oversee budgets and referee conflicts and somehow get the job done. He retired a year later, in the wake of our town tragedy, and died seven years after that, his body found by his only daughter, sitting upright in his bed, with no book in his lap, the television turned off, nothing on the radio, perhaps thinking in that silence of the things he'd done right and the things he'd done wrong, of teachers he'd correctly kept a grip on and of others, like me, he'd trusted to his vast regret.

Forty-five minutes later, at the end of my specialty class I asked if any of my students wanted to give a progress report on the paper he or she was working on. I'd expected Stacia Decker to go first and so had braced myself to receive a stupefying list of Adolf Hitler's already well-known crimes, but it was Eddie's hand that rose into the air.

I stepped from behind my lectern. "All yours," I said.

He came forward slowly, but with what struck me as an in-contestable determination to see it through. At the lectern, he opened the black notebook he seemed to carry with him con-tinually now, paused a moment, and began.

"My father's name was Luther Ray Miller," he said. "When I was five years old, he murdered a seventeen-year-old girl named Linda Elizabeth Gracie. I was home the day he did it."

I leaned forward slightly in the way I liked to see my own students lean forward, strain to hear, drawn toward me by the tale I told.

"She was tied up in the back of my father's van when it went up the logging road near our house," Eddie continued. "I was sitting on the porch of our house. I saw my father's van go up that road."

He glanced at his notes, then back up at the class, where Sheila Longstreet was sitting just in front of him, staring at him intently with her blue-moon eyes.

"I'm making a list of the people who knew my father," Eddie continued. "My mother is on that list. There are some teachers who knew my father and some people my father worked for, and kept a list of, and I'd like to talk to them." He drew a quick breath. "There may be some police records, too. These would be primary sources." He glanced down at his notebook. "I have newspaper clippings my mother keeps in an old scrapbook. These are secondary sources, but good for the basic information about what happened."

With that he closed the notebook and stepped away from the lectern.

"Can I ask a question?"

It was Sheila who spoke and she wasn't asking me. She was focused entirely upon Eddie.

He moved back behind the lectern, utterly surprised, and glanced at me. "Is it okay?"

"Sure," I said. "Go ahead, Sheila."

"When did you start thinking about writing this paper?" Sheila asked.

"Mr. Branch gave me the idea," Eddie answered. "And it seemed like a good idea, because I think about my dad a lot." With that a small floodgate released, and more flowed out of him. "I mean, I even see him sometimes. I'll be sitting on the porch, and there's this swing in the front yard, and I see him standing behind it, like when I was a little kid."

Sheila's question appeared to give others in the class leave to ask their own questions. Stacia Decker's hand lifted. Eddie acknowledged her with a nod.

"Does he seem like a ghost when you see him like that?"

"No, it's not like he's a ghost. It's like a memory, only with more shape."

Dirk and Wendell exchanged baffled glances, both clearly amazed that Eddie Miller, of all people, had managed simultaneously to raise the interest of a brain like Stacia and a beauty like Sheila.

"And sometimes, there's music," Eddie said. "Behind what I'm seeing, like in a movie."

I could see Eddie's mind moving through a series of very subtle machinations. Then he looked directly at Sheila.

"There was music the day I let you out," he told her. "I watched you go in the rearview mirror. Down Clearwater, remember?"

Sheila nodded softly, and something in her eyes, the way she stared at Eddie, suddenly got Dirk's attention.

"I could see my face in the mirror," Eddie added. "And then all of a sudden it was my father's face." He was still gazing at Sheila. "And he was looking at you in this really scary way, like I thought he must have looked at Linda Gracie." He drew his eyes from Sheila and faced the class. "And there was this . . . music . . . that was scary."

He continued to stand behind the lectern, the class utterly silent before him, expectant, attentive, wanting more, so that he suddenly no longer seemed completely invisible nor an outcast. For he had become, abruptly and miraculously, it seemed to me, a storyteller.

But it was a spell that lasted for only a second or two before it was rudely and purposefully broken.

"You think you're like your old man?" Dirk Littlefield blurted.

Eddie's eyes sprang over to Dirk. "No, I don't," he said.

And with that he stepped away from the lectern and headed down the aisle toward his seat.

I waited until he was safely in it before I resumed my own place behind the lectern. "Anybody else want to make a progress report?"

To my surprise, Sheila rose and stepped behind the lectern.

"We hear that little kids get killed sometimes," she began. "But it hardly ever happens that a little kid kills another little kid." She swept back her hair, though not in a coquettish fashion. "It happens though."

It was a dramatic opening, I thought, one she'd probably learned from my own lecture style, blunt-force introductions meant to grab the attention of the class, which hers, as I saw, quite obviously had.

Sheila went on to describe the murder of two small boys, four years old and three years old. The murders had occurred in Connors, Georgia, she said, and a book had been written about them. She'd found the book at the town dump, where her mother routinely went to retrieve "chipped cups and dishes and other stuff people throw out." With that, she'd returned to the murdered boys, the investigation that followed, and finally the arrest, trial, and conviction, in 1927, of Julie Ann Fogg, an eleven-year-old girl.

"You're probably thinking that these two kids were murdered at the same time," Sheila continued. "But they weren't. It was six weeks from one to the other. So it seems to me that maybe the first murder gave this girl a taste for it. So six weeks later she killed again, and who knows how many little boys she might have killed if she hadn't gotten caught." She smiled. "Does anybody have any questions?"

I looked out over the class. Stacia Decker was at full note-taking attention, as was her friend Debbie Link. Dirk was slouched at his desk, a notebook in front of him, idly drawing squares and rectangles. Wendell was fully occupied in tying his right shoelace, an action George Frobish seemed to find completely mesmerizing.

None of them had questions, so I raised my hand.

Sheila nodded.

"Do you think Julie Fogg was evil from the beginning?" I asked.

I expected a quick, unelaborated yes, but Sheila considered the matter for a moment then said, "Well, one thing bothers me. This was in the book. The writer went back to talk to a lot of people, and he found out that when Julie was just born and the nurse tried to hand her to her mother, her mother pushed her away and screamed at the nurse. 'Take that thing away from me!' That's what she told the nurse. 'Thing,' like it wasn't even a person."

Before I could comment on this, Dirk yelped, "So what?"

Sheila glared at him silently, a look that seemed briefly to put him off balance.

"I mean, she enjoyed it, didn't she?" Dirk demanded.

Sheila smoldered silently.

"You said it yourself, Sheila," Dirk taunted. "You said she got a taste for it." He looked at Wendell for approval and instantly got it. "And it tasted good to her." Now he glared at Sheila. "You did say that, right?"

"Yeah," said Sheila with a dull shrug.

"Well what else could it be but she liked it, and that's why she did it," Dirk said triumphantly. "Her mother didn't want her, so what? I mean, she didn't do it because she needed money or something. Or because she was mad at those kids. She didn't even know 'em. She enjoyed it. That's why she did it." He paused a moment, peering about, seeking, as always, a level of approval or admiration he would never in his life receive. "Right?" he demanded.

A few in the class nodded, but that was enough for Dirk. He smiled as if he'd achieved some kind of victory, then looked at Sheila like a man anticipating a kiss, though what he got in return was a look of such fiery rebuke I immediately stepped in to douse the flame.

"Okay, let's move on," I said, then quickly stood and nodded for Sheila to resume her seat.

"Anyone else?" I asked.

When none of the students responded, I shifted my gaze to Dirk.

"How about you?" I asked.

Dirk blinked quickly. "Me?"

"Well, you had a lot to say about Eddie's paper, and Sheila's," I said. "I thought you might want to give a preview of your own."

He knew what I was doing and why, and I could almost see a blue smoke rising from his ears. "I ain't ready yet," he barked.

I knew he wanted to get off the hook, but I had the line in hand and continued to tug at it.

"Have you at least picked a subject?" I asked.

Dirk's eyes swept over to Wendell like a wrestler in a tag-team match. "No, I ain't," he said.

Then he turned back toward me with the sort of glare that closes every pathway to understanding or any hope of reconciliation, and which in all the years that followed, never left his eyes when they looked on mine.

"You hear what I said?" he asked. "I ain't picked it yet."

Abruptly, as if on a signal, everyone rose and began gathering books and papers so that I realized that, for the first time in my career, I had not heard the bell.

SIXTEEN

As he would on many similar occasions, it was the old post-man who brought me news of death.

"Wendell Casey died," he said. "And Melinda Ford had a baby that she's named Edith after that woman on TV."

"Edith Bunker?" I asked, though that such a namesake might be chosen was beyond my imagination.

He smiled. "Like that woman on TV is what Lester said." He handed me a package and a couple of journals, along with my daily copy of the *Lakeland Telegraph*. "See you tomorrow, Mr. Branch."

The paper's obituary column informed that Wendell would lie in state at Gillette's Funeral Parlor, where he'd worked for many years, the man who showed up at the door, wheeling the velvet-covered gurney upon which the loved one would be borne away.

We had shared a dark experience, Wendell and I, and so the next day I paid a respectful call to Gillette's, where he lay amid a sparse display of flowers, all plastic, which the funeral home used when no fresh ones had been received, the sure sign of a lonely passing.

"Mr. Branch?"

I turned to see Toby Olson, once a fellow member, with Wendell, of my class on evil.

"Good to see you, Toby," I said. "I mean . . . Dr. Olson."

He smiled. "I'd been treating Wendell," he said. "He told me you were a frequent visitor."

"Yes," I said. "We talked things over quite often."

I'd run into him shortly after his release, a man seeking work and family after the grave interruption of his life. He'd found a job at Gillette's by that time, but the other thing he sought, family, was never his, and so he'd lived the rest of his days in a tiny trailer on the mudflat that was left after the Bridges was torn down.

"We talked of old times," I told Dr. Olson. "Past wrongs."

"All forgiven then?" Dr. Olson asked.

I nodded. "Between ourselves." I recalled the ripped Naugahyde recliner Wendell had used until he could no longer sit up comfortably, always with a beer in hand, puffing a Swisher Sweet.

"When did you see him last?" Dr. Olson asked.

"Only a week or so before he died," I answered.

Then I quoted Wendell's final words to me, said over the phone just before I hung up: "'So fast, Mr. Branch.' That's the last thing I heard him say." He'd been talking about that night, how it had all happened so fast. "'I never thought he should have gone to prison.'"

Dr. Olson's face turned very solemn. "Dirk's back in town."

"He's meant to be here," I said dryly. "Where'd you see him?"

"He works at the Wal-Mart. In the paint department." Dr. Olson glanced at Wendell's coffin. "I think of it all the time, Mr. Branch."

"Me, too."

My mind spun the wheel to which their faces were attached, some taken, some spared by chance.

Dr. Olson touched my arm. "Like the Bible says, it's a vale of tears."

He said this with such unalloyed sorrow that I saw immediately how deep it ran, the sympathy he had for all who live behind that veil.

"Will you be my doctor?" I asked.

"Don't you already have one?"

"A man can change, can't he?" I asked. "His doctor, I mean."

"All right, Mr. Branch, if you wish," he said. "And I want to thank you again, or your father, that is, for writing that wonderful letter to medical school. I'm sure his influence was very helpful." He smiled. "I'll always be grateful to you," he added. "And of course, Miss Ellis. She was the one who first mentioned medicine to me."

"I didn't know that," I told him.

"A fine person," Dr. Olson said.

Nora's face swam into view.

"The best I ever knew," I said.

———

She was standing at the front of the school as I headed for my car at the end of the day.

"I'm waiting for my bus," she said.

"Bus?"

"School bus," Nora explained. "My car's having a few problems so I'm going to hitch a ride with the kids."

"I'll take you home," I told her. "And pick you up tomorrow morning, too, if you want."

"No, my car should be fixed by now," Nora said. "But I'd love a ride to the shop."

"Done," I said.

We were already on Route 4, halfway to the Bridges, when I said, "You were right about Sheila, by the way. It was pretty obvious in class today that she's interested in Eddie Miller."

"But is he interested in her?"

"I think so, yes," I answered. "They had a little moment, if you know what I mean. Eyes meet . . . a hint of fireworks."

She smiled. "Have you ever had a moment like that?"

"No," I said. "You?"

Her eyes took on a strange steeliness. "Not exactly." Then in what seemed an act fraught with tremendous risk, she said, "But I did think of you a few times this weekend."

"And I of you," I told her, and suddenly felt that if there were more of soaring jeopardy in life than this, I had no notion what it was.

We talked on a little while of nothing in particular, then I said, "Are you doing anything for dinner tonight?"

"I have to take Morrell to the swings in the park. I take him every Monday night. He really looks forward to it."

"Okay," I said. "Another time. I'll call you."

"I don't have a phone," Nora said. "I had one once, but the ring scares Morrell, so I took it out." She smiled. "But about tonight, you could go with us, if you like."

No prospect had ever struck me as more appealing. "Morrell won't be afraid with me tagging along?"

"No," Nora said. "I told him about you, so he won't be scared."

"What did you tell him?"

"That you were kind."

And so at around six that evening I picked Nora up at her house in the Bridges. She sat on the passenger side, Morrell in the back, where he excitedly watched the scenery as we drove toward the town park.

As evening fell, Nora and I rested at the base of the Confederate Monument and watched Morrell pumping energetically in his swing. He was a full-grown man who looked about thirty, balding already, and moderately heavyset. The children in the park were clearly accustomed to him and joked and played with him as one of their own.

"He has such a good heart," Nora said at one point.

I could see her own heart embrace her brother and felt a terrible need, though perhaps it was more a hope, to feel that same embrace one day.

"The trouble is that most everything scares him," she added. She looked at me pointedly. "So wherever I go, he goes, Jack."

I nodded. "As well he should," I told her, and dreamed, both oddly and prophetically, of Morrell in the garden of Great

Oaks, playing with my father's collection of miniature Civil War soldiers, the living still on their feet, the dead toppled over, lying on their backs.

We left the park at around eight that evening, and it was at approximately that same hour, as I later learned, that Eddie arrived at the Shenoba County sheriff's office, the very building from which I'd retrieved him two weeks ago. He did not go there alone, however. Sheila Longstreet came with him.

She would later say that it all happened by chance, that after the last class of the day, she and Eddie had run into each other quite by accident. She'd been hanging around with Dirk and Wendell and Betty Groom, Wendell's sometime girlfriend. A light rain was falling, she recalled, and so they were huddled under the awning at the back entrance of the school. Wendell had just drawn Betty beneath his arm and had tried to stick his tongue in her ear, a scene from which Sheila had turned away in disgust.

"Yuck," she said.

Dirk looked at her sharply. "When did you get so prissy?"

His tone was angry, but Sheila simply shrugged, her attention now focused on the interior of the school, an empty corridor lined with gray metal lockers. She had still not turned back toward Dirk when she heard him say, "They got in a new hot rod at Ben's Auto."

Then it was Wendell. "Yeah?"

"Really nice, man. Red. I'd kill to have that thing."

"You'd have to." Wendell's laugh was edged in mockery.

Sheila shifted her attention back to Dirk in time to see him scratch a wooden match against the building's brick façade and light a cigarette. "Shit." He waved out the match and tossed it onto the rain-soaked ground. "I got to find a job."

She drew the cigarette from Dirk's mouth and took a puff. "They got work at the mills."

Dirk snapped the cigarette from her lips. "I don't mean that kind of job," he sneered.

"He means a bank job," Wendell said with a loud chuckle. "Or knock over some filling station, right, Dirk?"

Wendell continued to move through a list of possible "jobs," everything from burglary to kidnapping, as Wendell later testified, "some planter's kid."

It was the kind of talk that no one took seriously, least of all Sheila, who tuned out after a few moments, let her gaze return to the corridor, which was still empty save for a figure slouched against a locker, writing in his black notebook, alone as always, a solitariness she found at that moment—and would find to the end of her days—irresistibly alluring.

"Eddie just seemed all by himself," Sheila would later tell the jury, her oddly broken voice so low it barely carried to the jury box, "and I guess I wanted to show him that he didn't have to be."

And so, in an act she would later describe as "my turning point," she told Dirk that she had to get something in her locker, left him muttering about "a job," and walked back into the school. Eddie was still leaning against his locker, writing in the black notebook District Attorney Carlton would later lift from the top of the prosecution table and hold aloft in the stuffy courthouse air.

MR. CARLTON: Is this the notebook, Miss Longstreet?

MISS LONGSTREET: Yes, it is.

MR. CARLTON: And when you came upon Eddie Miller that afternoon, what did he tell you?

MISS LONGSTREET: He said he had a list of people he needed to talk to about his father.

MR. CARLTON: Did he show you that list?

MISS LONGSTREET: Later he did. But that day he just said he wanted to talk to this one cop . . . officer . . . police officer.

MR. CARLTON: Did he name this police officer?

MISS LONGSTREET: Yes, he did.

MR. CARLTON: And what was that name?

MISS LONGSTREET: It was Sheriff Drummond he meant. Eddie said that he was planning to go to the police station and see if he could talk to him.

MR. CARLTON: Did he tell you why this particular officer?

MISS LONGSTREET: Because Sheriff Drummond had talked to him before, and had talked to his father, and so he was on the list of people Eddie wanted to ask about his father.

It was Mrs. June Davies who greeted Eddie when he reached the administrative office of the sheriff's department, and later she would describe him simply as "a polite young man." She'd occupied a front office in the building, she told the jury, and had noticed Eddie's brown van make a lazy circle into the parking lot. As it did, she saw "that girl who disappeared" in the van's passenger seat.

But Sheila had remained in the waiting room just to the right of the reception desk, so it was Eddie alone with whom Mrs. Davies dealt that evening. He said he'd talked to Sheriff Drummond on a previous occasion, Mrs. Davies testified, and asked if perhaps Mr. Drummond had time to talk to him for what Mrs. Davies called "a school paper he was writing."

A trial transcript records what happened then:

MR. CARLTON: Did he tell you the subject of this paper?
MRS. DAVIES: No, he didn't.
MR. CARLTON: And was Sheriff Drummond physically present that night?
MRS. DAVIES: Yes, he was.
MR. CARLTON: Did you alert Sheriff Drummond as to the presence of Eddie Miller?
MRS. DAVIES: I did.
MR. CARLTON: Could you tell the jury what happened after that?
MRS. DAVIES: The sheriff said he'd talk to Eddie. He said that Eddie should meet him in a room down the hall.
MR. CARLTON: Which room?
MRS. DAVIES: Room 101.

The literary coincidence of the room's number would not have been lost on my father, as it was not lost on me when Eddie later wrote about it. Room 101 was the room to which

Winston is brought in *1984*, the place in which he is made to confront his deepest fear and in which he will betray his deepest love.

Eddie never made reference to this irony in any draft of his paper, however, and so described it bare of literary plumage:

Room 101 was almost square and there was nothing in it but a table and a chair. The light didn't swing from a cord the way it does in cop movies. Instead, there was a metal fixture with a fluorescent bulb that flashed and hummed the whole time because it was old and beginning to die out. The walls were light gray, and there was nothing hanging on them, not even a calendar, and that made me see that a room like this makes you feel that there's nothing outside it. There is only "here" inside this room, and if you want to go back to "there," outside this room, you have to say something that makes them let you go. For some people, that means telling the truth, but for others, like my father, it means telling lies.

For a little while, Eddie sat alone in Room 101. Mae Jeeter, a cleaning woman, saw him there as she made her way down the corridor. By that time, Sheriff Drummond was already on his way, coming toward her in the opposite direction, churning past her, as she said in her affidavit, "like a little smoking train."

Seconds later, as Eddie later wrote, Drummond opened the door to Room 101.

It was a face I'd seen before, but the light was somehow different this time, and I saw that there were little lines everywhere on his face. They shot out from the corners of his eyes and around the edges of his mouth, and there were even very tiny lines in between the deep ones that ran across his forehead. And so, when Sheila asked me what he looked like, I said that he looked "crisscrossed" because Mr. Branch had said that things look like other things and so when I write, I try to see things in that way, not what they look like exactly but other things they look like, and so that's what I did with Drummond's face, and saw an old scratched-up wooden floor.

The meeting, according to Mrs. Davies's testimony, could not have lasted more than ten minutes. Several people glanced through the closed door's small window and saw Drummond and Eddie together in the room, Drummond standing, his pipe in his mouth, his arms folded over his chest, Eddie in a chair at the end of the table. There was a black notebook on the table, and Deputy Brennan remembered seeing Eddie open it and point to a particular page "that Sheriff Drummond leaned over to get a look at."

At the end of the meeting, Eddie walked out of Room 101, down the corridor, where he nodded to Mrs. Davies, still at her desk in the administrative office, and returned to the reception area. Sheila Longstreet sat waiting for him. She'd had her own notebook by then, she later said, a spiral one with a dark red cover in which she'd begun to make an outline for her paper on Julie Fogg. The contents of her notebook were not at all like Eddie's, as she told the court, "because Eddie's notebook was filled with all kinds of things, not just notes about his father but other things too, notes about Lakeland, Shenoba County, what it was like, the people here, like he was writing about the whole Delta."

When Eddie came back into the reception area, he motioned that he was ready to leave. Sheila rose and walked to where he stood in front of the reception desk. Then they turned toward the door, and at that moment, following an impulse she found irresistible, she took his arm, a gesture she fully expected him to find electrifying, so that she could not have been more astonished when his attention seemed riveted on something other than herself.

"It was Sheriff Drummond," she later told the court.

He'd suddenly come into the reception area, where he moved to a distant corner and stood, smoking his pipe, his back pressed against the concrete wall as if by the force of an invisible hand.

"He just sort of smiled at Eddie," Sheila said. "And Eddie smiled back at him. 'He likes me,' he said."

"Eddie thought that Sheriff Drummond liked him?" Mr. Carlton asked. "Why did he think that?"

"Because Sheriff Drummond said so," Sheila answered. "Told Eddie he liked him, that he reminded him of his son."

A sentiment the sheriff himself confirmed to me later that same night. I'd just returned from dropping off Nora and Morrell when I learned about Eddie's journey to police headquarters. It came in a phone call and by means of a voice I'd heard before, and which had lingered in my mind since then, so that I recognized it instantly.

"Sheriff Drummond," I said.

"Evening, Mr. Branch," Drummond said. "I hope you're enjoying the fine weather we're having."

"I am, thank you."

"I hope I'm not disturbing your studies."

An annoying obsequiousness dripped from his every word. "How may I help you, Sheriff?"

"Eddie Miller came by to see me this afternoon," he said. "He tells me you're working with him."

"Working with him?" I asked.

"Helping him with that paper he's writing," Drummond said.

"Yes, I'm helping him."

"He wanted me to talk to him about his father," Drummond said. "Wanted me to give him official reports." He laughed in the jocular way of club members over drinks. "Of course, I would need your approval to do that, Mr. Branch."

"I see," I said. "Well, I'd certainly appreciate it if you could give Eddie whatever seems appropriate."

"Certainly," Drummond said, his manner so courtly it was all but clownish, a harlequin playing a gentleman, and so doomed to missteps.

"He said something about 'primary sources,'" Drummond said.

"That would be anything having to do with the initial investigation," I told him.

I could almost see Drummond nodding thoughtfully, as if he'd long had acquaintance with the term.

"And the confession, of course," I added.

"The confession?" Drummond asked.

"It was given to you, I assume?"

I meant simply that the written confession had been given to Drummond, but he confirmed a closer connection.

"Oh, yes sir," Drummond said. "Eddie's father spoke to me, personally."

"Then Eddie might want to know what he said to you," I told him.

For the first time, I sensed hesitation at the other end of the line.

"Well, Mr. Branch," Drummond said, "these are . . . ugly matters. And Eddie, well, he's just a boy."

"A boy who's lived under a shadow," I said. "The shadow of his father. I think that's what he's trying to lift."

"So it seems," Drummond said. "But such an ugly story." Again, there was a hesitation before Drummond said, "Because he . . . tortured her, Mr. Branch."

A chill went through me.

"He burned her with cigarettes," Drummond added. "The paper put it as a beating, but it was worse than that, and I'm not sure any boy would want to know such things about his father."

I considered this, then made my decision.

"I don't think Eddie needs to know that," I said.

"If you say so, Mr. Branch." Again, the somewhat forced clubby chuckle. "You're the teacher, after all."

"Is that all then?" I asked.

"Oh, yes," Drummond said, like a man suddenly aware of himself as an imposition. "And I'll certainly be giving Eddie any help I can."

"Thank you."

"Yes, thank you," Drummond said in what struck me as a completely realized imitation of Dickens's relentlessly fawning Uriah Heap. "And I hope you have a pleasant evening."

But as it turned out I didn't, because something in Drummond's excruciating manner left an itch in my mind. Was it real, this tone of humble service, or had he laughed under his breath as he'd hung up the phone, pleased to have covered another plantation boy in a waterfall of flattery?

It was a thought I found curiously disturbing, and so I walked to my reading chair, a huge square monstrosity that rested by the front window, plucked my volume of Suetonius from the table beside it, and tried to lose myself in the crimes of the ancient Romans. But try as I did, their outrages seemed very far away. I could read about them until I grew, in Yeats's melancholy phrase, "old and gray and full of sleep," and still discover nothing that was not discoverable in books. But in all the books I'd read for my class on evil, not one of them had raked my spine like Harry Drummond's voice, though exactly what I'd heard within it—whether a genuine pledge of assistance or merely some clever deceit—remained very far from clear.

Which is perhaps why I continued to replay it, the sound of Drummond's voice growing darker and darker with each rehearing, as if it weren't a voice at all but steps on a long, winding staircase that was forever spiraling down.

SEVENTEEN

Caligula heard voices. They whispered incessantly in his mind, urging him to ever-more fantastic acts of public eccentricity. At their instruction he donned animal skins and journeyed to the Colosseum to fight tigers and wild boar. At other times, following the same mad summons, he put on female clothes and jewelry and in that guise actually received emissaries from throughout the world.

My lectures on Roman tyranny were given over five days, and thus, as planned, ended on a Friday, predictably with Lord Acton's dictum that absolute power corrupts absolutely, especially when wielded by madmen and fools.

The lectures had gone well, and I'd been careful to pepper them with macabre details of imperial excess I'd culled from Plutarch and Suetonius. It struck me that had Mr. Rankin attended these lectures, he might actually have believed that I'd achieved the intellectual sweep I'd originally set for my course on evil. Puffed up by all that, as only a young man can be puffed up by small accomplishments, I'd felt like celebrating my own success and so I asked Nora to dinner at Broom's Restaurant, a favorite of my father's before he'd stopped going out.

"And let's bring Morrell along," I added. "He needs to see a little more of the world."

I picked them up at seven that same evening, and with Morrell looking quite contented in the backseat, we made our way to Broom's.

"Mr. Branch," Broom said as we came through the door. He was a little round cannonball of a man, a bachelor who'd migrated to Lakeland just after the war. His accent was not exactly Southern, but neither could it be described as foreign. He had dark skin and slick black hair, and these features, along with his sudden appearance among us and his never recounted past, made him universally suspected of being Jewish, though I doubt he'd ever gotten the slightest hint that such suspicion was routinely bandied about. Nor was the subject raised when, some years later, he was buried without comment in the Presbyterian cemetery.

He had greeted my father with the same overdone deference he now accorded me.

"Such a privilege to have you with us tonight, Mr. Branch," he said.

He led us to a nearby table, pulled out Nora's chair and waited for her to be seated.

"And you, sir," he said to Morrell.

Morrell stared at him blankly.

"That's your chair," I told him.

Mr. Broom suddenly got the idea. "Yes, yes," he said, pulling out the chair. "Please. Have a seat."

Morrell slowly lowered himself into the chair, though not without several backward glances to where Broom stood, grinning fiercely behind him.

Once seated, he gazed with dread and bafflement at the formidable array of plates and saucers, forks and spoons, all of them of different sizes, which must certainly have alarmed him even more.

"Okay, Norie?" he asked.

She gently patted his hand. "Yes," she said. "Everything's okay."

I smoothed the napkin across my lap, a movement Morrell appeared to find oddly captivating. "I had a pretty good week in class," I said. "It was all about the—"

"Me, too," Morrell said suddenly. He nodded toward his napkin, then copied every move I'd made, down to the quick swipe of the lap. Once done, he glanced back and forth to Nora and me, smiling all the while, convinced, as he seemed to be, that we were knit together now and would be that way forever.

"Well done," I told him. I reached over to touch his shoulder. He pulled away, and so I stopped. Then, with a smile, he leaned his shoulder toward me, and I grasped it for a moment as I thought a loving older brother might. "Good," I said, then let it go.

"He's not afraid of you anymore," Nora said.

"There's no reason for him to be afraid of me," I assured her. But of course, there was.

We were well into our dinners when I heard a stir at the front of the restaurant and noticed that the staff suddenly became alert the way they do when a distinguished figure enters the room. They had done it for my father, and now, as I saw, they were doing it for Harry Drummond.

He was alone, dressed as always in a jacket and tie. He took off his hat and handed it to Mr. Broom. They shook hands and Mr. Broom led Drummond to a corner table at the opposite end of the room, where he sat in what seemed a self-generated gloom, his hazel eyes perusing a limited menu of the usual Southern fare.

"Look who's joining us for dinner," I said. I nodded toward the far corner of the restaurant. "The esteemed sheriff of Shenoba County."

Nora looked over to where I indicated. "He's awful small," she said.

"Smaller even than he looks in my estimation," I said.

Drummond folded the menu and in a quick flick of his head glanced out the window to his left, where he held his gaze on the few cars parked in front. It was the face of a gargoyle, with beaked nose and razor-thin lips, and something about its stripped-down emaciation suggested a bone-hard capacity to come to judgment quickly, then follow that judgment to the end. Small evidence would turn conclusive in his mind, I decided, and he would dismiss anything exculpatory. Such men sometimes did little more than speak out of turn or jump the line. But others, less restrained by countervailing powers, had burned the art of Florence and put Jerusalem to the sword.

"Evening, Jack."

The hand on my shoulder belonged to Hugh Crombie. He was standing just to my right, his fingers trembling slightly when he let go and drew back his hand.

"Evening, Nora," he added with a nod.

His gaze drifted over to where Morrell sat, slightly drawn away, as was his usual posture when approached by strangers. He looked as if he were staring at a monkey in a zoo. I could almost see the shadow of bars transverse his face.

"This is my brother, Morrell," Nora told him.

Crombie looked at Morrell not as one he pitied but as one whose life seemed pointlessly sustained. I thought of something Stacia Decker had said to the class in the course of giving a progress report on her paper on Hitler, how he'd labeled people like Morrell "useless eaters," and later had them herded into sealed trucks where they were gassed with carbon monoxide.

"Shake hands with Mr. Crombie," Nora told Morrell.

Morrell looked at Nora as if to confirm that he'd actually been told to do such a thing. She nodded a gentle okay, and with that assurance, Morrell cautiously offered his hand to Mr. Crombie.

Mr. Crombie took Morrell's hand and shook it. "Pleased to meet you," he said.

Morrell drew back his hand and sunk it beneath the table.

Crombie looked at me with an expression of subtle warning that I should know better than to mingle my high blood with one so base as Nora's, that its issue would surely be another like Morrell.

Nora clearly saw this warning, too, though she said nothing about it.

"Well, I hope you two have a lovely evening," Mr. Crombie said. He looked at Morrell. "You, too, of course."

"Say, 'Thank you, sir,' Morrell," Nora told him.

Morrell drew his eyes away from Mr. Crombie as if from a hard, unforgiving light. "Thank you, sir," he muttered shyly.

Mr. Crombie nodded crisply, then made his way to the far corner of the restaurant and sat down at Drummond's table. He was clearly expected, and the two men immediately hunched over the table in what seemed quite urgent conversation.

"Okay, Norie?" Morrell asked, nodding toward the dessert menu.

"Sure, take a look."

Morrell picked up the menu as he'd seen me do, and pretended to read it.

"Look," Nora said. "They have ice cream. You like ice cream."

I heard all this as voices in another room. For my attention was focused on Drummond. "I don't trust him," I said.

Nora looked up from her menu. "Who?" she asked.

"Drummond," I answered, then told Nora about our previous conversation, his questions, the little hesitation I'd sensed despite his grand pledge of assistance.

"But why wouldn't he help Eddie?" Nora asked. "It's just a high school paper."

She'd asked this absently, and added nothing to it, but her question was still playing in my mind when we left the restaurant. Drummond and Crombie still huddled in what I'd begun to imagine as a dark conclave, myself against them, as if they were twin dragons that I, in my vaunted knighthood, had to slay.

Even so, I said nothing more about them as I drove Nora and Morrell back to their little house in the Bridges.

Morrell rushed in, leaving Nora and me together at the bottom of the stairs. The night air was warm and smelled of honeysuckle. Across the street the ruin of Wanda Ruth's once-fabled bordello now leaned like an old whore against a railroad siding.

"Want to sit awhile?" Nora asked when we reached her door.

I knew she meant the rickety swing that hung from rusty chains at one end of her porch.

"Yes," I said.

We sat down in the swing, our bodies a few inches apart, the distance couples maintained in those days.

She glanced across the unpaved road, to the old abandoned railroad flats that stood, gray and forlorn, like people in line for food or shelter.

"Do you ever think of leaving here?" I asked.

She laughed. "Where would I go, Jack?" She glanced out into the night, the battered neighborhood that surrounded her. "The question is, what are you doing here? Don't you have some girl from Vanderbilt to court?"

"No, I don't."

I leaned over and kissed her. It was long and slow and when she finally drew away it was with a languid backward drift.

"You've probably always heard that Bridges girls are loose," she said.

I started to answer, but she lifted her hand to stop me. "Well, I'm not," she said firmly. Her gaze informed me of an inviolable fact. "And I come with Morrell. I've made that clear, right?"

"You make everything clear, Nora," I said. "In this case, more than once."

She took my hand and stared me dead in the eye. "Wherever I go, he goes. I'm all he's got, and somebody's got to take care of him."

"And someone always will," I assured her. "And that someone will be you. Regardless of where you live. Or with whom you live. I understand, Nora. Morrell is part of the package."

He came through the door at just that moment, and like a small child he nestled himself between us, kicking at the floor to get the swing going.

I put my arm around him but kept my eyes on Nora.

It was a gesture that could not have pleased her more.

Morrell looked at me, then at Nora. "Nice," he said.

I headed home at just after eleven that evening. At that hour, Lakeland was deserted, all the shops closed, their windows dark. Something in the way we'd all sat in the swing, the simple sweetness of it, both bathed me in light and fired me with energy. It was all still coursing through me when I got home and so although I went directly to bed, I remained awake. The air seemed touched by kindness, and from time to time, remembering some small bit of whispered conversation that had passed between Nora and me while Morrell slept soundly and without fear between us, I felt happiness almost physically, as a deep internal warmth, a calming of all agitation, the opposite of hunger. I had expected it to come with fireworks, as it did in books and songs, come with a ferocity that drove men to kill their brothers and women to leap into raging streams . . . but what a quiet thing it was.

By daylight, everything smelled better than it ever had. There was a shine on the table, the chairs, the windowsills. Nothing looked drab or worn or without luster, and the morning light came straight from heaven and seemed—like me—as yet untouched by darkness.

PART III

EIGHTEEN

So whom does a man tell when he falls in love with a woman save the person to whom, before her, he was most devoted.

"I think I'm in love," I told my father.

I'd waited as long as I could, though I'd felt I might surely burst before the clock struck nine and I was reasonably certain he'd awakened.

"With that girl from the Bridges?" my father asked.

"Yes."

"Nora," my father said in a tone near reverential, so that I knew he fully understood how momentous I found this particular moment in my life. "I'm very happy for you, Jack."

I expected him to add something to this, some words of joyful celebration, but instead there was a pause. When he spoke again, his manner was matter-of-fact. "I'd like to see the orchard."

I was still floating on a wave of happiness, and so such a strange announcement pulled me up short. For the orchard had never been more than a hardscrabble piece of land at the far-thermost reaches of our property. To my knowledge, it had no value, either real or sentimental. In fact, it could hardly be called an orchard at all, since the pecan and crab apple trees planted on its limited acreage had scarcely ever borne fruit.

"But there's nothing there, Dad."

"For me there is."

"All right," I said. "I'll be right over."

I picked him up at the house a few minutes later. He was leaning against one of its high, white columns, his hand grasping the brass-handled cane his grandfather had once used, according to Great Oaks legend, to thrash a carpetbagger. Despite the spring warmth, he wore what he called his "parade-ground jacket," though its faded fabric and frayed collar seemed less fitting to a soldier on parade than the war-weary veteran of a failed campaign.

"I haven't been out in the light in quite some time," he said as he got into my car.

This was true. Since the "incident," he'd not only stopped going out in public but had also adopted a vampirish affection for dimly lighted rooms. He never threw open the curtains of the library or the study, and I had only rarely found him in the garden or strolling the grounds.

"So, you're in love," he said. "Good." His hand gripped the cane more tightly. "And better it should be a girl from the Bridges than some creature of the cotillion ball."

"But wasn't my mother a girl of the cotillion?"

My father smiled. "We danced the quadrille in many a grand room," he said. "But I should not have forced a grand tour upon her."

He'd rarely spoken of their marriage, save the final episode of it, how he'd fallen to the "bottoms," and sought relief in a year's tour of Europe, he and my mother journeying first to New York then across the waves to England, and from there making their way to Paris. It was there she'd discovered herself pregnant, so they'd remained in the City of Light until, somewhat prematurely, I'd been born, a birth much anticipated at Great Oaks, as my father always emphasized, and which would have ended their Parisian idyll quite happily had not my mother later perished in a fever on the crossing, an event that, each time he thought of it, threatened to return him once again, as he said, "to the depths."

"There was never another like her, Jack," he added now. "Such beauty and intelligence. Such flashing eyes."

For a moment, I had an image of them in their youth, my father in evening clothes, my mother in her gown, dancing in one of the great ballrooms of the Delta.

Briefly my father seemed lost in that same romance. Then, like one slapped back to reality, he suddenly glanced out over the grounds, his expression entirely changed. "Youth, as they say, is another country."

"Was yours wild?" I asked lightly.

He shrugged. "No more than most," he answered.

"No visits to Wanda Ruth's?"

He smiled. "Where did you hear of that particular establishment?"

"From Nora," I answered. "She was raised just across the street."

"In that case she must have seen quite a few plantation boys."

"They were the only boys Wanda Ruth catered to, evidently."

My father made no effort to deny this, nor add to it. "Youth is meant to be misspent, I suppose."

"And its doings covered up if necessary, as well," I added. "Nora told me that Wanda Ruth's body was still warm when the cops arrived to clean things up."

My father rolled down the window. "Where does that fit on your scale of evil, Jack?" he asked. "Doing what must be done to save a family name?"

"As I recall, hypocrites were put on the eighth circle in the *Inferno*," I told him.

He loosed the scarf from around his neck. "Which is most likely no hotter than a Delta summer."

He didn't speak again until I stopped the car beside the old barbed-wire fence that enclosed the orchard. It was sagging and rusty and in that way seemed at one with the ragged trees and weedy grounds.

I started to get out of the car.

"No need to walk around," my father said. "Being here is enough." He looked out to where twenty or so scraggly trees grew in a desolate field. "It reminds me of Lincoln's face in the last photograph that was taken of him."

I realized then why he'd asked to come here. He was near the end of his biography, and thus seeking a metaphor, perhaps some physical image that would give him a sense of Lincoln's last days, the full weight of his burden.

"Like this orchard," he added. "Ravaged."

He leaned forward slightly, as if trying to see some phantom figure among the trees, a tall, lanky man, ghostly in his stovepipe hat.

"Are you sure you don't want to get out?" I asked.

He shook his head. "He was so tired, Jack," he said softly. "His last days."

His eyes were glistening, and I felt the urge to draw him into my arms, but I knew that he'd recoil from that. And so I pretended not to notice this sudden seizure of emotion and quickly changed the subject. "I saw Hugh Crombie at Broom's when Nora and I were there last night. He was talking with Sheriff Drummond."

It was an image of vague collusion that, in turn, gave rise to the yet stranger notion that I might do well to prepare for some future deviousness on his part.

"He gives me a strange feeling," I said. "Drummond."

My father faced me, his head lifted, eyes dry, the crack in his composure now thoroughly resealed. "What sort of feeling?"

I didn't actually know what the feeling was, and so merely grasped for a word. "Unwholesome."

My father shrugged. "There are a great many unwholesome people in the world, Jack." He was staring out into the orchard again, focused now on a peculiarly decrepit line of trees, crooked branches, bare of leaves. They seemed gathered like starving old men. "And we all become so in the end." With that, he sat back slightly, as if stricken by a disturbing vision. "They're building an old-age home in Jackson. They call it a facility. I think I should take a look at it."

"Why?" I asked. "You're not old. And besides, no Branch has ever been put in a home, and certainly you won't be."

He looked at me with a strange, sad indulgence, as if I'd made a hasty pledge. "I think I should take a look at it, Jack."

But more than thirty years would pass before I actually took him there, and even then only at his aged, addled insistence, never with a view actually to moving him to such a place. By then he was very frail and so a wheelchair had been provided in which I propelled him through the "facility's" various rooms, almost all of which were painted in pastel yellow or light blue. Some of these rooms were equipped with televisions that seemed never to be turned off nor to experience a change of channels, while others had been given over to card tables and shelves stuffed with board games. There were a few potted plants, not quite plastic, not quite rubber. The air had smelled of medicines and the walls were dotted with decidedly sunny landscapes in whose relentless cheerfulness I sensed only the beleaguered optimism of those who know better but will not face it.

"Lincoln's face, yes," my father said softly, his attention once again fixed on the battered field before him. "It was like this, near the end, a ruined orchard."

He fell silent for a time, and during that interval I saw a strange exhaustion settle over him, so that he sat slumped, shoulders bowed, a ragged quality in his eyes. "He lost his son, you know."

"Yes," I said. "Little Edward."

"I don't mean Lincoln," my father said. "I mean Drummond. He lost his son in the war. His name is on that plaque in front of the sheriff's office." He drew in a long breath. "'The last full measure of devotion,'" he quoted. "What a poet Lincoln was." He looked at me. "He actually wrote poetry, did you know that?"

"No, I didn't."

He turned away, surveyed the orchard, moving from tree to tree until his attention finally settled upon the twisted branches of a single crab apple tree. "Lincoln took cocaine for his melancholy," he added. "You could buy it from a druggist in those days. The druggist's bill is in the archive. Of course, he may have bought it for his wife instead. So the mystery continues."

"How might you solve it?"

"Why should it matter?" my father asked.

"For the record," I said.

He waved his hand. "A man doesn't need to know everything. Especially about a revered figure. Like that boy you're helping. He should be careful, the questions he asks about his father."

"Why?"

He looked at me intently, from what seemed behind the veil of a grave experience. Then slowly and prophetically, he said the scariest thing I'd ever heard: "Because the answer to a heartfelt question, Jack, will always break your heart."

NINETEEN

Years later my father added this:

> There is a reverse quality in heartbreak, the fact that it may
> in time return what it so swiftly took away, like a shadow
> that as the years go by begins quite unaccountably to shed
> its own peculiar light.
> JEFFERSON BRANCH, Last Letter to My Son

Now, in my old age, with nothing to await but the postman's daily visit, such talk of heartbreak rings somewhat hollow.
There is an overheated preciousness to it, a whiff of magnolia
blossoms. And yet, each time I read my father's final letter to
me, it brings to mind the darker truth that destruction sometimes comes to us not in a sudden fall but in a slow descent,
taken in faltering steps, one decision at a time.

Take, for example, Dirk Littlefield's destruction.

In memory, repeatedly, his hand raises, his voice calls.

"How about you?"

He had spoken abruptly at the very end of the class period,

harshly, as if both threatening and preparing for trouble, like someone breaking a bottle on a bar.

"Me?" I answered stiffly, determined to remain unruffled by his attitude, which had always been disrespectful.

Dirk glanced at Wendell, then looked back at me, his mouth twisted in a smirk. "Are you going to write a paper, Mr. Branch?"

Every negative impression I'd ever had of him, and there'd been a great many before that moment, now suddenly coalesced, and I saw him as the very symbol of the sheer, ignorant belligerence of that portion of humanity that irredeemably smothers beneath the folds of its own grim intransigence. With his slicked-back hair and grimy fingernails, he stood not only in his own way but in the way of anyone else who might seek a higher path. Low, he sought only to stay low, I thought, and to make sure others stayed low, too. In his small, round eyes, I saw every obstacle he placed in the way of his progress, the hatred he bore for anything that might, however briefly, allay the bitterness he nurtured at the very center of himself. I knew he would spend his days demonizing every effort to reform him. But worse, he would slap down the hope of others, then stand over it, arms raised in triumph, as if he'd slaughtered a great beast.

"A paper like you're making us write," Dirk added. "Pick some bad guy and write about him." A smile crawled onto his lips. "I mean, we'd all like to know who you think is evil." He turned to address the class. "Right?"

A few heads nodded and Wendell released a little chuckle, which he stopped when my eyes whipped over to him.

"I mean, the rest of us have picked somebody," Dirk continued. "So I think you should tell us who you'd pick."

It was an open challenge and in some way I felt my standing with the class demanded that I take it up. "I don't care what you think," I said. "I'm the teacher, and you're not. I give the assignments and you carry them out." As if turning from an unpleasant odor, I returned my attention to the other members of the class. "Any other questions?"

There weren't any.

"All right, class dismissed," I said.

They filed out in the usual pattern, Eddie the last to leave, with Sheila just in front of him.

It seemed the perfect moment to have a private talk with him.

"Eddie, may I speak with you a minute?" I asked.

He turned to me casually, with none of his earlier apprehension. He trusted me now, I saw. He would do what I said.

I started to speak, but suddenly glimpsed Dirk watching us from just down the hall, a shadowy figure staring at me with a maliciousness I gave back to him in full force, convinced that he saw me as his enemy, and thus determined to be exactly that.

And so, in a second gesture of towering dismissal, I turned from him and put all my attention on Eddie Miller, so that it was only in the corner of my eye I saw him whirl around and stride down the hall, carrying Wendell in his wake like debris in a funnel cloud.

"I'm working hard on my paper, Mr. Branch," Eddie assured me. "See?"

There were bits of paper sticking out of his notebook, some unevenly torn, notes hastily written for inclusion later.

"Yes, terrific," I said. "Actually it's the paper I want to talk to you about."

Eddie stood quite still, his eyes motionless but strangely expectant.

"Has Sheriff Drummond contacted you?" I asked.

Eddie shook his head.

"Because he's assured me that he'll give you any papers about your father's case you want," I said.

Eddie smiled. "Thanks, Mr. Branch." He opened his notebook and displayed a list of names. "I'm doing my first interview today," he said. He pointed to a name with a long list, but at an angle that made it impossible to read.

"And I have pictures, too," he added.

He flipped a few pages, and I saw that he'd taped perhaps twenty photographs onto various pages. Some were of his father at different ages, and there were one or two of his mother, and even a couple of himself. But there were others I didn't recognize, though only one grabbed my attention.

It was a black-and-white photograph of two boys, both dressed in badly soiled shirts and jeans, posed within the hazy summer light of what appeared to be a large greenhouse. I recognized one of the boys as Luther Miller.

"Who's the other boy?"

"That's Noel Drummond," Eddie said. "Sheriff Drummond's son."

"How do you know that?" I asked.

"I recognized him from my father's high school annual," Eddie answered. "They were in the same class." He had returned his attention to the picture, a photograph in which, as

I noticed, his father appeared far less wolfish than in the earlier pictures I'd seen of him, the smile on his face less cunning, something other than a predator's gleam in his deep-set eyes.

"Your father seems happy in this picture."

Eddie continued to gaze at the photograph as if he were looking for some key within it, a clue to what his father later became. "Is it okay to have pictures in my paper?" he asked.

"Yes."

He held his eyes on the photograph a moment longer. "I don't know where it was taken."

I looked at the picture again. Through the filmy greenhouse windows I could make out the indistinct reaches of a large garden, bordered by a brick wall, and off to the right, a rather imposing statue, blurry but still clear enough to discern the figure of a nude woman carrying a large pitcher. It was obviously the garden of one of the great houses of the plantation district, and though I didn't recognize it, I knew someone who might.

"I think I can find that out for you," I told Eddie. "Miss Ellis cleaned houses with her mother. They went all over town. This kind of garden looks like it might be one of those big houses out in the plantation district." I smiled. "And if she doesn't recognize it, my father might."

Before I could ask, Eddie peeled the picture from the notebook and offered it to me.

"I'll let you know what I find out," I told him as I slipped it from his fingers.

Eddie smiled softly. "Thanks, Mr. Branch."

This might have been the end of it, a simple, decent pledge

to help him locate the garden in the picture, but I added a drop of something darker to the brew.

"Be careful when you talk to Drummond," I said.

Eddie looked at me quizzically.

"And before you go to him, come to me," I added. "I may be able to help you more."

And so later that same day, I went looking for Nora and found her standing outside the school library, searching through her purse. I got right to the point. "I spoke to Eddie Miller this morning. He has a picture of his father with Harry Drummond's son. He doesn't know where it was taken, but I thought you might recognize the place."

In fact, she recognized it immediately.

"Oh, sure," she said. "The biggest flower garden I ever saw. All kinds of roses. In summer the whole place smelled like perfume." She handed the picture back to me. "It's the Brantley place."

"The Brantley place?" I asked. "That's practically next door to Great Oaks."

"He has some kind of disease," Nora told me. "Mr. Brantley."

"Muscular dystrophy," I said, which I knew because my father had occasionally paid a call on Mr. Brantley, though he'd never taken me along and so I'd never seen the house or garden.

Still, it seemed easy enough to establish contact: simply telephone Mr. Brantley, tell him who I was, mention the photograph, that I had a student who was working on a paper and would like to speak with him.

It would be a simple matter to do this, of course, and should have had no accompanying charge attached, and yet I felt a subtle thrill at the prospect of helping Eddie, shaping him, adding new skills as we went along, until step by step, witness by witness, we would at last—Eddie and I—draw back the veil of his father's life, and in doing so, as I still hoped, release Eddie from the lethal grip of his murderous sire.

TWENTY

I don't know why, but on the way home from school that afternoon, I hit upon the odd fact that the Brantley plantation and Breaker Landing were almost exactly a mile in opposite directions from my father's house. Another straight line could be drawn from Luther Miller's shed to Breaker Landing, where Linda Gracie had left her car, to the upstairs room where my father toiled over his life of Lincoln and dutifully made entries in *The Book of Days*. These were meaningless geometrical configurations, and yet, years later, still seeking some pattern in the scheme of things, I would plot the position of Dirk's house and Nora's and Eddie's and Sheila's, along with the small wedge of blood-soaked earth upon which it all, in my dark graph, seemed inevitably to converge, and find that Great Oaks, by then little more than a crumbling ruin, rested, like honor in truth, at the dead center of it all, the overheated core of the explosion.

But though the past, once passed, is easy to navigate, we blindly move into our futures by little steps and missteps, always in the dark, as Henry James once said, doing what we can. So it happened that almost at the instant I was considering the little geographical connections between my family home and the various "scenes" connected with Eddie's paper, I glanced to the left and there it was, the town library.

It was little more than a basement beneath the courthouse, with a cement floor and metal shelves. The front room was empty when I entered, but I could hear the sounds of a woman's footsteps in the next room. I waited at the front desk until she appeared, tall, elegantly attired, with graying hair gathered in a bun at the nape of her neck.

"Hello," I said as she came up to me.

"Why, Jack," she said. "I don't recall you ever coming to the public library." She smiled. "But of course, you have such a fine one at Great Oaks."

It was then I recognized her as a woman with whom my father had had, to use the polite Southern phrase, "brief concourse" at some point during one of my vacations from boarding school. She'd probably been in her late thirties at that time, her hair less streaked with gray but with the same beautifully sculptured face and penetrating eyes that I'd sometimes glimpsed in old photographs of my mother.

She offered her hand. "Amy Hunter."

"Yes." I shook her hand. "I remember you."

"Such a grand, grand house," she said. "And a lovely gentleman, your father. We were sweethearts once. Long before your mother, of course." She waved her hand. "But I fear it was only my eyes that attracted him," she added with a quick smile. "Jefferson is first drawn to people by their eyes."

I'd never heard this, but I could see why he'd been drawn to hers. They were of a deep green in a way that seemed both forbidding and enticing. It was easy to image broken ships beneath their surface.

"How is your father doing, by the way?" she asked.

"He's fine," I told her, though she, of course, knew better. The "incident" was not something that could be covered up, and my father's subsequent withdrawal only deepened the suspicion that he would live forever in its physical and emotional aftermath.

"He's writing a biography of Lincoln," I added.

She was quite obviously puzzled by the choice. "Lincoln? But there are already so many biographies of Lincoln. What do you suppose he's looking for?"

"I don't know," I admitted. "But he's quite occupied by it."

There was no place to go with this, and so Mrs. Hunter primly tucked her left hand in her right. "So, how may I help you?"

"I was wondering if you keep back issues of the local paper."

"Oh, yes, of course," Mrs. Hunter said. "Are you looking for anything in particular?"

"Whatever you might have on the Coed Killer," I told her.

Now it was Mrs. Hunter's turn to look surprised. "What a terrible thing," she said.

"Yes, it was," I said.

"He's been here, you know," Mrs. Hunter said. "The son."

"Eddie?"

She nodded. "Just a couple of days ago. He said he was

working on a paper about his father. Very charming boy. He
asked if I had any 'secondary sources.'"

I smiled. "He learns quickly, Eddie."

"So it seems," Mrs. Hunter said.

With no further word, she turned and led me into the adjoining room. There was a long metal table with a few chairs.
A naked lightbulb hung above it so that had the walls not been
lined with books, it would have seemed little different from
some grim interrogation chamber.

"Have a seat," Mrs. Hunter said. "I'll bring out the issues
you're looking for."

They arrived only a few seconds later, bound together in a
huge book that seemed almost too heavy for Mrs. Hunter to lift.

"There," she said as she lowered the book to the table. "Let
me know if you need anything else."

With that she returned to the equally dimly lighted front
room where I could hear her going about her work.

I had read and long ago returned the clippings Eddie had
given me. They had related the story only as far as his father's
arrest. But there'd been nothing in them of what happened
later, though that record, as I found as I began to flip through
the back issues of the *Telegraph,* was fully detailed.

According to the paper's account, Luther Ray Miller had
been taken into custody at three thirty in the afternoon. He
had been brought to the sheriff's office, where he'd been in-
terrogated by "Sheriff Drummond, himself." According to
Drummond, Miller had denied any involvement in Linda
Gracie's murder.

Until when?

Until the following day, as the next day's paper reported, at which time Drummond had questioned him again. This time he'd confessed, been returned to jail, and that night murdered by a fellow inmate identified as Marl Brogan, "a local figure in the Ku Klux Klan."

After that, all reference to Luther Miller's life and death ceased. His name vanished from the paper, like his body from the earth, so that he became invisible, save in the grim legacy he'd bestowed upon his son.

I started to close the book, disappointed that I'd found nothing more than what I'd already learned from the scrapbook, when something caught my eye.

It was on the second page of the issue whose full front page had been devoted to Luther Miller's murder. It appeared in a feature called "Yesteryear" in which "historical photographs" were meant to "jog the memory of our readers." In the photograph, my father is standing on the cement steps of Lakeland High with what appears to be an entire class gathered around him. The caption asked a question that was anything but heartfelt: WHOM CAN YOU NAME?

I'd never seen this photograph, though I'd seen many similar ones in my father's old high school annuals, as well as the few pictures he'd selected, framed, and hung in his upstairs office, all of which he'd later taken down and replaced with various Lincoln portraits.

And so had I not looked closer, or had already seen other pictures, I would probably have noted only that my father

looks happy in his role, happy with his work, all those faces behind him, most of them smiling.

But not all.

She stands at the far end of the back row, and even then a
little off to the side, separated from the rest. There were no
names attached to this photograph, but I didn't need one to
recognize the face. There were the same sharp bones and
sunken cheeks, the same look of melancholy resignation,
though in one so young, it struck me as even more oddly
haunting. The air around me grew warm as it had been that
night, and through it she drifted toward me in a cloud of cigarette smoke, Eddie's mother, a woman, as I now clearly saw,
who'd somehow been old and ragged even in her youth.

So was this the aspect of small-town life that formed
both its charm and its horror, I wondered suddenly, the fact
that those who live their lives in so confined a space must incessantly bump into one another? Here it was before me,
encapsulated in a photograph, the terrible closeness of it
all. Within that closeness, the parameters of the Delta, my
father had taught the Coed Killer, as well as his victim and
his wife.

And now I taught his son.

I knew that there were others who might feel only distress
at the claustrophobia of living one's entire life in a small place,
surrounded by familiar faces whose sons and daughters would
bear an almost equal familiarity. Here on the Delta, one saw
the work of lineage in eyes of similar shade and skin of similar tone. Why, I wondered, would anyone ever wish for a more

alien or disconnected life? Why would anyone seek to live in such a way as to know only a single generation?

It was precisely at that moment I knew I'd never leave my ancestral home, that always and proudly on the tree of my forebears, I would be a branch.

It was perhaps due to my sudden acceptance of this closeness that it seemed completely fitting to find Eddie's van sitting in my driveway when I arrived home from the library. He got out when he saw me pull in behind him.

"Oh, hi," I said, then got directly to the issue that I thought most likely on his mind. "I showed the picture you gave me to Miss Ellis. The house belongs to—"

"Mr. Branch," Eddie interrupted urgently. "It's Sheila. She's in the van."

I glanced toward the van, saw only an empty passenger seat.

"Where?" I asked.

"In the back."

In a chilling vision I imagined Sheila not as herself but in the form of Linda Gracie or some nameless woman from the *Minsk,* tied up, broken, staring down at her hands.

"She's okay, but she's scared," Eddie added as he turned and led me to the rear of the van and opened the door.

She was crouched in the corner behind the driver's seat, just as Linda Gracie might once have been, a grim coincidence, I was sure, that had not escaped Eddie's notice.

"Sheila?" I asked softly. I stood at the open back door of the van, peering into its dark interior, not sure if I should move any closer to her. Eddie was just behind me, his hands limp at his sides, so that he looked helpless and uncertain, caught in a situation he found impossible to fathom.

I lifted my hand toward Sheila. "Come on out," I said softly.

She shook her head. "I can't, Mr. Branch." She dropped her head and her long black hair hung almost to the floor of the van in a beautiful, trembling curtain.

"What happened?" I asked.

Sheila lifted her face, and I saw her moist eyes. "Dirk," she whispered.

The light was dim at the back of the van, but there was enough of it for me to see her face in full. Her white skin glowed unblemished and unwounded. Her lips were full, as always, but not split or swollen.

"What did Dirk do?" I asked.

"He said I was going to get hurt."

"Did he hurt you?"

She seemed suddenly struck by a cold blast. Her shoulders shook and her hands trembled.

"If he did, you have to report it," I told her.

"What'll happen if she reports it?" Eddie asked.

"He'll be arrested," I answered. "He'll be put in jail."

"He'll get out, though," Sheila said. "Eventually, he'll get out." She stared at me brokenly. "It's just women at home, Mr. Branch. Just me and my mother."

I knew what this meant, that there was no man in her

house, no father to stand up to Dirk Littlefield, threaten him with even worse harm than he had threatened her with, a promise made in the dead of night by the kind of man who means every word he says and who therefore could with complete conviction assure Dirk Littlefield that should he come for him again, it would be to deliver that rough justice for which the Bridges was well known.

"But there are laws, Sheila," I told her.

"Not for Dirk," Eddie said. "He doesn't care about the law. He's like my father."

He appeared to me in a sudden apparition, Luther Ray Miller slouched against a tree, smoking idly as he stared at us, the Coed Killer, a man not so much surrounded by darkness as made of it. I glanced at Eddie, oddly certain that he'd seen him, too, but Eddie was focused entirely on Sheila.

"Tell Mr. Branch what happened," Eddie asked her gently.

She spoke in the low, oddly broken voice she would later use when asked the same question by Mr. Carlton.

"He came to my house and wanted me to go for a ride with him," she said. "I didn't want to, but he said it was okay, he wasn't mad at me or anything, he just wanted to talk."

She'd thought they might go to Jake's, she said, but Dirk had turned into Glenford Park, then swung onto one of the old logging roads that twined through it, bumping and joggling all the way until he brought the car to a stop.

"Dirk said there was an old shed up there," Sheila told me.

I glanced at Eddie, and he nodded, so I knew it was the same shed to which his father had taken Linda Gracie.

"He told me to get out," Sheila said. "I wouldn't do it, so

he came around and opened the door and yanked me out." She drew the blanket from her legs and I saw that both of them were badly scratched. "I fell, and he jerked me up and pushed me ahead of him. He said, 'You need to see what's coming to you, Sheila.' That's all he said until we'd gone up the road and got to the shed."

At the door of the shed, Sheila had stopped, frightened, but Dirk had pushed her inside it.

"He told me that this was where he killed her, where Eddie's father killed that girl." She looked at Eddie. "I don't know how he knew where it was, but he did."

Dirk then turned and closed the door behind him, Sheila went on, demanding to know what was going on "between you and that killer's kid." She had told him that there was nothing between them, which was the truth, she said, "at least in that dirty way Dirk was thinking." But Dirk had not believed her. She'd been seen "snuggling" with Eddie at the sheriff's office, he said.

At that point, Sheila had bolted for the door of the shed, but Dirk had grabbed her arm and whirled her around.

"He pushed back me into a corner," she said. "He said Eddie was just like his father."

I looked back to where Eddie stood in the night air, his hands deep in his pockets, peering at Sheila in a way that struck me as oddly mesmerized, as if he were hearing the terrible details not of Sheila's encounter with Dirk Littlefield but of his father's with Linda Gracie.

"Dirk said Eddie would do the same to me one of these

days," Sheila added. "The same his father did to that girl. That it was in his blood, that meanness. That he hid it, but one day it would come out." She paused, nearly breathless. "Then he pulled me up and took me back to his car and drove me to Eddie's house and pushed me out. 'Tell Eddie what I said,' he told me. 'Ask him what he's going to do about it.'"

"Do about it," Eddie repeated, his voice low, taut, so I knew exactly what he was thinking.

"I think we should take Sheila home," I told him.

He didn't move.

"Eddie," I said. "Did you hear me?"

He nodded, but his gaze remained intently on Sheila. "Mr. Branch is right," he told her. Then he stretched his hand out toward where she still crouched at the front of the van, in what had perhaps been the exact place and position Linda Gracie had once occupied. "Come," was all he said.

The irony, of course, was overwhelming, Eddie offering his hand to one captured by her fear in the very place where his father had inspired nothing but soul-searing terror.

She came out slowly, but she came out, as if drawn by the pull of Eddie's quiet summons. When she reached him, she lowered herself into his arms, and held him for a moment in the fierce grip of that rare love she'd dreamed of all her life, as she would later admit to Nora, but would never know again.

We went in my car, but I didn't get out when we reached Sheila's house in the Bridges. Instead I remained behind the wheel, watching silently as Eddie escorted her to the door. He lingered there a moment, then returned to the car, utterly silent as I pulled away, headed back to my house.

"You want to hurt Dirk, right?" I asked him. "You want to beat him up. Beat him to death probably."

Eddie said nothing.

"But you're small, and he's big," I added. "And even if you were the same size, he has Wendell with him all the time, so it would be two against one, wouldn't it?"

Eddie kept his eyes on the road.

"So you're thinking, 'What can I do?'" I continued. "'What can I do to get even with Dirk Littlefield?'"

Eddie turned toward me. "Wouldn't you be asking yourself that question, Mr. Branch?"

"Yes. I would."

"What would you do?"

I felt the urgency of his question, as well as the importance of my answer. This was one of those moments, I decided, when a wrong word could do incalculable damage, and so I paused briefly before I gave my answer, thought things through as I thought my father would have done in the same situation.

"I'd write my paper," I told him finally. "That's what I'd do."

We were passing the entrance to Glenford State Park, and on impulse I pulled a little way into the park, guided the car to the side of the road, and stopped. "Eddie, you can tell the world all about your father. That's the way to get out from under him forever. You can fix it so he can never be used against you the way Dirk is using him."

I told him all this as we sat facing each other beneath the

dim streetlights at the entrance to Glenford Park. It was a flow of words that must have poured over him in an overwhelming torrent, urging him to take up his own sword of words and cut his way out of his father's skin, perhaps out of Lakeland, slash his way to some far country, unspecified at the moment, but surely the very one to which my own father had urged me to go and into which neither Eddie's father nor the Dirk Littlefields of this world would be able to pursue him. The torrent flowed and flowed, Eddie silent, attentive, listening, while my verbal cataract washed over him, all the things I'd learned from history and literature, all the wisdom handed down to me from my father, the full cannonade of my eloquence delivered in volley after volley until a kind of surging wave broke over me and I finally ended it with a soft, urgent plea.

"The paper is your chance for salvation, Eddie," I told him. "Don't let Dirk or anyone else take it from you."

He nodded. "Okay, Mr. Branch," he said, a response that was so quiet compared to the thunder of my argument that I took it as tentative and uncertain, a wall that needed shoring up.

"You're not alone," I assured him. "You'll never be alone."

With that I started the car, pulled onto the main road, and drove him back to my house. Through that long drive, he remained silent, but I could see that he was going over what I'd told him.

"Well, good night," I said when we stood again in my driveway, Eddie's van huddled glumly just to the right, its rear door still open.

He started to turn, but didn't.

"You said Miss Ellis knows where that picture was taken?" he asked.

"Yes, she does. It was in one of those big houses in the plantation district."

"Do you know who lives there?"

I paused as if I were in my classroom, staring at him from behind my lectern, let the pause linger for full effect, and then . . . "I know everyone who lives there," I told him. "Don't worry. I can get you in."

TWENTY-ONE

That same evening, I heard his voice for the first time in many years.

"What is this boy looking for?"

Anthony Brantley's voice was soft and gentlemanly. It was stronger than I expected, since I knew that he'd been steadily weakening for many years. At home from boarding school or college, I'd occasionally seen him in town, always pushed along by a stooped old Negro who seemed in every way devoted to him. His mother had been equally devoted, but had died some years ago, so that he now lived in the great house with only a dwindling number of servants to provide whatever comfort remained his.

"His father," I answered. "Eddie wants to know more about him."

"The Coed Killer's son," Brantley said. "That's what they call him?"

"Yes," I said.

"A terrible thing to bear such a legacy."

"Which is why this paper is so important to him," I said.

"Well, I doubt that I can be of much assistance to this boy," Brantley said. "His father only worked here for one summer. That was many years ago when he was just a teenager."

"Anything might help," I said.

"All right," Brantley said. "Would tomorrow afternoon be convenient? Say, around four?"

"I'm sure it would be," I told him.

"Fine," Brantley said. "I'll be in the garden. Philip will show you in."

The next morning I told Eddie about the call. He was clearly eager to talk to Mr. Brantley, and so I arranged to pick him up at his house at a quarter to four. "I'll be waiting on the porch," he said.

But when I arrived at Eddie's house, I found his mother stationed there instead.

She rose instantly and strode down the stairs. I was barely out of my car when she reached me.

"Eddie's all fired up 'bout this paper," she said. "Asking all kinds of questions."

I smiled. "That's what writers do," I told her.

Mrs. Miller considered this a moment, then said, "You think Eddie's smart?"

"Yes, I do."

She stared at me intently. "So you think there's something to him? That he could make something of hisself?"

"I'm posing that possibility."

"Posing the possibility," she repeated, though with none of the mockery she'd offered to me at our first encounter. "Eddie says you're a mighty good teacher."

"Well, I try to—"

"Main thing is this," she interrupted, "Eddie's doing good." She sank her hand into the pocket of her dress, grabbed a pack of cigarettes, popped one out, and lit it. "Nobody figured he could, but he's doing good." She waved out the match. "'Cause of you."

I swelled with pride. "Thank you."

She thought a moment before she spoke again. "Take care of him, 'cause . . ." She stopped and with a slow, hesitant movement, reached out and wrapped her fingers around my hand. "'Cause all in the world I got is him."

I saw her last in the local hospital. Many years had passed, and I'd come to check in on my father, who'd taken a fall. I was on my way out when I glanced in one of the rooms, idly, expecting to see an unknown figure in a hospital bed, but my eyes were keen enough to recognize her lean profile.

Her hair had gone completely white and hung over her shoulders in two silver drapes. Attentive hands had recently washed it and spread it out in a wave across her barely lifting chest.

"Mrs. Miller," I said softly as I stepped up beside her bed.

She shifted in her bed, oddly alert, though less to a voice than to something she thought unreal.

"Good evening," I said quietly.

She smiled softly, her eyes still closed. "Eddie?" she whispered.

I breathed in that ancient dust. "No."

Her eyes opened very slowly, squinting in the shadowy light. "So smart, my boy."

My eyes glistened. "I'm so sorry," I told her. "I'm so very sorry."

She died that night, a death that would not normally have been covered by the local paper, just a "truck-stop waitress and short-order cook," as the paper described her, and thus one whose passing the paper noted not because of anything famous or infamous that she had ever done but only because she'd married badly, and by that means become, as the paper said, "the Coed Killer's wife and the mother of his son."

"My mother doesn't have much to tell me," Eddie said as we headed east on Route 4, a road that would take us through the prosperous suburbs of North Hills before we reached the sacred precinct of the old plantations. "She doesn't think she knew him. It surprised her what he did. She said it came out of the blue."

I thought of something my father had once said, *There are no strangers like married strangers.*

"Maybe Mr. Brantley will be of help," I told him.

He appeared heartened by my optimism, and it struck me that this easy hope was perhaps necessary, though certainly not sufficient, to draw a Bridges boy from the grip of the Bridges. Still, I saw it as a plus for Eddie, the way he quickly grabbed for light, one step out of the pit into which he had been born.

"I wanted to show you this, Mr. Branch," he said.

He'd brought something besides his notebook this time, a small pasteboard box whose top flaps he now drew open to reveal what lay inside.

"My father had some books," he said. "My mother showed them to me."

He drew the books out one by one, all of them cheap paper-backs, usually with women sprawled across rumpled beds or lean-ing sultrily against lampposts, almost always in sleeveless dresses with at least one spaghetti strap hanging loosely off the shoulder.

"They're not very good," Eddie said. "The stories, I mean."

"They're called pulps," I told him. "And you're right, they're not very good."

"One was, though," Eddie said. He dug into the box and produced, to my surprise, a paperback edition of a Raymond Chandler novel. "This one had a pretty good story, and I liked the way it was written."

"What did you like about the writing?"

"That it didn't seem . . . fast."

I smiled at this development of taste, the fact that Eddie could distinguish between novels, appreciate a writer's choice of words.

"You should start a journal, Eddie," I said. "It's great prac-tice for writing."

"Like a diary?"

"Only with more detail," I said. "Not just what happens, but what you think about it. My father has one. He calls it *The Book of Days*. He's been writing it for years."

Eddie nodded softly. "Okay, Mr. Branch. If you think it's a good idea."

The alacrity with which he'd accepted my suggestion thrilled me. "Good," I said. "Good."

We reached the Brantley plantation a few minutes later,

passed through its graceful wrought-iron arch and down a long shaded road that finally made a lazy curve around to the house. It was large and grand, and Eddie stared at it with all the amazement of someone who suddenly found himself standing in front of the Eiffel Tower or in the shadow of the Sphinx.

"I take it you've never been out this way," I said.

"No," Eddie said. "I mean, down the regular road, but never off of it. They're a long way back, these houses. Too far to see them from the road."

He looked out the window to his right and held his gaze on a great white portico that might have been a stage set for *Gone With the Wind*, stately and august, and which exuded power like a musk.

Philip turned out to be a young black man, though I would have said "Negro" then. He was dressed not in the formal attire of a butler or house servant but in a plaid shirt and blue jeans. He had short hair, and a thin mustache, and his eyes twinkled with a curious irony, as if he found his role of escorting us into the back garden somewhat comic.

It was so strange a presentation, so different from anything I'd seen in the plantation houses before, that I asked Philip how long he'd worked at the Brantley plantation.

"Since I was a boy," he said. "But I'm only here to help Mr. Brantley for a few days."

"So you work at some other house in the Delta?" I asked.

"No," Philip said with a slight smile. "I attend Morehouse College."

"Oh," I said, embarrassed by the lowly station I'd assumed he occupied. "I'm sure you'll be very successful."

Philip nodded politely. "That's Mr. Brantley's hope, as well."

At the entrance to the garden, he stopped, peered out at the man who sat bolt upright in a wheelchair. "Mr. Brantley has trouble moving his head, so please sit in the chairs directly in front of him."

He'd been asleep as we approached, but roused himself to receive us.

"Mr. Brantley," Philip said softly, "your guests have arrived."

"Yes, yes, thank you, Philip," Mr. Brantley said. He smiled softly. "Good afternoon, gentlemen."

He was only in his midfifties, but his long years of steadily deepening debilitation had carved trenches in the corners of his eyes and across his forehead. I had little doubt that he'd once been quite handsome, his features so finely wrought they seemed almost feminine. But there was a decidedly masculine look to his eyes, which were dark and sheathed in that gloom my father had described once in Lincoln, the product, as he wrote, "of worlds and worlds of pain."

"Please, sit," Mr. Brantley said quietly. "Welcome to my home."

We took the chairs we'd been instructed to take. Eddie sat to my left, his notebook in his lap, an accessory Brantley was quick to notice.

"So, you're writing a paper on your father," Brantley said. "Would you like a lemonade?"

"No thank you, sir," Eddie said.

Mr. Brantley turned to me. "Something stronger?"

"No, nothing. Thank you."

"Straight to business then," Brantley said. He slumped very slightly to the right, as if to get a better view. "I understand you have a photograph."

I'd given it back to Eddie by then and so it was Eddie who drew it from his notebook and presented it to Brantley, quite careful, as I noticed, to place it very near his right hand, so that he barely had to move in order to grasp it.

"Ah, yes," he said when he looked at it. "That was a lovely summer day." He lifted one of his shoulders as if attempting to shift the bone in its socket, bones that responded to him only vaguely, in tiny increments of movement. Once in position, he peered at the photograph a moment longer. "He was very bright, your father," he said to Eddie. "I sensed that he had a high intelligence. And he was very charming. He seemed . . . appreciative of everything, the favors he received."

This was obviously a good thing for Eddie to hear, but its good news had hardly settled in when a shadow fell over Brantley's face.

"But as they say, he was like rotten mackerel in moonlight," Brantley said. "He both shone and stank."

Eddie opened his notebook and began to write.

Mr. Brantley seemed somewhat reluctant to reveal what he said next, though also compelled to do so. "The fact is, my mother discovered that he stole from us. When she confronted him, he changed his stripes quite suddenly, and became quite a different boy. Very devious, cunning. He blamed the missing articles on one of the servants. Philip's father, as a matter of fact. He claimed to have seen him in the act." He shook his head. "That was absurd, and my mother told your father so. Then she forbade him from returning here and told him that his name would be put on a list of those never to be hired by the families of the plantation district."

I had never heard of such a list, though it didn't surprise me that it existed.

"She told Philip to escort Luke to the door," Mr. Brantley continued, "but even that wasn't the end of it, I'm afraid. Not for Luke Miller, who could always make a bad situation worse." He shifted slightly then described a further outrage Eddie would later render in an early draft of his paper:

My father wouldn't let anybody go with him to the door, and when Mrs. Brantley tried, he pulled his arm away and spit on the floor, right at her feet. When Mr. Brantley told me this, I remembered other times, how he was always spitting something out, tobacco from the cigarettes he smoked or a piece of gristle, or some fat he couldn't chew enough to swallow. These were real things, physical things, but I think he also spit out chances he had in life and opportunities people gave him, but which he just spit out. If he'd lived, he might have spit out my mother and me, might have spit out Lakeland and gone somewhere and later spit that place out, too, because it was natural to him just to spit out and be done with anything that crossed him or that he didn't like. Maybe it was his whole life he was trying to spit out.

"Then he ran for the door," Brantley continued. "He didn't even close it. He was running too hard, too fast. He ran all the way to the road, I guess. From there, he probably thumbed a ride, or just walked all the way back to the Bridges." He waited, watching closely as Eddie continued to write in his notebook. Finally he said, "But he must have had another side, your father."

Eddie looked up from his notebook and waited.

"Something Noel Drummond saw." He settled his gaze on the photograph once again. "The other boy in the picture. They were friends, you know. Very close friends." He lifted his head slightly, a movement accompanied by a wince. "Philip?" he called.

The young man appeared at the doorway to the garden. "Could you bring me that album from"—he stopped, glanced at the picture—"1939."

Philip retreated back into the house, and for the next few minutes Brantley inquired about Eddie's education, where he'd gotten the idea to do a paper on his father, how far along he was with it. Through it all, Eddie remained entirely self-possessed, so that I had a brief vision of him as I hoped he might one day be, poised and graceful, with impeccable manners and flawless grammar, the marks, though not acquired by breeding, of a gentleman.

Philip arrived with the album. It was very thick, the pictures inside it secured in plastic sheets.

"You can take it with you," Brantley told Eddie.

Eddie was clearly hesitant to do any such thing. "I'm afraid to," he said.

"Why?" Brantley asked.

"Something might happen to it," Eddie said.

"Not in your hands," Brantley said.

Philip again offered the album to Eddie.

"I'm afraid to," Eddie repeated.

"I know, but I want you to take it," Brantley said. "You can return it to me when you're through."

Eddie looked at me for advice.

"I think Mr. Brantley trusts you," I told him, thinking at that moment, and more fully than ever before, that I did, too.

We took the album to Breaker Landing and sat together on a bench beside the water. The pictures spoke of a time that seemed to me both recent and oddly vanishing, of garden parties populated by young girls with tightly curled hair and young men in light summer suits of fine linen. They sipped from large tumblers of lemonade or iced tea or bourbon, glasses that sometimes sprouted stalks of fresh mint. Anthony Brantley stood tall and slender among them, usually surrounded by a gaggle of laughing girls or other boys as picture-perfect as himself. From time to time servants appeared carrying silver trays heaped with meat and cheese. They wore white bolero jackets with brass buttons and neatly pressed black pants. Once I noticed a little boy in similar dress, carrying a crystal bowl filled with chocolates and sprinkled with pale petals. This, as Eddie saw and pointed out, was Philip as a child.

Toward the middle of the album, two boys suddenly appear, Noel Drummond and Luke Miller. In these few photographs they are in work clothes, the loaders and haulers of buckets of ice. They are often together, carrying tables or large metal tubs. In one photograph they sit atop the garden wall, their brown-bag lunches beside them. Luke squarely confronts the camera like one unpleasantly surprised, but determined to put his best face forward.

Eddie concentrated on this particular picture for a long time. "He was just an act," he said finally. "So nobody could see what he was really like."

"Do you think you know what he was really like?" I asked.

"Everybody says the same thing," Eddie said. "Everybody I've talked to." He offered a few names, people who'd worked with his father, a few for whom he'd worked. "They all say he could be nice when he needed to be, but that deep down, he wasn't. My mother says that, too."

It was the classic portrait of a sociopath, of one who may smile and smile, yet be a villain, but I knew that there were darker things still.

"Do you want to know everything, Eddie?" I asked cautiously.

"Yes, sir," Eddie said.

I said nothing else but returned to the album and turned the page.

There were a few more photographs, but only one of Eddie's father, standing at the garden gate, a tin bucket dangling from his right hand. After that, he vanishes altogether from the photographic record of that summer. Winter arrives, and there are no more garden parties. But the festivities continue unabated in the many sumptuous rooms of the Brantley plantation, dinner parties and costume parties, the last of which was held in the library, the walls high with books.

In one of them, a man sits in a far corner, with a little boy on his lap. He is dressed in dark pants and a snow-white jacket. He is around thirty, with sleek black hair. He wears a black, Lone Ranger–type mask, but it isn't sufficient to conceal his identity from me.

"That's my father," I said.

Eddie stared at the little boy, perhaps no more than three or four, but dressed in a perfectly fitted miniature tuxedo, his light hair neatly cut and combed, enormous brown eyes, looking for all the world entirely comfortable amid such splendor, ordained by blood to enjoy its pleasures and wield its powers.

"And that," I said, "is me."

TWENTY-TWO

Abraham Lincoln was a man who in his twenties sank into such overpowering gloom that friends feared death by his own hand, and thus held vigil over him and once locked him in a room. He was a man who frequently wept in public and could be brought to tears by maudlin verse. He was a man often found alone, seated, bent, his face pressed into his open hands, the very posture of funereal grief. He was a man darkened by rain and cold, a gray autumnal day of a man who mourned lost love and his dead son, and who felt beneath every lively vibration that life on earth affords—the tremor of youth, the shiver of love—an undertow of doom.

JEFFERSON BRANCH, *Sorrow's Last Full Measure*

I had arrived at the age of twenty-four and had never in the least, or for the briefest instant, felt that undertow. Even the aftershocks of the "incident" had lasted only for a time, and seemed far away. Then, as I drove Eddie back home from the Brantley plantation, he made a chance remark, and in the asking of it, a word sounded in my mind.

"What was the word?" Nora asked after I'd told her all this.

"Forbear," I answered. "When's the last time you heard any-one say that?"

I recalled the moment I'd first heard the word. I was seated in my father's lap. He was reading to me from a collection of thrilling stories suitable for boys. He'd reached the point where the youthful hero was opening a door that would, quite obvi-ously, reveal the solution to the mystery. *The door creaked as it opened, and the light from the corridor crawled across the floor to reveal* . . . Here, my father stopped and refused to read more until the following morning. It was a lesson in patience, he said as he rose, book in hand, and headed out of the library. I fol-lowed after him, protesting vociferously, *I want to know, I want to know,* until he grew uncharacteristically agitated, lifted his hand, and sternly silenced me. "Forbear, Jack," he said. "Forbear."

"From then on it was a very dark word to me," I added. "I don't know why, but it has always struck me as a word that comes just before some terrible thing happens."

It was a Sunday afternoon. We were walking in Glenford Park, with Morrell strolling a little distance behind us, kicking at stones or slapping at weeds with whatever stick he found along the way.

"So what did Eddie say that made you think of it?" Nora asked.

"That Sheriff Drummond had written him a letter," I said, "pledging his cooperation. Eddie's already set up an interview with him."

We sauntered on for a while, down a wide unpaved trail that had probably once been another of the old logging roads that crisscrossed the park. Nora listened as I went on about how pleased Eddie was that Drummond had contacted him, that he considered him an important "source."

"So, why . . . forbear?"

I struggled for an answer as the path wound to the right to reveal a parking area amid a narrow stand of trees.

"That's it," I said, oddly unsettled by the fact that I'd come across it at just this moment in our conversation. "That's where they found Linda Gracie's car."

Nora stopped and we both peered through the trees at the little square of paved ground to which Linda Gracie had unaccountably come on the last day of her life.

"This is where she met Eddie's father," I said. I recalled the characteristics of that chilly late-autumn day, the low gray clouds, the rain, not a good day to visit a park, go for a stroll. "A secret meeting." My gaze drifted over to the very spot where she'd parked, a shaded area in a far corner, obscured from view on every side but one. "He tortured her, you know. He burned her with cigarettes."

Nora shivered. "How do you know that?" she asked.

"Drummond told me," I said. "But I asked him not to tell Eddie."

Nora peered at the empty parking space where, twelve years earlier, Linda Gracie had brought her car to a stop. "And now you think he will?"

"No, I'm sure he won't . . . unless I tell him to."

She looked at me. "Are you going to do that, Jack?"

"Yes," I said. "Because Eddie's really looking for the truth about his father. Not some . . . image. But the truth. However brutal it may be." I glanced out into the woods. "But I don't think he should be alone with Drummond when he hears it."

Nora's solution was typically simple and direct. "Then go with him," she said. "And he won't be."

And so I did, though only after Eddie agreed to the idea, which he did quite enthusiastically, keen, as I could see, on having me evaluate his interviewing skills, give him tips on what he did well or badly.

"That would be great, Mr. Branch," he said when I floated the idea of accompanying him on his interview.

"Well, I can only do it if Drummond doesn't mind my coming along," I cautioned.

Which, as it turned out, he didn't.

"You're more than welcome to come with him, of course," Drummond said when I telephoned him. "A boy needs guidance," he added in a wholly benevolent tone. "Especially a boy without a father."

"There's one more thing," I said. "He needs to hear the truth."

Drummond said nothing.

"All of it."

For a moment he hesitated, his own judgment clearly quite different from mine. "All right, Mr. Branch," he said.

He appeared in the same acquiescent mood when we arrived at his office two days later. By then, Eddie and I had discussed his interview with Drummond. I'd offered a few suggestions on how he should go about questioning him, that he should be polite, of course, but also watchful of any defensiveness on Drummond's part. He was the sheriff, after all, I told him, and in charge of the investigation. Any problems in that investigation, any suggestion of incompetence, however slight, might cause Drummond to "swerve from the straight-and-narrow truth."

"Hello, Mr. Branch," Drummond said as we came into his office. He offered Eddie a pleasant smile. "Good to see you again."

"Thank you, sir," Eddie said politely.

"Could I offer you gentlemen refreshment?" he asked. "We have a Co' Cola machine that keeps them very cold." He looked at Eddie. "Is that the way you like them, son?"

"Yes, sir," Eddie said.

He ordered three Cokes, and while we waited for them, he talked of trivial things, the weather, Ole Miss football, whether Eddie played for the Lakeland Lions. Through it all, he was entirely amiable and open, a pleasant twinkle in his otherwise somewhat milky eyes. Often his gaze drifted over to me, as if gauging my reaction to whatever he was saying, an odd tic I'd seen before in people uncertain in their station.

The soft drinks arrived. Drummond lifted his bottle with a flourish, as if it were a glass of bubbling champagne. "Mighty refreshing," he said, after the first sip. "Some people prefer RC." His eyes slid over to me. "But I am a steadfast devotee of Coke."

He seemed pleased by "steadfast devotee," as if this arch

usage gave evidence of actual formal education. Then he caught my gaze and stiffened slightly, a child lightly struck by a teacher's ruler. A tiny, self-conscious smile flitted across his lips. "Well," he said, "I suppose we can get started."

"Yes," I said.

He shifted his attention to Eddie, who, as I saw, returned a warm look to him, and in whose soft heat Drummond seemed oddly to take comfort. "I know you've probably read whatever was in the papers," he began. "Have you talked to your mama?"

"Yes, sir."

"What has she told you about what he did?"

"Nothing that wasn't in the paper," Eddie answered.

Drummond drew in a long breath. "Well, I probably don't have that much more to tell you." He looked at the notebook on Eddie's lap. "But anything you want to ask me, I'd be glad to answer."

Eddie glanced at his notes and repeated a question I'd suggested he ask.

"What was your impression of my father?"

Drummond took the meerschaum pipe from the rack on his desk and began to fill the bowl with tobacco from a cheap leather pouch. "A gift from my son," he said when he noticed Eddie looking at it. "Came all the way from Rome, Italy." He shot me a cautious glance and seemed to expect some response.

"Very nice," I said crisply. "You were about to give your impression."

Drummond returned immediately to the subject at hand. "Impression, yes," he said, turning back to Eddie. "What was my impression?" He lit the pipe and took a few short puffs. "That he was mad inside. Always mad inside. So he had to keep control of himself, to keep from bustin' open."

He'd been mad at Linda Gracie, Drummond went on, watching as Eddie took notes, pausing to let him catch up, intervals during which he glanced toward me as though to ask if the interview were to my liking, his answers adequate and to the point, laudably responsive.

At one point, Eddie asked, "When he finally confessed, did he tell you why he did it?"

Drummond's face turned grave. "It was the old story," he said. "She had thrown him over. That was why they met in the park. She was afraid he'd act up, and people would find out that she'd been seeing him."

From there Drummond went on with the few sketchy details he said Luke Miller had told him, all of it hardscrabble stuff, a boy essentially cut loose and left to the winds, but one who struggled to claw his way out by working hard, though always reduced to the most menial labor. He'd done bad things, of course, and Drummond made no attempt to conceal them. There'd been thievery and other deceptions. He'd charmed people into lending him money and accepting bad checks.

"It had all pretty much caught up with him by the time he met Linda Gracie," Drummond said. "I figure he saw her as a way out, so when she threw him over, it was sort of the end of the line for him."

Through it all Eddie dutifully took notes, asking questions

only when Drummond's narrative came to an end, often abruptly and after a winding route, like a driverless car at a precipice.

Finally, he reached the moment of Luke Miller's confession.

"He knew what he'd done," Drummond said. "And he knew I knew what he'd done." His pipe had gone out by then. He did not relight it, but placed it softly in the ashtray on his desk. "My boy tried to help him, you know," he added as if it were a final footnote. "But he cheated Noel, too." With that, he opened a drawer and took out two envelopes. "I thought you might want to see the official report," he said as he handed one of the envelopes to Eddie. He offered the other one to me. "And seeing as you're helping Eddie, I thought you might want a copy, too, Mr. Branch."

I took the envelope. "Thank you."

Drummond looked immensely pleased with how things had gone. "Is there anything else I can do for you?" He glanced back and forth between Eddie and me. "You have any other questions?"

Eddie shook his head. "I guess not," he said.

"I do," I said.

Drummond looked at me.

"Before the murder," I said, "was there anything else?"

"Anything . . . else?" Drummond asked, clearly giving me a chance to change my mind.

I looked at him pointedly, as I thought my father would, a general to a foot soldier. "That Luke Miller did . . . before he killed Linda Gracie."

Drummond stared at me a moment, then looked at Eddie. "There is more," he said. "Bad things." A wave of sympathy suddenly swept out from him, quite mighty, as it seemed to me, in so small a man. "Real bad."

Eddie opened his notebook, placed his pencil at the ready. "Go on," was all he said.

Which Drummond did, very quickly, so that within seconds we stood together on the steps of the building, Drummond on the step above mine, which gave him added height, and which I saw as the usual gesture of a little man who wanted, against nature, to be larger than he was.

Drummond offered his hand. "Give your father my regards," he said.

"I shall."

He turned to Eddie and put out his hand. "You're a fine boy," he told him. "I have no doubt you'll go far." Then, like a bird unexpectedly descending from a distant sky, a strange tenderness settled over Drummond's face. "You'd come to me, wouldn't you?" he asked. "If you ever needed help."

Eddie suddenly looked as if he were cradled beneath Drummond's arm, willingly and comfortably cradled, with no need to look further for support. "Yes, sir," he said. "I would."

But why?

That was the question I incessantly asked myself as I drove Eddie back to his house that afternoon. Could he not see that

Drummond was a small man with many small devices and ludicrous pretensions? Could he not see the very mannerisms that made me cringe?

But I said none of this to Eddie, nor did he mention Drummond until we reached his house.

"It was hard for him," he said, "telling me those things."

"Yes," I said dryly. "Very hard." I looked at him. "Are you okay?"

"Yes, sir," he answered quietly, though I could see a certain darkness descending over him.

"We could take a drive," I suggested. "Get something to eat."

He shook his head. "My mama wants me home."

"Okay," I said.

He offered a thin smile. "Well, thank you, Mr. Branch." He tucked the envelope Drummond had given him in his notebook. "I'll read it tonight."

I returned a smile. "So will I."

And which I did a few minutes later, alone beneath the gooseneck lamp in the front room of the little house I occupied.

It was written on a police form that bore no identifying number. The name Luther Ray Miller was printed out at the top, along with the time of his arrival at the Shenoba County sheriff's office and the number of the cell in which he had been detained. Below this spare information, Drummond had written a brief summary of his interrogation of Luther Miller on the evening he was brought in for questioning. The narrative was written in a prose that was pedestrian to say the least, though the sheriff had obviously labored over each tortured line, the sort of writing one sees in those for whom written language is a slithery serpent they can only after mighty effort finally uncoil.

> **Luther Ray Miller was taken into custody as a result of a police inquiry having to do with the disappearance and presumed foul play and whereabouts of Linda Elizabeth Gracie, after a report of suspicious activity having been made to the Shenoba County sheriff's office which was forwarded to me according to procedure. Mr. Miller was taken from Cell 4 and escorted to Room 101 which is the interrogation room of said sheriff's office, which commenced at three thirty and ended at five fifteen, Miller having expressed hunger and needed a break, which I gave him.**

It both amused and amazed me that this entire rabbit warren of language had been constructed to reveal little more than the single banal fact that Luther Miller had been questioned by Drummond for less than two hours.

Nor did Drummond's writing style gain felicity as the narrative unfolded.

> **After having ordered hamburgers from Jake's and eaten and been ready to go on, Mr. Miller was seated at the desk in Room 101. He looked calm and composed and when he was offered a cigarette, he said no to it and that he was of a**

mind to talk and was ready to do so since he couldn't see any use in stringing things out as he figured he was caught and said so.

Thus, as I gathered from this thorny nest of words, Luther Miller, now gorged to the full with Jake's hamburgers, was prepared for more conversation with the astute and wily sheriff of Shenoba County, though not before Sheriff Drummond detoured into an awkward flashback.

Now before this, I'd asked him if he knew why he was here being questioned. He said he thought it maybe had to do with some house break-ins that he'd heard about taking place in the plantation district, which there was none to my knowledge. When I informed him that him being in custody had nothing to do with that, but had to do with the disappearance of Linda Elizabeth Gracie, and at which earlier time he had become agitated, and claimed that it was news to him, and that he didn't know anything about Miss Gracie's whereabouts. When I asked him if he went to Glenford Park he said no but said his property did lie at the edge of the park. I asked about the shed, and he said he used it for storage of the tools of his trade, which was yard work. When I asked if he knew Miss Gracie, he said no, but we had evidence that he did, including people saying so, which I told him. At which point I showed him what we'd found, Miss Gracie's belongings, and that she'd been found, and that there was lime on her body and we found lime in his shed, and a shovel with lime on it in the shed, too, which was his shed and his shovel and his lime. Then I said, "Luke, it's the end of the line," and he looked like he understood this, like this line had been ending for a long time and he knew there was no point holding on to it anymore. He bowed his head and kept it down awhile before he looked up again. "I was mad," he said, because Miss Gracie was through with him and told him he was no-account, and talked to him like a dog, and so he hit her and then hurt her even more, and finally decided to kill her because she was too beaten up and hurt to let it go, so he knew if she lived she'd tell. I said okay, and this would all be written up for him to sign and he said okay he'd sign it, and we shook hands like gentlemen and I sent him back to Cell 4.

The odd thing, as I noticed, was that Drummond had not had Miller returned to his cell. Instead, he'd drawn a line through Cell 4, and in his own hand, a script that bore the same large looping script with which he'd written my name on the envelope he'd just given me, had penciled in "Cell 2."

I sat back and looked at the single sheet of paper that, according to Drummond, was the only record that existed of Luther Miller's time in the county jail. It wasn't signed by anyone but Drummond and there was no indication of when it had actually been written.

I recalled Drummond as we'd all stood on the steps of the sheriff's office an hour or so ago, his parting offer of assistance, *You'd come to me, wouldn't you,* and in that instant felt a hint of something sinister so that I suddenly hit upon a different evil from any I'd lectured on before, evil done at a distance, and because of that all the more cleverly malignant, an evil full of drama and collusion, deeds done by marionettes controlled by fiendishly manipulative puppeteers. I could hardly wait for the next morning, the opening words of my new lecture already fully formed within my mind.

TWENTY-THREE

"He is known as Iago," I began after my students had settled into their seats on Thursday morning. "And he is perhaps the most evil man in all of literature."

From here I detailed Iago's jealousy of Othello, the terrible suspicions he aroused against Othello's wife, the saintly Desdemona, the murder to which these false suspicions finally led, and at last to a general discussion of this particular kind of evil, not the hand that holds the knife but the one that cleverly places it in the hand of another.

By the time the class neared its end, I was ready to pose my question for discussion.

"What is worse, do you think?" I asked. "A man like Jack the Ripper, who does terrible things himself, or a man like Iago, who willfully deceives the innocent, and by that means instigates murder without committing it himself?"

I stared out over the students in the classroom, waiting for a lifted hand. But none of the students appeared engaged by the question, nor even by the preceding presentation.

Rather than press the issue, I simply moved on to my next example, one fittingly biblical, and thus far more recognizable to my students.

"All right," I said. "How about the case of a man who wants another man's wife? Let's say the man is a king, and the other man is a soldier in the king's army."

Celia Williamson's face suddenly glowed with recognition. "I know that one," she said. "The king is David. And the soldier is Uriah."

"And what did David do?" I asked.

"He sent Uriah to the front lines in a war," Celia answered. "So he would be killed and then David could have his wife."

"Uriah's wife, yes," I said. Again I looked out over the class. "Would David have been more or less evil if he'd killed Uriah himself?"

The class stared at me silently.

"I mean, by not murdering Uriah himself, David involved another man in his crime, right?" I asked.

There was no response.

Dirk seemed to see that I was struggling, and his gloating gaze increased my sense of awkwardness and ineptitude, so that I felt like one of those boring teachers with whom I shared lunch each day: Mr. Kendall with his medieval war maps or Mrs. Donahue endlessly reciting in high chirping voice the cloying verses of "The Lady of the Lake."

It was a blow to my pride, and perhaps even to my faith that I had found, at least to some extent, my calling. And so I made a dive for the jugular by eschewing learned references altogether.

THOMAS H. COOK

"Suppose a corrupt cop arrests a man," I said. "He questions the man and tries to break him, but the man won't break
because he's innocent."

I detected mild interest, which urged me to continue on
the same track.

"Or suppose a man who's been arrested comes up with
something that threatens the cop," I said. "So the cop decides
to get rid of him."

I glanced back and saw, or thought I saw, Eddie lean forward very slightly.

"They're in a room, these two, the cop and the man accused
of murder," I continued, my tone becoming yet more dramatic.
"The cop can't kill him right there, can he?"

A few heads responded with nods and shakes.

"What then can the cop do?" I asked.

Stacia Decker lifted her hand. "He could take him somewhere else and kill him," she said. "Some deserted place."

"Everyone would see him do that," I said. "You can't just
take a prisoner out of a crowded police station then show up a
few minutes later without him."

"Maybe wait until it's late," Stacia said, still trying to hold
on to the scraps of her argument.

"A prisoner has to be signed out," I said.

Stacia shrank back, defeated.

"Maybe the guy who signs him out could be in on it," Debbie Link offered hesitantly.

"That would double the number of conspirators," I said.
"Which doubles the danger of getting caught. Besides, the cop

232

would have to find another cop who would be willing to do that. Which might be hard to find, right?"

With more nods and shakes of the head, several students allowed that this was true.

"Poison his food," Wendell Casey suggested.

"What would a detective be doing with a prisoner's food?" I asked him.

Wendell didn't bother to answer, and along with him, the class fell silent.

I waited a beat. "Let's use the Bible story. Suppose this cop were David and his prisoner were Uriah, what would David do?"

Suddenly Sheila Longstreet's hand was in the air.

"He would send the prisoner some place where he'd be killed," she said.

"By whom?" I asked.

"By another cop?" Sheila asked tentatively.

I shook my head. "No," I said. "But how about another prisoner?"

As if I'd planned it for just that moment, the bell rang starkly, ending any further discussion of the issues I'd raised. Within seconds, the students had gathered up their things and were heading out of the room, Eddie the last of them, though less in the pose of a straggler now than a student deep in thought, so that as he reached me, I expected him to engage me further, perhaps reveal his own feelings about the report Drummond had given us.

But to my surprise, he made no effort to extend our conversation, ask any questions, or request further guidance. Instead he simply nodded as he went by, and within seconds had become one with the faceless crowd of students that choked the corridor.

Once he disappeared, I returned to my desk with a vague sense of unease that I sought to relieve by reviewing my notes in the hope of finding exactly what had gone wrong in the lecture, pacing, examples, or the like.

But in fact it would be many weeks before I returned to the lecture I gave that day, and even then, I would be returned to it distantly and matter-of-factly, a figure in the witness box:

MR. TITUS: This was all supposition, wasn't it, Mr. Branch? This whole business of David and Uriah, of putting Sheriff Drummond in the place of David and Luther Miller in the place of Uriah?

MR. BRANCH: I didn't say anything about Sheriff Drummond.

MR. TITUS: But the implication was clear, wasn't it?

MR. BRANCH: It was a Bible story.

MR. TITUS: But a rather carefully charged one as far as Eddie Miller was concerned, this whole business of Luther Miller maybe being set up to be murdered by Marl Brogan.

MR. BRANCH: I didn't say any of that.

MR. TITUS: Prior to that day, had Eddie Miller ever given you any indication that he believed his father was innocent?

MR. BRANCH: No.

MR. TITUS: Had he ever suggested to you that he was a victim of any conspiracy?

MR. BRANCH: No.

MR. TITUS: All right, when did you next see Eddie Miller?

I didn't see him again until the end of the day. Nora and I were sitting in the grove that separated the school from the parking lot. She'd brought a small album of photographs, old and tattered, the only record of her family's history.

"Take a look," she said.

The sense of unease was still lingering within me, but I opened the album as if I were eager to find what lay inside it.

"My history," Nora said quietly. "My . . . blood."

One by one Nora's ancestors greeted me from their rickety porches or barren fields or outside the doors of the cotton gins and red-brick textile mills where they'd labored. They were dressed in the work clothes of their time, men in flannel shirts and trousers, or sometimes in bib overalls, women in hand-me-down dresses made, as was still common only a few years ago, from old feed sacks or bolts of cloth ordered from the local milliners and delivered wrapped in brown paper and tied with string.

"That's my uncle Fred, and that's my aunt Dottie," she said with a curious pride as she pointed out some lanky field hand, "and that's Aunt Mable," a large woman whose face was barely visible beneath the heavy shadow of an enormous bonnet. "They worked the old Boss Bryant place."

It was clear that through all the passing generations Nora's kin had toiled on the lowest rung of labor, tilled the earth's most barren fields, then trudged home to the tumbledown shacks of the Bridges. As I turned the pages of the album, it struck me that Nora had brought it to me because she'd come to a place where, by her lights, another aspect of the air between us had to be cleared of some foul debris. As always, her point was blunt: If I shared the merest tincture of what the Hugh Crombies of the world believed, then I should leave her now, close this chapter in both our lives, so that each of us, chastened by experience, could move on to relationships less likely to be encumbered by gross misunderstanding.

"What do you think of my kinfolk?" she asked.

"What do you expect me to think?"

She faced me, forthright as a hammer. "You know what I mean, Jack."

Rather than answer, I turned the final page of the album and came at last to Nora's father.

"His name was Jedediah, but people called him Jed, of course," she told me. "My mother died of TB when I was five and Morrell was twelve. He raised Morrell and me, along with a couple of cousins his dead brother left behind. Four of us in all, with barely enough money for one."

In the photograph, Jedediah Ellis looked skeletal and exhausted, slumped in the same swing in which I would later kiss his daughter.

"Why does it matter so much, Nora?" I asked. "Your people? Mine? Eddie's?"

I nodded toward where he could be seen making his way toward the parking lot, his gait steady, even a little bold, his black notebook held like a shield beneath his arm. He was alone, but Sheila stood a few feet away, waiting for him, lifting her hand toward him as he approached.

Then he stopped as if someone had called his name, stood still for an instant, a boy frozen by a thought. It passed, and he came to life again, smoothed back his hair, and continued on, Sheila now strolling beside him as they drifted obliviously past where Dirk stood in the bed of the beaten-up Ford pickup that was the hated symbol of his low estate, and from which he watched them even as he labored at the intransigent coil of an old rusty chain.

MR. BRANCH: The next time I saw Eddie was at the end of
    that same school day. He was with Sheila Longstreet.
MR. TITUS: Headed where?
MR. BRANCH: Toward his car. Dirk was standing not far
    away, looking—
MR. TITUS: How Dirk looked is not for you to tell the
    court.
MR. BRANCH: Evil.

But because I had lived all my life in a haze of good fortune, I did not say, *Forbear.*

PART IV

TWENTY-FOUR

Time changes everything but the past. Take Lakeland, for example. Its home-owned shops and restaurants are now lost in antique mists. When they appear to me at all, it is through a scrim of memory, and therefore ghostly and abandoned, like orphans left on church steps. It was once utterly Southern, with its courthouse square surrounded by shops built from timber sliced and shaved at the local sawmill. Now it is an "American" town, more or less indistinguishable from any other of similar size. The old shops have given way to franchise operations that sell the same wares one would find in Providence or San Diego. Our "local handicrafts" are made in China. The townspeople line up in Japanese cars at the end of the day and receive their dinners in paper bags handed to them by teenagers wearing paper hats. Their children are overweight, unlettered, and for the most part untested. They watch movies on iPods and read almost not at all. Worse still, from an old man's point of view, is that they have been taught that love must be offered without judgment, and thus grow up strangers to a sense of shame.

My father taught me differently of course, and so I still live under what he called "the dust of unrightable wrongs." When he wrote that phrase he was talking about slavery. But when it circles through my mind, I think of Eddie.

"Do you think he could have been saved?" I asked Wendell not long before he died. He was lying on an old foam sofa, the table next to it littered with pill bottles and beer cans. He shook his head. "Not after Dirk got all fired up." He winced. "Be glad when it's over."

"How bad is the pain?" I asked.

"You get used to it," Wendell said. He smiled. "Remember how you once said that life is just a matter of getting used to pain." He reached for one of the orange plastic pill containers. "In court, that's where you said it."

I remembered the moment. Mr. Titus had asked a final question: "Will you ever get used to the pain, Mr. Branch?" In response, I'd offered the world the final product of my experience: "Getting used to pain is what life is."

"Anyway, it'll be over soon," Wendell said. "Toby says I only got about a month to go." He squinted to read the label on the bottle. "No, Eddie couldn't have been saved," he said, returning to my earlier question. He looked at me and saw, perhaps, a field of ravaged lives. "Wasn't none of it your fault, Mr. Branch. You didn't know."

I recalled the terrible thing I "didn't know," but said nothing about it.

Wendell swallowed the pill with a gulp of beer. "Dirk was just bad to the bone."

Wendell was three weeks dead before I actually saw Dirk for the first time since he'd been sent away, a black sheep returned, still unwanted, to his fold. His hair had dulled to a lusterless gray, almost the color of his eyes, and his face was worn, with deep crevices that ran down from his nose to the sides of his mouth. Jagged furrows cut horizontally across his forehead as if plowed there by a farmer who cared nothing for the land he tilled.

"Like some old lemon car," Wendell added, "more wrong with it than just the brakes or the clutch." He looked at the clock and reached for another pill. "Made of nothing but bad parts."

I grasped for one saving grace. "Do you think he loved Sheila?" I asked.

Wendell shrugged. "Well, at least he didn't do nothing to her that time in the car."

The "time in the car" had come out during the trial, Mr. Carlton cautiously leading Sheila through a series of events whose grim aftermath still unnerved her.

> Mr. Carlton: Were you surprised to see Dirk that evening?
> Miss Longstreet: Yes, sir. I didn't know who it was at first. Because he was driving this hot rod he'd been wanting. On a test drive, he said, but he was going to buy it he told me.
> Mr. Carlton: Buy it?

MISS LONGSTREET: Yes, sir. He wanted me to go for a drive
  with him. But I said no. Because the last time I went for
  a drive, he took me to that shed.
MR. CARLTON: The incident you previously described?
MISS LONGSTREET: But Dirk promised it wouldn't be like
  that. He just wanted me to take this test drive with him.

And so reluctantly, because her heart was open and she was
a trusting person, Sheila Longstreet got into Dirk Littlefield's
red hot rod with its shiny wire wheels and gleaming exhaust
pipes, and drove away with him, leaving her mother staring
fretfully out the curtained window of the house they shared.

It began as a leisurely drive into the countryside, she told
the court, through orchards and fields, the phantasmagoric
landscape of the Delta. Dirk spoke of his plans, she said, which
were vague and dreamy, something about moving to Jackson,
going to mechanic's school. He didn't mention their recent es-
trangement, nor anything about their previous encounter at the
shed.

They drove with the windows down, Sheila said, and Dirk
let his arm dangle outside the car, driving with his other hand
poised at the top of the wheel. He seemed determined to show
command, that he was still the Dirk whose girl she'd once been,
intent now on getting her back, an effort to which she responded, as she told Mr. Carlton, "in a bad way."

MR. CARLTON: What way was that?
MISS LONGSTREET: I told him no.
MR. CARLTON: That you wouldn't come back to him?

MISS LONGSTREET: Yes, sir.

MR. CARLTON: How did he react to that?

MISS LONGSTREET: He jerked the wheel and turned the car back around.

MR. CARLTON: Back toward Lakeland?

MISS LONGSTREET: Yes, sir, but we didn't go there right away.

MR. CARLTON: Where did you go?

MISS LONGSTREET: The plantation district.

It was approaching dark when they turned onto the long, serpentine road that winds among the old plantations, the grand houses of the Rankins, the Brantleys, and, of course, Great Oaks. Through the long drive, Dirk said very little until he suddenly caught sight of a particular house, and at that point drew the red hot rod to a halt and peered out at a mansion whose snow-white columns rose majestically beyond a grove of oaks.

MR. CARLTON: Which house was this?

MISS LONGSTREET: It was Mr. Branch's house.

MR. CARLTON: Jefferson Branch?

MISS LONGSTREET: Yes, sir. Mr. Branch's daddy. A big house. Mighty nice.

The evening shade had deepened by then, and so Sheila saw lighted windows in the distance, all of them upstairs, as she told the court, so that I knew it was my father's office she'd glimpsed that night.

"You know who lives there, don't you?" Dirk asked.

Sheila shook her head.

"Mr. Branch's old man," Dirk said. "He's a drunk. Tried to kill hisself. Dug a ditch right up the side of his head." His eyes slid over to Sheila's. "Never goes out is what that cross-eyed guy at Sander's grocery told me. Has everything delivered. Pays in cash."

They talked on about other things the "cross-eyed guy" had said, the splendor of Great Oaks, how much it must take to run such an estate. Then, according to Sheila, Dirk suddenly mentioned Eddie.

MR. CARLTON: What did Dirk say?

MISS LONGSTREET: He said it was creepy the way Eddie was always hanging around Mr. Branch, getting help with his paper.

MR. CARLTON: Is that all he said about Eddie and Mr. Branch?

MISS LONGSTREET: Yes, sir. After that he started talking about how he was going to buy this car we'd been riding around in, how he was going to find a way to get the money for it.

MR. CARLTON: What way was that?

MISS LONGSTREET: Just a way, that's all he said. I figured it was something bad.

MR. TITUS: Objection. Opinion.

JUDGE MILLSTONE: Sustained.

And so Sheila never told the court what she suspected Dirk intended to do in order to get the money he needed for that

fiery-red hot rod. For it was now Mr. Titus, Dirk's defense attorney, who took over the questioning, bent upon exploring a
different area of the case, closing in upon that final, fatal night.

MR. TITUS: Miss Longstreet, when you and Dirk went on
　　that drive, did Dirk at any time threaten you?
MISS LONGSTREET: No, sir.
MR. TITUS: Did he threaten Jefferson Branch?
MISS LONGSTREET: No, sir.
MR. TITUS: Did he threaten Eddie Miller?
MISS LONGSTREET: No, sir.
MR. TITUS: There was no mention of Dirk beating anybody
　　up, was there?
MISS LONGSTREET: No, sir.
MR. TITUS: And certainly no mention of murder, isn't that
　　right?
MISS LONGSTREET: No, sir, he didn't mention killing
　　anybody.
MR. TITUS: In fact, the only thing that was really clear is
　　that he didn't care much for the way Eddie Miller was
　　always getting special help from Mr. Branch, correct?
MISS LONGSTREET: Yes, sir.
MR. TITUS: But you didn't see anything wrong with what
　　Mr. Branch was doing with Eddie, did you, Miss
　　Longstreet?
MISS LONGSTREET: Wrong?
MR. TITUS: Wrong, yes. You didn't see anything wrong with
　　it, did you?
MISS LONGSTREET: I guess not.

In all her lengthy testimony, this was the only answer Sheila gave that later struck me as hedged in doubt, as if she'd already begun to consider a dark motive for the help I'd offered Eddie, a process, as I later discovered, that had continued through the years, but which she only addressed once, as it were, face-to-face.

She was in her forties by then. It was a spring day when I came upon her picking through a local yard sale.

"Hello, Sheila," I said.

I'd come up behind her, so that when she turned abruptly, she stepped back suddenly, almost fearfully.

"Sorry," she said. She patted her chest rapidly. "You scared me, Mr. Branch."

Time and loneliness and the long drip of disappointment had weathered her into a raggedly composed middle-aged woman.

"I've moved over there." She nodded toward a tangle of squat brick public-housing units that some years before had been built on the very land the Bridges had once so grimly occupied. "It's just me since my mama died."

For an instant I couldn't look into her eyes, and so glanced down at the small item she held in her right hand. "You've found something, I see."

She shrugged. "I got a bunch of them at home. Little glass animals." She lifted her hand and opened her fingers to reveal the glass figure of a unicorn. "It's like the one the girl had in that play they did last year at the high school."

"*The Glass Menagerie*," I said. It had been the senior play of

Lakeland High the year before. "I didn't know you went to plays."

She looked once again misjudged and underestimated, exactly as she had looked so many years ago, when she'd approached me as I sat reading in the bleachers. Once her perfect beauty had blinded others. Now they were blinded by her disarray.

"I just meant . . . ," I began.

She folded her fingers delicately around the unicorn. "Eddie loved me," she said. She lifted her head like one making a defiant stand. "And he wouldn't have loved just any girl."

"Yes, I know."

"You were just his teacher," she said in a tone that struck me as oddly unsettling, some errant piece of the puzzle still missing from the picture.

I could tell she wanted to say more but didn't know how, or if she should, so that it came from her in a small explosion. "Nothing like Dirk said you was maybe up to."

"What did Dirk say I was 'up to'?"

Even then she could not bring herself directly to repeat so unseemly an accusation. "I mean taking up with Eddie like you did . . . and you not married and all."

It was an idea she'd never mentioned in court but which Dirk had planted in her mind, a grim seed of suspicion she had never managed to uproot.

"I was only Eddie's teacher," I added, now staring at her intently. "Nothing else, Sheila. Only his teacher."

She suddenly smiled her old sweet smile. "Well, nice seeing you again, Mr. Branch," she said.

"You, too."

She turned and strolled out among the sprawl of discarded things, weaving through a bramble of old dishes and lamps before she finally reached the road.

I saw her only rarely after that, and on those occasions she wore the same bedraggled clothes, her hair a gray tangle, her eyes webbed with wrinkles, so that I never again recalled her in the full beauty of her youth, her flawless white skin, the long black hair that must have blown so freely in the wind as Dirk pulled away from my father's house that night, going faster and faster as he angrily sped back toward the Bridges.

Years later, seeing him in my mind as I sat that final time with Wendell, the two of us veiled in the gloom of his trailer, among the clutter of his many medicines, I had only one question left.

"Did you know what Dirk was going to do?" I asked.

Wendell looked as if I'd suddenly accused him of a crime. "Course not," he said. "If I'da known, I wouldn'a gone with him." He appeared to see the story unfold before him. "Even tried to stop him." He seemed to see a thick darkness cut suddenly by two bright beams of light. "Just like Miss Ellis done."

TWENTY-FIVE

She was never more beautiful than the day we picnicked at Glenford Lake. It was late May and the flat surface of the water mirrored a cloudless blue sky. At Nora's insistence we'd all worn bathing suits under our clothes, and at the water's edge we quickly stripped down to them, Morrell and I rather shyly, Nora in a happy, heedless rush.

She made a quick turn and dashed toward the water, crashing into it and striding forward up to her knees before making a headlong dive. When she came up again she shook her hair, and it is there I freeze the frame, her face wet and glistening, silver lines of water cascading down her neck and shoulders. Had she not continued to look human, I would have thought she had no fate.

Morrell and I approached the water more cautiously, Morrell even more timorous than I was of the chill.

"Oh, come on in," Nora called. She was already far out, waving us into the water, then disappearing again beneath its surface.

Morrell looked at me. "It's cold."

"Yes," I said. "But we'll get used to it."

He smiled. "Okay," he said. "Okay, Jack."

But we never made it into the water. I never went deeper than my knees, and Morrell stopped even before that. It was just too cold, so cold that I marveled that Nora wasn't shivering when she came back on shore.

"I don't know how you stand it," I said as I wrapped the towel around her. "It's a punishing cold."

She laughed. "That's the point, Jack."

She sat down in the grass, stretched out to let the sun dry her, watching with great amusement as Morrell and I slipped back into our clothes. I sat down, but Morrell remained standing, his attention focused on a line of ducks, a mother and three chicks paddling along the waterline.

"They don't sink," he said. "Davey sank."

I looked at Nora quizzically.

"Our little brother," she said. "He drowned here."

"They're floating over him," Morrell blurted suddenly. His gaze was still focused on the ducks. There was a frightened glitter in his eyes. "They're . . ."

"No," Nora said. "Davey's not in the water. They pulled him out."

Morrell's gaze followed the ducks as they drifted farther out, toward the deep water at the center of the lake.

"Davey's in the ground," Nora said. "You know that, Morrell." She turned back to me. "We better go," she said. "It's coming back to him. He gets upset."

And so we packed up and drove back to Nora's house, where we picnicked on her front porch, pretending for our own amusement that we were still at the water's edge. After that, because Morrell still seemed agitated, we took a drive, first through town, then out into the surrounding area where, on a whim, I took the long, lovely road that led into the heart of the old plantation district.

Perhaps I had always intended to do what I did at that moment. Perhaps the thought came to me suddenly.

"How'd you like to meet my father?" I asked.

Nora looked truly surprised. "Now?"

"Why not?"

"But I'm not wearing—"

"You're wearing what you always wear," I interrupted.

"What about Morrell?"

"I want Morrell to meet him, too," I said.

She seemed to take all this for what it was, the next step, traditional and time-honored, the presentation of the intended.

"Okay," she said.

We drove down the road that led to Great Oaks. It was only a short ride, but all during it Nora filled Morrell in on what was happening, that the house we were going to was "Jack's father's house," and that we were going there to meet "Jack's daddy." Morrell watched the house grow large as we closed in upon it, but he seemed less fearful of it than I'd expected him to be.

"It's like when we go out to eat," he said.

"Exactly," Nora assured him. "Nothing to worry about."

The drive was circular, and beautifully maintained, so different from the disrepair into which it later fell, its proud columns now cracked and chipped beneath a stranglehold of clinging vines, the surrounding grounds gone back to the wild, with tufts of crabgrass and dandelion springing up haphazardly beneath a weaving undergrowth of misshapen oaks.

"It's the family pride," I told Nora as I brought the car to a halt before the tall white columns. "They once threw great balls here," I added. "For all the plantation neighbors. Jefferson Davis came here more than once." I looked at her. "Where did it go, all that glory?"

"It went to war," Nora answered with striking clarity, and not a whit of sentiment. "Where glory always goes."

And I thought, *She is the one.*

The miracle of which must have fully registered in my eyes.

"What?" Nora asked, when she looked at me.

All I could do was smile. "You," I said.

She laughed. "Stop it."

With that she got out of the car, opened the back door, and offered her hand to Morrell. "Okay, brother," she said. "It's time to meet our betters."

And so it was an odd tableau that greeted my father when he opened the door, I to his right, an unknown young woman in a cheap blue dress beneath my arm, a childlike man in bib overalls clinging to her hand.

"I'd like to present Miss Nora Ellis," I said to him with full formality. "And her brother, Morrell."

He was still in his bathrobe, a book in his hand. For a moment he seemed lost as to what he should do. Then a warm smile bloomed on his face. "Welcome to Great Oaks," he said to Nora and Morrell. "I'm honored to have you as my guests."

The next hour was surely one of the grandest of my life.

Like a lord of the manor, my father escorted Nora and Morrell through the downstairs rooms of the house, the great dining hall with its satin drapes, the sitting room with its massive sofas and chairs and footstools, the library, where we lingered over port. He talked a little about me and a little about Lincoln, but said nothing of himself or of my dead mother. Instead, he made his usual beguiling turn and focused on his guests, asking questions about Nora's life and Morrell's, then continuing the discussion of themselves by means of follow-up questions and asides that kept them to the subject of their own experience.

It was like turning the gilded pages of *The Holy Book of Southern Manners,* watching its hallowed rules come to life before me, my father a standing miracle of antebellum charm, his every gesture meant to put his guests at ease. In fact, everything about Nora and Morrell appeared to captivate him. The Bridges held nothing but enchantment. He marveled at every humble detail, the sweet odor of cotton poison on her father's clothes, the dawn risings of innumerable cousins from their crowded beds, boiling water for a bath, the fiery taste of cheap whiskey, the family and bar brawls that sometimes spilled out into the muddy streets.

It was an act of course, and I saw instantly that Nora realized this, too. But she continued with her stories all the same in a softly informative tone, tales told not to entertain my father or designed in any way to garner his approval but, rather, to educate him, cut through his wall of manners, breach the fortress of his charm, and show him, once and truly, what it meant to be a Bridges girl.

"There was a joke my mother once told me," she said. "The plantation boys told it to one another."

"Oh, good," my father said. "I love jokes."

"It was before there were phones in the Bridges," Nora said. "So the joke was, 'How do you call a Bridges girl?'"

"How?" my father asked, faking anticipation.

Nora's eyes chilled. "SooEEEEEEEEEE!"

It was the call farmers made to summon pigs.

My father's lips parted wordlessly, with no hint of a smile.

"You're right," Nora said to him quietly. "It's not funny." Her gaze remained fixed on my father. "So thank you, sir, for not laughing."

My father's full approval of Nora shone in his eyes. "Come," he said rising from his chair and indicating the stairs that led up to the never-visited inner sanctum of his office. "I want to show you where I commune with Lincoln."

I drove Nora home through an evening as beautiful as any I had ever known. Morrell sat with us on the porch for a while, then wandered back into the house and turned on the radio.

"He turns on the radio when something's bothering him," Nora said.

"Davey?"

"Probably," Nora answered. "He was there when it happened. He has pictures of it in his mind."

We talked on for a time, in the cool and quiet of that soft spring night. In the deepening darkness, the smell of Bridges cooking wafted from the tumbledown houses that surrounded us, meats cooked in lard or bacon fat, boiled potatoes and collard greens, a fare that varied little from day to day, and which never included the ethnic staples of the North, never pasta of any sort, never anything cooked in wine or sherry, nor seasoned with savory or tarragon or herbes de Provence.

Nora drew in a long, oddly troubled breath. "It's peaceful here this time of day, but it can get rough at night. Drinking and fistfights, the ritual beating of the wife."

"God," I whispered. "You Bridges people sure are trash."

She abruptly drew her hand from mine, got up and sat in the swing, drifting slowly forward and backward, her bare toes softly moving in whispers across the smooth cement porch.

"What is it?" I asked.

"I don't like that word," Nora said. "Trash."

"I didn't mean it," I told her. "It was just a joke, Nora."

She gazed out over the battered landscape of the Bridges. "We're all tangled up together." She pressed her feet against the floor of the porch and stopped her flight. "Eddie's come to that conclusion, by the way. Sheila says his paper isn't about his father anymore. It's about the Delta. Growing up here, taking it in."

Which explained, I realized suddenly, the odd places where I'd spotted Eddie in recent days, sitting in the town park, on the steps of the courthouse, in the bleachers of the old ball field, sometimes with Sheila but more often alone. I'd noticed his notebook growing, too, bulging with photographs and small slips of paper, all of it carried in a frayed military pack he'd no doubt bought for pennies at the town army surplus store.

"Sheila thinks he should make a book out of it," Nora said. "She thinks he could be a great writer." She laughed. "But then she's in love with him, so naturally she thinks he's Shakespeare."

"Another small-town boy," I said. I looked out over the rows of wooden houses, their littered yards and cluttered porches, the little that remained of Wanda Ruth's palace of delight. "I grew up in never-never land," I told Nora. "But something real lives here."

Nora's eyes flashed visibly, two small white fires. But she remained silent, and in that brief silence I got a presentiment of heaven, that if it existed at all, it was not a place of gold or glory, raptures or ecstasies, but just the eternally felt presence of a loving heart.

As if summoned, Nora rose from the swing, padded over to me softly, lowered herself beside me, and tucked her arm in mine.

"It's time, Jack," she said.

I looked at her. "For me to go?"

"For you to stay," was all she said.

TWENTY-SIX

And so, the next morning, when I faced my class, I found it hard to talk about evil. But I'd written that day's lecture weeks earlier, still liked what I'd written, and so proceeded.

"In Dante's *Inferno*," I began, "the lowest circle was reserved for traitors." I flipped the switch on the overhead projector and a man dressed in full eighteenth-century finery flashed onto the screen. "His name was Benedict Arnold."

From there I detailed Arnold's life, focusing on his great abilities, his fine looks, the many sterling attributes that were his. On the overhead projector, I displayed this fine figure of a man in various portraits I'd assembled for the lecture, sometimes in formal dress, with waistcoats and undervests, sometimes in various military uniforms. I let the class bask in the splendor of his good fortune, his highborn friends and lovely, wealthy wife.

"Throughout his life," I said, "Benedict Arnold had known nothing but good fortune. It had come to him by birth. He'd inherited high intelligence and good looks. He'd been born into an esteemed and wealthy family. He had every gift a man could possess, save the one that might have spared him infamy."

This was high-flying language, and I could see that it had soared over the heads of my students. So I brought myself and them back to earth.

"As a man, Benedict Arnold was vain and easily offended," I continued. "The British took note of this, and played upon it, and in the end, at America's most desperate hour, won him over to their side."

From there I described Arnold's clever deception, how he'd contrived to win command of West Point, then immediately handed it over to the British, an act of treason Arnold himself believed sufficient to destroy all hope of American independence.

"But like many a traitor before him," I continued, now wading deep in patriotic gore, "Benedict Arnold suffered from a terrible misjudgment." I paused and let their anticipation build. "When two great forces vied for his devotion," I concluded, using words that would accuse me for the rest of my life, "he chose what was old and dying over what was trying to be born."

On that trumpeting note, I brought my lecture to an end. "Any questions?"

There weren't any, and so I moved on with my class plan.

"Okay," I said. "How about reports on the progress of your papers. Anyone ready to give the class an update?"

Stacia Decker's hand shot up.

I sat down at my desk and watched as she took her place behind the wooden lectern and informed us yet more fully about her paper on Adolf Hitler. Celia Williamson followed with Judas, then George Frobish with Joseph Stalin, his information culled, he said, from "the stuff my daddy gets in the mail."

Toby Olson was the last to raise his hand.

"Yes, Toby."

Self-effacing as he would remain all his life, the future Dr. Olson took his place behind the lectern. "I'm going to write about Frankenstein." He glanced down at the single page of notes he'd brought up with him. "Not the monster. The doctor. Because he didn't want to create the monster to help people. It was just that he wanted to be famous." He looked at me. "That's all I have to say, Mr. Branch."

"Fine, Toby," I said. "Good choice. Different."

He took his seat.

"Anyone else?" I asked.

I glanced toward Eddie, but his hand remained on the top of his desk.

I looked at my watch. "Okay, we have a few minutes before the bell. Just work on your papers, and I'll ask for more updates tomorrow."

When the bell rang, they gathered their papers and headed out of the room. Eddie was nearly to the door before I said, "I hear your paper has expanded."

He looked at me quizzically.

"The subject of your paper," I explained. "It's about more than your father now."

He nodded. "Yes, sir."

"Don't forget about the deadline, though," I warned him pleasantly. "Are you almost finished?"

"I guess," Eddie said. "But there's one person I can't talk to. I mean, on that list I made."

"Who is it?"

"Marl Brogan," Eddie said. "He's in prison at Willard's Bluff, and they won't let you in if you're not eighteen or a relative."

"How do you know that?"

"Mr. Drummond told me. He tried, but they said no."

"So even Drummond couldn't get you in?" I asked.

Eddie shook his head.

This didn't surprise me, for though sheriff of Shenoba County, Drummond cut no great figure in the affairs of the Great State of Mississippi, his position little more than servile to the families who actually ran it. Even a young son from such a family, as I well knew, had more authority than he.

"Don't worry about Sheriff Drummond," I told Eddie.

I thought of my own fortunate connections, the doors that would open for me because I was a Branch. "Let me see what I can do."

What I did was make a phone call to Holton Wainwright, my fraternity brother in college. His father had been governor of the state for the last eight years, and thus the man who oversaw the penitentiary system. I told Holton where I was teaching, the assignment, the fact that Eddie Miller, known locally as the Coed Killer's son, had chosen his own father as the subject of his paper. I added a few details, then moved on to the matter of Luther Miller's death at the hands of Marl Brogan.

The whole conversation took only a few minutes, after which, by only a few minutes more, Holton called back with the happy information that the doors of Willard's Bluff Prison would be open to me.

"But is Brogan willing to talk to Eddie?" I asked.

"Willing?" Holton laughed. "Jack, Marl Brogan is in the custody of the Great State of Mississippi. He's a mule in a stall. He moves when we poke him, otherwise he stays put."

As for prisoners' rights, I learned, there weren't any. Brogan would speak to whomever he was told to speak to because he had murdered another human being and by that act, according to the thinking of the day, had forfeited any tender consideration for his feelings.

"Just show up at Willard's Bluff and tell them who you are," Holton said.

Man to man and class to class, I said, "You're an officer and a gentleman, Holton."

In the code of our brotherhood, he added, "Beneath the apple blossoms, Jack."

Meaning, together at the next Gettysburg, where this time we would win.

I knew that without me Eddie would not be permitted inside Willard's Bluff, so there was never any question but that I would go with him, a drive of just over seventy miles.

"We could go this Saturday," I told him in the hallway later that day.

He was clearly surprised not only by my offer to accompany

him to Willard's Bluff but by the ease and speed with which I'd been able to remove the obstacles that had thwarted Drummond and so must have seemed enormous to him, the complex apparatus of state government, penitentiary regulations, questions of security, even Marl Brogan's permission, all such considerations brushed aside by a simple fraternity connection.

On the way to the prison, I took the opportunity to give Eddie a few pointers.

"When you meet Brogan, act as if you like him and think he's important," I said. "You have to charm the people you need, the people you want to get something out of."

Eddie nodded, then opened his notebook to a particular page and studied the few lines he'd written there.

"Why is that page of such interest?" I asked him lightly, merely as a way of making conversation.

"It's the one with questions," Eddie said. "For Mr. Brogan. I think it's better to memorize them, so I'm not always looking at notes."

With that he closed the book and looked out at the passing countryside, the rounded hills, distant barns and farmhouses, animals grazing in grassy fields. Something about him struck me as alien to the landscape, born here, but set apart not only by what his father had done but by his own indefinable rootlessness, or failure to root, as if his native soil were inhospitable to his growth.

I took a page from my father's book. "Maybe you should leave this area," I said. "Lakeland. The Delta. Maybe even the whole South."

He gave no hint that such advice had struck a chord.

"Go up North, maybe," I added for no particular reason

save that the North had always beckoned a certain kind of Southerner, particularly those of literary bent. "Some big city. New York, someplace like that. You could start over. Get away from all this . . . history."

Eddie could not possibly have found this a realistic idea, of course, but my own good fortune had inflated my hopes for him, made it as boundless as it was romantic. In its grip, I imagined Eddie living in New York, down in Greenwich Village, where poets recited to a jazz accompaniment and everyone seemed to smoke cigarettes in underground bars. I gave this vision full voice. "Maybe you could be a writer," I said. "You seem to like it. Doing research. Talking to people. Maybe journalism. Working for a newspaper or a magazine."

Eddie smiled softly, but clearly without the slightest belief that such a possibility might be his.

And so I offered something more realistic, a proposal he might actually be able to take seriously. "We could look at colleges for you. There are scholarships." I added another touch of reality to the possibility that I could see Eddie beginning to entertain. "And my father knows people. He could write you letters of introduction."

The network to which I alluded was something Eddie could hardly have grasped save distantly, like a beckoning mirage, and yet, as he listened, he seemed to see such a future take shape, though only vaguely, as in a dream.

"Of course, there'd still be living expenses," I said. "But . . ." I stopped, thought it through, decided it was possible. "But I might be able to help you with that, too. My father, I mean. A loan, of course. I don't mean charity."

Eddie said only, "Thank you, Mr. Branch," but I let myself believe that my impulsively stated dream for him might actually have taken root, that lifted on its wings, Eddie would eventually escape from the low estate that otherwise awaited him, the heavy weight of living his whole life among people who knew him only as the Coed Killer's son.

And in my vaulted pride I allowed myself to touch a little of what I thought God must have felt on the last day of creation, when He looked upon His work and declared that it was good.

TWENTY-SEVEN

"Life reverses the myth of creation," my father said.

It was a day in late summer, as we sat in the now generally untended garden of Great Oaks, watching a languid breeze rock the ragweed and dandelion that flourished where carefully nurtured roses had once held sway. I shifted an arthritic shoulder. "How so?" I asked.

"The myth starts in darkness and ends in light," my father answered. "Life goes the other way."

"Not for him," I said, nodding toward where Morrell, his large head fringed in short white hair, squatted in a patch of shade, playing with my father's once-prized collection of hand-painted Civil War figures. He glanced up when he noticed our eyes upon him, grinned briefly then returned to his play, toppling a plumed Nathan Bedford Forrest, a sure sign that the general had been shot.

My father shook his head softly. "Forrest wasn't killed in the war," he said, still the great Lincoln biographer, a stickler for historical accuracy.

"And so went on to become the first Grand Wizard of the Ku Klux Klan," I added.

Which Marl Brogan later joined, I thought, my mind clearly determined to keep the dark thread of my story forever weaving in the air around me.

A bell sounded the postman's arrival at my door, bringing his customary load, along with his usual tidbits about marriages and births, news he delivers in brief bulletins, himself, in his own lights, the self-styled historian of the Delta.

"Marl Brogan died." He touched a crooked finger to his cap. "Crawford said you'd be interested."

Crawford was the town postmaster, and he'd always seen it as his duty to indicate tidings he thought particularly significant to the final son of Great Oaks.

"Do you know who he is?" I asked. "Marl Brogan?"

He shook his head. "Don't ring a bell, Mr. Branch." He said nothing else, and appeared anxious to be on his way.

"Good evening, then," I said, since there was clearly no point in further discussing news that, though curiously momentous to me, meant little to anyone else.

But he'd brought the daily paper, too, so that, once seated again in the garden, I learned that Brogan had reached the age of seventy-four, still at Willard's Bluff because he'd committed additional outrages while in prison, assaulting fellow prisoners as well as guards and staff, his prison term extended again and again, utterly unable to control his own malevolent impulses.

Yes, I thought, malevolent impulses. Marl Brogan had been nothing but a ball of those.

As Eddie must have perfectly understood the day he met him. And yet there'd been a moment of true sympathy, as I once again quite vividly recalled. It had been brief but oddly deep, and I always replayed that moment when I remembered that day—which I often did—for it was surely, as I knew too well, the point when my story suddenly veered off the well-worn and predictable path and into the dark wood where nothing was as it had seemed, or ever would be again.

And on that thought, I was there again, approaching Willard's Bluff Prison, Eddie in the passenger seat, the black notebook in his lap.

"It's small," he said as the prison walls rose before us. At the time, it was his only mention of what Willard's Bluff looked like, though later he would compose a more detailed picture of the place:

> There were vines all over. They hung down from the trees and climbed up the walls, where someone had cut them so that they didn't go over the walls, because if they did, the prisoners might use them for ropes and hoist themselves up and out of prison. At the prison gate, everything had been cut away, so that only honeysuckle was left, thin green vines dotted with small white flowers that Mr. Branch called "trumpet-shaped." These little white flowers bowed when we brushed by them, and when they did that, they looked humble, like prisoners.

At the gate, I told the guard my name, why I'd come, and, of course, mentioned the clearance I'd gotten from the governor.

Predictably the gate opened and Eddie and I were ushered up a wide set of stairs that led to the warden's office.

"So, you're a friend of Governor Wainwright."

He was a big man, with a sleek bald head and cheeks I might have described as rosy under less austere conditions. He'd clearly dressed up to receive me, a dark three-piece suit, complete with vest buttoned top to bottom over his large, rounded belly.

"Of his son, actually," I corrected. "We were roommates in college."

"And fellow members of the Kappa Alpha Order, I believe, as was your father before you."

"Yes," I said.

"Whose spiritual founder was Robert E. Lee."

I smiled. "There was a portrait of him in the dining room."

"As well there should have been," the warden said. He thrust out his hand. "Homer Preston."

I shook Preston's hand, trying not to wince at the pressure of his grip.

Preston turned a beaming face to Eddie. "And you're the boy writing a paper, I take it?"

Eddie nodded.

"Well, Marl's not feeling well," Preston said. "As a matter of fact, he's been in the prison infirmary quite a few times over the past weeks." He looked at me, and his eyes glinted with suspicion. "It may well be fakery, of course. The food is better in the infirmary, as are the mattresses. But when a prisoner claims to be ill, we have him taken there rather than expose the rest of the prisoners to whatever ailment he may or may not have contracted."

I expected this to lead to a polite apology for having had us come all this way, only to find Marl Brogan too ill to receive us. But instead, Preston stepped around me and over to the door. "Right this way, gentlemen."

The warden led us out of his office, back down the stairs through a series of checkpoints until we reached the doors of the prison infirmary.

"This is Dr. Kuykendall," Preston said by way of introducing us to a very tall man with steel-gray hair. "He's in charge of the infirmary."

"I'll leave you to your business now," he said with a second hearty handshake. He looked at Eddie. "Good luck with your paper, son." He turned to me. "Fine thing, being a teacher." I could see that he found it a sacrificial calling, so much less than the many, far greater professions that had no doubt been within my reach. "Mighty fine thing."

"Thank you."

With that, Preston turned and left us.

"Mr. Brogan is kept apart from other prisoners," Dr. Kuykendall warned us. He wore round, plastic-framed glasses, and behind their thick lenses were eyes that seemed very still, as if weighted down by the grave things they had seen. "He has a very violent temperament, always getting into fights with other prisoners. For that reason, he's not allowed in an open ward."

"He's in solitary?" I asked.

"Most of the time," Dr. Kuykendall said. "Even in the infirmary." He turned and directed us into the bowels of the hospital, a scene Eddie would labor to describe in one rewrite after another, until at last he settled on this:

The prison hospital at Willard's Bluff was quiet except for a few sounds, small sounds you wouldn't notice anywhere else. I heard sheets flapping from open windows and the creak of unoiled wheelchairs and bedsprings screeching. When a prisoner turned onto his side, it sounded like someone whispering under the sheet. In a place like this, stillness has a sound, or maybe it's a weight. I thought of the *Inferno* because Mr. Branch had talked about it in class that week, but this seemed different. In the *Inferno* people moved and flopped around. But here, everything felt walled in, with nothing going on, just people waiting in a place they'd never be let out of. To them, death must have looked like open space.

Brogan had been placed in a locked room at the far end of the infirmary. Once inside it, Dr. Kuykendall drew back the thick plastic curtain that surrounded his bed, but only slightly, merely enough room for us to step within its folds. Then he closed it, and we stood beside Marl Brogan's bed, in a silence Eddie later described as "hard" in the sense, I think, that he suddenly found himself standing before a man who seemed connected to life by nothing but a fierce malignant spark.

Brogan's face was almost perfectly round, with ears that sprouted like dried mushrooms from the side of his head. His lips were full and faintly purple. His hair was a dull yellow and cut very close to his head, little more than a brittle fuzz. But these merely physical characteristics paled before the "feeling" of Marl Brogan. It was unhappiness in its pure state, beyond what pain can do, or disappointment, a core unhappiness that drew light from the air, and which I mistook, following Dante, as nothing less than a total loss of hope, not only in oneself or one's circumstances but in the whole benighted scheme of things, all that had ever been or would ever be.

"Who are you?" he barked.

"My name is Jack Branch," I answered. "And this is Eddie Miller. Luke Miller's son."

He looked at Eddie, and for a moment everything went very still. Then he returned his gaze to me and a strange, primitive vehemence wafted up from him like heat from a sun-baked stone.

"Your daddy taught at Lakeland," he said.

I offered him a courtly smile. "Yes, he did."

"Wore a bow tie," Brogan added. "Prissy."

I stared at him sourly. "I wouldn't call him that."

Brogan didn't argue the point. "You this boy's teacher?"

"Yes, I am."

Brogan stared at me silently for a moment, and during that brief interval I sensed a misery that was rooted not in the hopelessness of life itself, as I'd earlier speculated, but in the fact that even pure malignancy was helpless against it. Marl Brogan could slaughter whole villages, commit untold atrocities, and still fail to calm the rage inside himself.

A single, spiky eyebrow arched upward like a bristling worm. "What you looking at?" he barked.

"You," I answered stiffly, determined not to be cowed by such an apish creature.

Brogan laughed into a cough, saw the cough to its rattling end, and laughed beyond it. Then he turned to Eddie. "So you're Eddie Miller."

His tone was impossible for me to read, and thus, I assumed, impossible for Eddie, and so I intervened.

"Mr. Brogan," I said, "Eddie is writing a paper about his father."

Tiny, demonic fires glittered in Brogan's eyes.

"He has a few questions for you," I added.

Brogan's smile looked as if it had been sliced across his face. "Your old man still alive?" he asked me.

"Yes."

Behind the smile I saw teeth that were sharp and jagged, like a broken bottle.

"Ain't teaching no more though, is he?"

"No, he isn't teaching anymore," I said.

A diabolical sparkle flickered in his eyes, watchful, observant, but maliciously so, like a seeker of filth searching ever deeper into the sewer's depths.

"What is he up to now?" Brogan asked. "If he ain't teaching no more."

"He's writing a biography of Lincoln," I said matter-of-factly.

Brogan's body appeared to coil, like a snake with a lizard in its sights. "Shit." He glared at me. "I bet you're one of them wants us to go to school with niggers."

I stared at him coldly.

Brogan laughed. "No skin off your nose what happens, right? Your kids won't ever have to go to school with 'em.

They'll go to some fancy school, like you went to." He turned to Eddie. "His daddy wouldn't put his little boy with us scum from the Bridges. But now I bet he wants my kids with niggers." His eyes shifted over to me. "It don't ever come down to your own, the things you do. You run off and send off, but we set right here."

I squared my shoulders and turned to Eddie. "I don't think we're going to do any good here," I told him. "This man—"

"No, wait," Eddie said. He looked at Brogan. "Why did you kill my father?" he asked softly.

For a moment Brogan didn't face him, but instead continued to stare at me, his eyes like a vise slowly squeezing in. Then he drew his gaze away, and turned to Eddie. "What are you looking for, boy?" he asked.

A terrible challenge dripped from every word he said, and for a moment Eddie hesitated. Then very quietly, he said, "Just why you did it."

"Why?" Brogan asked. He looked at Eddie pointedly. "Do you really want to know that?" His tone turned oddly tender, a man holding back with what seemed all he had of self-control. "'Cause it ain't good, what I got to say."

"Yes, sir," Eddie said. "I want to know."

"All right," Brogan said. "I kilt him because I don't hold with what he done to that girl, like she was just some trash." He faced Eddie squarely, like a man, eye to eye. "Treating her the way he done, and her a little thing couldn't put up much fight." He shrugged. "So I figured he maybe oughta know what it feels like, being treated that way." He raised himself up slightly, as if to give added weight to what he said. "Fact is, your daddy turned out mighty weak, so it didn't take much to bust him up." He smiled. "Sort of weak and sickly, like Old Man Branch."

"That's enough," I blurted.

Brogan looked at me as if I were the largest tiny thing he'd ever seen, inhumanly small, but monstrously inflated. "Even a little prissy," he said. A jagged smile cut around his mouth. "And I can see you're just like him."

"I hope so," I said, chin uplifted, proud of both my father's high estate and selfless service, and proud, as well, of mine.

Brogan stared at me a second or two longer, then turned toward Eddie, so that for a moment I thought he was about to say more about Luke Miller, give his son some small pinch of hope that his father was something other than a monster. But instead he said, "All right, take care, boy."

For a moment they seemed curiously connected, a tie I found oddly unsettling, though not as much as Brogan's parting words to Eddie, offered with a jerk of the head back toward me. "And don't get fooled by the likes of him."

TWENTY-EIGHT

And don't get fooled by the likes of him.

As I drove Eddie back to Lakeland, I wondered if those words were circling in his mind, empty words, of course, but words that hinted that something sinister lay behind them.

For a long time Eddie said nothing about our meeting with Brogan. Instead, he watched the landscape sweep by or flipped through the pages of his notebook. His silence struck me as forced, a way of avoiding the issue of Brogan's banal but strangely incriminating remark.

"I hope you don't let what Brogan said bother you," I said finally.

Eddie shrugged. "It's just the truth," he said.

I was shocked not only by Eddie's response, but by the casual way he'd offered it.

"Just the truth?" I asked. "What truth? Marl Brogan doesn't know one thing about me."

"I mean what he said about my father," Eddie said.

I felt a wave of relief that he'd been speaking of the "truth" of his father's unwholesome nature rather than the notion that he should mistrust "the likes" of me.

"I've almost finished talking to people," he added as he opened his notebook again. He studied a list of names, most of them crossed out. "I still have Mr. Crombie."

"Mr. Crombie only sees the worst in people," I said.

Eddie offered no response to this, and I wondered if perhaps the work itself had begun to wear him down. After all, he'd found nothing remotely redeeming in his father, no hint of goodness upon which he could hang a shred of respect.

"What about my father?" I asked. "He was one of your father's teachers. You should talk to him. He might know something no one else has told you. Something good . . . or at least enlightening, about your father."

He appeared to consider this in small steps, like a detective thinking through the bits and pieces of a case, putting tiny shards of evidence together, building a picture of the crime. Then he said, "I guess so, Mr. Branch."

I felt that he had met a crisis and overcome it, and I rejoiced in having helped him do it.

I said nothing else about my father as we made the drive back to Lakeland, but I knew what the next step in his inquiry would lead him to, and that I would help him go there, as I had helped him all along. Driving through the deep green countryside, I thought of the Confederate orphan, the little boy I'd dreamed of helping, and knew, without doubt, that he was Eddie.

———

And so, when Nora asked me how I was doing, I answered quite truthfully that I was in great spirits because I'd never loved teaching as much or more deeply felt its power to guide a human life.

"My goodness," she said. "How . . . effusive."

It was Saturday night, after the trip to Willard's Bluff. We'd gone to dinner and returned, the two of us now seated on the steps of the front porch, Morrell inside the house, contentedly asleep in front of the droning radio.

It was then she asked, "So, what do you think Marl meant?"

I'd told her about the trip to Willard's Bluff, the strings I'd pulled to arrange it, all done with an open heart, and so there was nothing in the "likes of me" against which Eddie should have been warned.

"I don't have any idea," I answered. "But whatever it was, I don't think it had any effect on Eddie. He still completely trusts me."

She glanced away, peered out into the little squares of light that shone weakly in the Bridges.

"Have you ever thought, Jack, that maybe you've gotten too close to Eddie?"

"No," I said. "Do you think I have?"

"Well," Nora answered tentatively, "you're just his teacher, not blood kin or anything."

I leaned back and challenged her. "If you think I've gotten too close to him, what do you think I should do about it?"

She gave her answer boldly. "I think you should let Eddie do the rest of the work himself," she said.

"But I've already told him that he should talk to my father," I told her. "Shouldn't I at least help him with that?"

"No," Nora answered.

"But how can I refuse to—"

"You should tell Eddie that you'd be glad to take him to your house, introduce him to your father, all that stuff," Nora said. "But that you think he should do that kind of thing himself from now on. Like it's part of his training. He's the one who's writing the paper, so he should call your father, ask to talk to him. You tell him that he needs to learn to do things like that on his own. If there's a question to be asked—of your father or anyone else—then it's up to him to ask it."

And I thought, *Yes, she's right.*

"Okay," I said. "I'll tell Eddie to call my father, set up a meeting, ask him whatever questions he wants."

What I didn't know as I lounged with Nora the remainder of that evening was that he already had.

It was at our once-a-month "dress for dinner" that I learned exactly what Eddie had done.

My father and I had spent the last hour in the great dining room. He'd served coq au vin with roasted potatoes and a colorful vegetable puree. Dressed in a dark suit and bow tie, he'd talked almost entirely of Lincoln, rendering Gideon Welles's eyewitness account of Lincoln's death, how "the giant sufferer," as Welles called him, had been too tall for the bed, and had therefore been laid diagonally across it.

Then a long silence, followed by what seemed a curious

conclusion. "Ah, Jack, how hard it is to please our fathers." He seemed briefly lost in self-examination, his eyes very still and directed inward. "Especially if he's a tyrant, as mine was."

I was surprised to hear this. "But you always seemed so happy with each other."

He glanced over at the portrait of his father. "Harmony is oppression's sweet disguise," he said wearily. He studied the portrait a moment longer. "Nothing mattered to him but Great Oaks," he said. "That the Branches should own it forever."

"Don't you want that, too?" I asked.

He shook his head. "All I ever wanted, Jack, was to be a writer."

"And you are one," I told him. "You're writing a biography of Lincoln. And each day you write in your journal, don't you?"

"My journal?"

"*The Book of Days.*"

My father waved his hand, as if dismissing these daily entries as mere excrescences, unworthy of consideration, a work of vanity, perhaps futility, never to be more.

"I wanted to be a novelist," my father said. "A mighty writer with a mighty theme." He appeared to return to some particularly frightful moment in his life. "But even little verses were beyond me. You read one of my poems once."

I remembered the moment well. I'd come home from my freshman year at college, and after dinner, my father had produced a few verses he'd written for the occasion, and which he'd seemed to think quite good.

"You held it in very low regard, remember?" he added.

I'd tried to disguise my true feeling, the fact that I'd found his poem cloying to say the least, but he'd seen through me, caught the embarrassment, even pity, I'd felt for his poor efforts. After that, he'd never shown me anything again.

Now he said, "But my father wanted only that I should produce an heir, and I, of course, sought his high regard." He smiled. "Which I finally gained when you came along." He glanced again at my grandfather's portrait. "It is a cruel thing, Jack, to have a cruel father. As that boy well knows."

"What boy?"

"Luke Miller's son."

"Eddie?" I asked. "What brought him to mind?"

"I suppose I was just recalling our conversation."

"What conversation?"

My father was clearly surprised by the question. "The one I had with Eddie," he answered. "What a burden it must be to carry such an evil legacy. The Coed Killer's son."

"When did you talk to Eddie?"

"Yesterday," my father said. He rose. "Shall we have a port?"

Within seconds we were in the library, my father at the liquor cabinet, pouring each of us a glass.

"A very fine boy, Eddie," he added. "Very . . . intense."

We touched glasses and drank.

"When did he come here?" I asked.

"Friday afternoon," my father answered. "And I must say, he has lovely manners. He called before coming over, behaved like a perfect young gentleman. If he hadn't been dressed the way he was, I'd have taken him for one of your Kappa brothers." He took another sip. "There's nothing . . . desperate about him. Which is good, because desperate boys do desperate things. They kill for love, or make a third charge at Cold Harbor." He seemed to retreat to his research. "Grant writes like Hemingway, did you know that? So eloquent in his understatement. He is the true father of modern American literature, Jack." He shook his head. "I wish I had his gift for that, to say things simply, and let them go at that."

My mind was on a less distant subject.

"What did Eddie ask you?"

"My impression of his father. Which wasn't very favorable, I'm afraid. To the extent that I recalled him at all, he seemed something of a schemer. Always trying to curry favor, but with something distasteful at the bottom of it all. A manipulator of affections."

"You told him that?"

"Yes, I did," my father answered. "Because he seemed to seek the truth." He downed the rest of the port, took his glass, walked back to the liquor cabinet, and poured another round. "There's something about that boy, Jack. A sweetness. I noticed it in his eyes."

I had seen only loneliness and isolation, but if my father had glimpsed something more, then so be it. "His life has been hard," I said.

My father nodded. "There's something strong in him, too. Something that can survive great trial. Like a crab. You can yank it across the ocean floor, jerk it out of the water, slam it against the bottom of the boat, and still, Jack, it won't let go. Even when it's only grabbing a hook." He returned to his chair and eased himself down into it. "There is grandeur, I think, in the simple grasp of things."

He said this with a flourish of the hand that was theatrical enough for the stage, and it struck me that my father had always held a kind of celebrity status for me, lowering now but still radiant, like someone famous long ago.

He lifted his glass and twirled it slowly in his fingers. Reflected light played on his face in a mirror-ball effect. "He asked if I thought he should keep a journal," he added.

"That's because I mentioned *The Book of Days* to him."

"Why on earth would you have mentioned that?" my father asked.

"I told him I thought it a good idea for a writer to keep a journal."

"A writer?" my father asked. "Is that what you have in mind for him?"

"Maybe."

"And you, dear Jack, will be present at the creation," my father said as if the scheme had suddenly come clear to him. "A teacher who discovers a brilliant boy, nurtures his genius." He nodded toward my nearly empty glass. "Care for another?"

"No, thank you."

My father smiled. "A sipper, not a drinker, Jack," he said. "It's good you didn't inherit my appetite for alcohol." He returned to his chair, and drew in a long, deep breath, like a swimmer readying himself for an airless dive. "Nor the 'bottoms.'"

That was when I saw it, a tiny glimmer in my father's eyes, quick, barely visible, a tiny marker of some deep-seated sorrow. I glanced toward the van Gogh self-portrait and felt a sudden urge to connect the red dots that marred it, though I also knew that my father had never felt a need to confess anything about the "incident," preferring to discuss Lincoln's melancholy rather than his own.

When I returned my attention to my father, he was staring at me very intently. "Eddie Miller," he breathed as he slowly drew the glass to his lips. "Such a fine young man."

I left Great Oaks an hour or so later. I was quite tired and so I went directly to bed, hoping for a long, restful sleep. Instead, I found myself thinking about the mood of dread my father had so often described. It came upon him on otherwise indistinguishable days, I knew, a sense of something dark and bloody gathering round him, "a black aura," as he'd often called it. All the Branches had felt it, he said, equally distributed among the men and women, a darkness that came upon them, lingered for a time, then departed. But though a Branch, I'd never shown the slightest hint of this affliction. And so, that very night, when I felt its slight downward tug for the first time, it was with a curious sense of induction, as if I'd passed through some Kappa rite of passage and was now officially a member of the tribe.

And so I called my father.

"I know what you mean now," I said. "About the 'bottoms.'"

My father said nothing, so that I heard only the strains of the Brahms Violin Concerto in the background.

"It's a sense of impending trouble, right?" I added. "Of something waiting in the wings?"

"Not at all, Jack," my father said. "Nothing is waiting in the 'bottoms.' Everything is already there. Pressing down and down."

This was far more severe than anything I'd felt, and my father seemed almost amused that I'd brought up so small a discomfort as the one I'd described to him.

"What can you do about it, then?" I asked. "Something as serious as that."

"Slowly or quickly?" my father asked. He had clearly been drinking since I'd left, but even so his words rang entirely clear.

"Slowly," I answered.

"Whiskey."

"And quickly?"

"A gun."

I laughed, because despite the deadpan tone of my father's voice I'd taken his last answer as a joke.

But I was wrong, for his next line was delivered in full solemnity. "You don't have the 'bottoms,' Jack."

This was said with great certainty, and followed by a pause, very dramatic, though I couldn't tell if it was calculated for effect or truly the product of the caught breath that preceded what he said next: "But I fear Eddie does."

TWENTY-NINE

Why would my father have said such a thing, I wondered. What had he seen in Eddie that I'd missed?

These questions were still playing in my mind the following Monday morning. And so, when I saw Eddie coming down the corridor, I decided to engage him.

"So, I understand you spoke with my father," I said.

He nodded.

I congratulated him on his self-reliance, the way he'd forged ahead without me. It was teacher-talk to some degree, but it was also a way of probing for the dark side my father had glimpsed but which had eluded me. I'd seen Eddie's isolation, his shyness, his uncertainty, all of which had become less noticeable as he'd worked on his paper. But for all that, I'd seen no hint of the black mood that swept in upon my father and which had seemed, only two nights ago, to have briefly fluttered around me.

"My father was very impressed with you," I told him.

Eddie said nothing, a silence that suddenly struck me as

perhaps melancholic, rather than merely the expression of shy people or those who were simply soft-spoken.

"I hope you enjoyed yourself at Great Oaks," I added.

Again he nodded silently.

"Eddie?" I asked. "Is something wrong?"

His voice held nothing but a chill. "Do you think you can inherit it?" he asked. "Being really bad."

"No," I told him. "I don't. But why that question?"

"Something your father said," Eddie answered. "About a 'family disease.'"

"He meant depression," I told him. "All the Branches have it."

"Do you?" Eddie asked.

I thought of the slight sense of dread that had come over me, how quickly my father had dismissed it.

"No," I said. "At least not in the way my father suffers."

Eddie nodded. "I saw that," he told me. "When I talked to him." He seemed almost to age before me. "He has a lot of pain."

It was, he said, something he'd "written up" at home later that night, a description I was to read only after our story had reached its end:

I asked Mr. Branch about my father and he said that he re-membered that he was always alone, and that each time he was caught in some bad thing, he'd try to appear innocent, but knew he wasn't innocent, and never could be, because there was something in him that was dark and that he knew he had this darkness but not how to get rid of it.

At which point, my father, in Eddie's rendering, had turned characteristically philosophical:

He said that he'd been unprepared to help my father, and that unpreparedness was the sad part of life, that nobody is ever ready to make the choice he has to make or do the thing he has to do, and this sounded like something anyone could say because that's the way it is, but he said it very slowly, and there was a beat to the way he spoke, so that how he said it sounded better than what he said, like they were the words of a song.

But that morning, as we stood in the hallway together, I knew only that in some vague way Eddie had seen something in my father that had moved him, perhaps even taken him briefly out of his search for his own father, and directed his inquiry toward mine, a veering from the path that his next remark made clear.

"He wants me to come back," he said. "He said he'd like for us to talk again."

My father had given me no indication of such a wish when I'd spoken to him about his talk with Eddie, but he often kept such things to himself. It was part of a general secretiveness that was as much a part of his nature as his drinking and depression, and which had always been symbolized by the way he kept *The Book of Days* locked in a cabinet, wrote in it only late at night, and refused to let anyone have the slightest glimpse of it.

"Come back to Great Oaks?" I asked.

"Yes, sir," Eddie answered. "Do you think he'll ever get better?"

"No," I told him. I shook my head heavily and sadly, as if coming to grips with truly mighty things. "I don't think anyone can help him."

"But someone should try," Eddie said gravely.

Which was, as it turned out, precisely what Eddie did.

But I learned that only later. As for that day, I made no further effort to engage Eddie, but merely headed to my classroom, where he took his usual seat, Sheila steadfastly at his side.

"Okay," I said. "Let's get settled."

I waited for the customary interval of shifting about, reaching for notebooks and pens, scratching and stretching, a delay in getting started that my boarding-school teachers would never have tolerated. But these were Lakeland students, Bridges kids, as I continually had to remind myself, fidgety and distractible, a predisposition to inattentiveness that Mr. Crombie thought—as he'd stated flatly and often—inseparable from their lowly blood.

"All right," I said. "Let's begin."

I'd decided to give the entire class over to progress reports on their term papers.

"Okay," I said. "Who wants to go first?"

They came forward without hesitation, led by Stacia Decker, as always. She'd discovered that Hitler was likely an illegitimate child, and speculated that the early trauma of this experience, the fact that he'd never known his father, had worked "like acid" on his character. "He got burned by being illegitimate," Stacia declared, "and so he burned the Jews."

This was worse than rudimentary psychohistory, but at least Stacia was putting one thing with another, and so I said, "Very interesting, Stacia, a Freudian analysis."

Her face went blank.

"From Freud," I said. "A theory that history is really individual history, not a product of great forces as Marx—"

"Who?"

Stacia had now returned to her desk and was scrambling to make notes.

"Karl Marx," I said.

Again, a total blank.

"He believed that history was determined by great economic forces," I informed her.

"Marx is in my paper," George Frobish blurted. "Stalin loved him."

"Yes," I said dryly. "I'm sure he did."

From there, the reports came forward like weary workers in a factory line, Celia Williamson on Judas, whom she said one local religion placed next to Jesus, "because betraying Christ was his job and he did it and died for it"; Toby Olson on Frankenstein; and at last Wendell Casey, who'd chosen Dracula because he'd liked the movie, though he hadn't known the movie was from a book, as he proudly put it, "by the English author Stroker."

"Stoker," I corrected.

He looked at me like a little boy scolded. "Right, Stoker," he said. "Brian Stoker."

"Bram," I corrected again. "Bram Stoker."

Wendell slumped from behind the lectern and took his seat. "Next?"

No one volunteered, and so, responding to an inexplicable but generalized feeling of hostility, I chose the one student in my class I truly despised.

"Dirk?" I said. "Time to hear from you."

Dirk shrugged. "I ain't chose yet."

"Then you need to choose," I said firmly.

Dirk's gaze didn't rise from the pattern of gouges and pen markings that peppered the top of all the ancient, battered desks of Lakeland High.

"Some people have been reading and gathering notes for several weeks now," I told him sternly. To rub it in, I linked two names in a way I knew would sear the moment in his mind: "Sheila, for example. And Eddie. They've already chosen their subjects and are working hard on their papers."

Dirk said nothing.

"So it's time now for you to choose your most evil person," I told him firmly.

His gaze remained downcast, but his voice hardened. "Maybe I'll choose you," he said. "How about that, Mr. Branch?"

Nora was shocked.

"What did you do when he said that?" she asked.

It was later that same day, and we were standing in the corridor outside my class, watching as the last of the stragglers made it to their assigned rooms.

"Nothing," I answered. "I just stared at him for a minute so the class knew I wasn't going to be cowed by him. Then I said, 'Disapproved,' and gave him a cold little smile."

"Good," Nora said. "You know what Mr. Crombie tells new teachers? 'Don't smile 'til Christmas.'"

I laughed. "He has something there, you know."

She nodded. "Did Eddie make a progress report?"

"No," I said. "But he's working hard. He went to my father on his own and got the interview. My father was pretty impressed with him."

Nora was pleased, of course. "See, I told you. He should handle things himself from now on."

"As a matter of fact, I think he made a real connection with my father," I added.

This also pleased her, though she clearly read something unpleasing in my face.

"How so?" she asked.

"I don't know," I told her. "But that's part of the mystery, isn't it? Who likes whom?"

"So you're surprised they got along like that?"

"I'm not surprised they had a nice chat," I said. "But I'm surprised my father invited him back to Great Oaks for another one."

"Why?"

"Because Eddie's so uneducated," I answered. "And my father and I always talk about intellectual things."

Nora shrugged. "Maybe he's tired of that," she said.

———

Her response had been typically frank, and though she'd made it casually, with no unsettling import intended, I found it disconcerting, the notion that my father had begun to tire of the type of conversation that had always been ours, studded with erudite references, and almost always directed at what he called "the mighty questions." In that sense, it seemed to me, I'd only followed his lead, talked in the way and about the subjects that were likely most to please him.

In this, I thought, I was at one with my father, since he'd always labored to please his own father. Such was the circle of life as it applied to the Branches, one I'd found no need to break.

But as my father had once said, to every answer we must append "the eternal 'and yet,'" that hedge against certainty that forces us to admit that life remains guesswork at best.

As Nora and I chatted on it was that "and yet" I pondered, then continued to ponder for the rest of the day.

My father had granted Eddie a full interview, *and yet* asked him back to Great Oaks. He had spoken of this interview with me, *and yet* had revealed almost nothing of its content. I had known my father all my life, *and yet* it was Eddie who'd suddenly seemed curiously stricken by his suffering.

These matters were still vaguely flitting through my mind when the last bell rang and I headed for the faculty parking lot. As usual, Eddie was among the students who were heading for their cars.

"Eddie," I called.

He was standing with Sheila, the two of them now the only students in the throng who'd ceased to move forward.

"Give my regards to my father if you see him before I do," I told him.

I expected him to mention when that next meeting was to take place, but instead he said, "I will, Mr. Branch," then turned, Sheila on his arm, and joined the moving river of other students toward their cars.

"Nice kid."

I turned to find Hugh Crombie at my side.

"We had a nice talk about his father," Crombie added.

I couldn't imagine Hugh Crombie having a "nice talk" with anyone.

"He's not trying to make a saint out of the bastard," Crombie added. "Which is what I figured he'd do. Maybe even try to convince himself that he didn't kill that girl." He smiled, his eyes all but twinkling as he singled Eddie out of the surging throng. "Made of stronger stuff than I thought, that boy."

"Yes," I said. "He is."

Crombie was practically beaming. "Nice to be surprised."

Not always, as I discovered later that same day.

I'd headed home directly after school, read for a time, but listlessly and with oddly little interest, so that I'd finally put the book down, stretched out on the sofa by the front window, hoping to grab a short nap before I rose and prepared dinner.

But sleep eluded me, and so, after a time, I got up, made a quick dinner, then once again picked up my book. It was a novel of some sort, though I no longer recall either title or author, which is testament of a sort to the vague distraction that had settled over me during the day, and which urged me toward human contact. Had Nora had a phone, I would have called her, talked through my steadily growing unease.

Instead, I called my father.

His failure to answer after the first ring did not disturb me. Nor the second, nor even the third, since he was at times preoccupied with his writings, and thus slow to answer. But there was a fourth ring and a fifth, and at the sixth I thought of our last conversation, the only swift treatment he knew for the "bottoms," *a gun.*

I felt a sharp blade of anxiety, put down the phone, and rushed to my car. Evening had fallen by the time I got to Great Oaks, but no lights were on, not even the one that burned continually in his upstairs study.

I knocked, but there was no answer at the door, and so I opened it and went it.

"Dad?" I called.

There was no response, so I called again, my voice still echoing through the house as I stepped into the foyer.

I checked the library first, and after it, all the rooms downstairs. Finding them empty, I walked out into the garden, where I found a stack of books by a chair, along with an empty tumbler and a half-filled bottle of bourbon.

I went back into the house and climbed the stairs to my father's study, its door ajar, the room itself in a gloomy light until I turned on the lamp that rested on his desk. The room brightened, and I saw the hundreds of pages of his Lincoln biography, along with stacks of note cards and boxes filled with correspondence, a vast and no doubt steadily accumulating messiness from which it seemed impossible that a finely etched portrait of Lincoln could possibly emerge. The large mahogany cabinet where he kept *The Book of Days* rested next to the window, as it always had, doors closed, under lock and key. A standing desk was next to the cabinet, so that I got a vision of my father at work, alone at the desk, recording his days one by one with ancient pen and ink.

All was as I had seen it often enough before, with only the deepening clutter to suggest any passage of time within the room. What was missing was my father.

I'd just gone back downstairs and stepped out of the house, hoping the cool air might give me some idea as to my father's whereabouts, when I saw a single light in the distance. It closed in upon the house very slowly, so that several seconds passed before I saw my father emerge from the darkness.

"Where have you been?"

"I just went out for a walk about the grounds," my father said, as if his straying from the house was not a wholly new behavior. "Lovely night, isn't it?"

He was dead sober, with no wobble in his walk, no slur in his speech.

"It's awfully dark out there," I said.

"I have light enough," my father said with a quick smile.

"What were you doing out there?" I asked.

"Just thinking," my father answered with an almost playful shrug.

"About Lincoln?" I asked, hoping now to engage him in conversation.

"No," he answered lightly. "About Eddie."

THIRTY

Out of natural courtesy he received, but did not appropriate. It was like a gift placed in the palm of an outreached hand upon which the fingers do not close.

The lines were from *Billy Budd,* and I found it ironic, given that I'd begun to reread the book on the very day I'd first noticed Eddie and Sheila beside the brick colonnade, that my father read them to me only a few minutes after we'd gone back into the house, both of us now seated in the library.

After reading them, my father looked up at me. "Eddie's like that," he said. "He's like Billy Budd. He has the same natural courtesy along with an admirable capacity to receive something without greedily appropriating it as his own."

I made no effort to disguise my surprise at this grandiose portrayal. "So you had another meeting with him, obviously," I said.

"Yes, this afternoon," my father said.

"And was it fruitful?"

"I think so," my father answered. "And you know, while we

were talking I found myself thinking that Eddie's grandmother might once have worked here at Great Oaks."

"Really," I said. "When was that?"

"It had to have been in the late twenties," my father said. "I was away at college by then, so I saw her about the place only that one summer." He appeared quite pleased to have recovered this memory. "I do recall a very pretty girl named Adela, however. Which, as it turns out, was the name of Eddie's grandmother."

"But how do you know it was she who worked here?"

"Actually, I don't," my father answered. "It was just something that came up."

I leaned forward slightly. "So, in this conversation with Eddie, did you recall anything about his father?"

"We didn't talk about his father," my father told me. "Instead, I mentioned the orchard, the one that's like Lincoln's face." He smiled at what seemed the memory of a pleasurable exchange. "And in response, Eddie said a strange thing." He appeared curiously moved. "That it reminded him of his mother's face."

"Well," I said. "I've taught him that things look like other things, so he's just applying—"

"They all have the same ravaged look, it seems," my father interrupted. "Lincoln, Eddie's mother, the orchard. Chewed up by life." He rose, and by means of a route so often taken that it had gently warped the floor, he made his way from his great chair to the liquor cabinet at the other end of the library. "I told him I liked that better . . . chewed. Because it's more active. Life as an animal that chews up great souls."

"I wouldn't call Eddie's mother a great soul," I said.

"Really," my father said. "What's she like?"

"Bitter," I said. "A Bridges woman."

"A Bridges woman," my father repeated. Without opening the cabinet or pouring a drink, he returned to his chair and eased himself into it. "Have you read much of this paper Eddie's writing?" he asked.

"Only bits and pieces," I answered.

"How far does it go back in his life?"

"All the way, I suppose. He was five when Luke Miller killed Linda Gracie."

It was clear that the murder story at the center of Eddie's life had little interest to my father.

"But what you've read of the paper, it's good?"

"It's okay," I said. "Not great, by any means. But at least it's not . . . embarrassing."

Something in my father's eyes chilled. "Well, one certainly wouldn't want to be embarrassed by one's writing," he said stiffly.

"You think I'm being harsh?" I asked.

"I think the heart is a better reader than the head," my father answered.

"But one has to—"

My father lifted his hand, so that I saw how much the subject pained him. "Anyway," he said as he leaned back into the chair and released a long breath, "Eddie's young, so he has plenty of time to find his way in life."

I smiled, seeking now only to soften my father's mood. "May we drink to that?" I asked.

Thus we did, first the one glass, then another, and another, as the night wore on. Through it all, we spoke no more of Eddie, but instead retreated to the familiar ground of intellectual subjects, the Greeks and Romans, the Civil War, and, as ever, Lincoln, though even in this last, most grand of subjects, my father's interest ultimately waned, his mind preoccupied with other matters, though he gave no hint of what these matters were.

But this was not the abiding mystery of that evening, one I hadn't guessed until, as I drove home that night, I suddenly found the lines of the road blurring, straight roads curving, heard the grind of my tires on dirt sidings rather than the pavement, then, almost in a single fluid motion, saw a face appear before me, small and pinched, eyes beneath a snap-brim hat that, like the face, appeared to be blinking red and blue.

"Evening, Mr. Branch."

I stared at him through a tunnel of greased air.

"It's Sheriff Drummond."

"Ah . . . ah . . ."

The door of my car breezed open and a wind lifted me to my feet.

"Let me just get you into my car, Mr. Branch."

On a cushion of air I floated toward the blinking light.

"We'll just have you sit a spell."

I descended to earth, where all was silent, save a soft crackling, and a voice.

"This is the sheriff, I'm gonna be busy on Route 4 for a time. Ten-four."

The world was a gossamer veil wrapped around my ears and eyes.

"I got a thermos of coffee, Mr. Branch."

Steam.

Heat.

Then in a slow, slanting decline I drifted downward into nothingness.

I awoke at Great Oaks, sprawled across the sofa in the parlor. Outside, dawn was just breaking, bathing the grounds in a golden light. I rose, moved unsteadily to the window, and looked out at the estate. A light dew sparkled on the grass and shimmered in the trees. For a moment I luxuriated in the sheer beauty of it, then something sharper pierced me and in that instant I felt the pull of the generations of Branches who'd stood at this window and peered out at this dawn. It was a transcendent emotion, fierce and searing, and in which I felt that mingling of blood and soil, man and his ancestral lands, about which Southern poets had so often sung. This is what it means, I thought, to belong to a place.

It was intoxicating in its sweetness, and I might have lingered in its emotional eddies for some time longer had I not heard the sound of footsteps overhead.

I knew it was my father padding about in his study, and so, a son with apologies to make, I climbed up the stairs to face him.

He was sitting at his desk, the room strewn with boxes, though they were considerably different from the ones I'd seen the night before. In fact, as I realized after a quick rub of my eyes, they were shoe boxes filled to overflowing with a vast number of multicolored papers of differing sizes.

"Father," I said.

He looked up from the large mound of papers he'd piled onto his desk.

"I wish to apologize for my behavior," I said. "It was unseemly not to know when I had reached my limit."

To my surprise, my father appeared to greet what I'd done as a welcome lapse in my rigid sense of decorum. "I always wondered what your limit was, Jack," he said.

"I'm sure no Branch has ever been detained for public intoxication," I said.

"That's true," my father said. "The Branches hold their liquor."

"I believe I remember Sheriff Drummond."

My father nodded. "He was kind enough to bring you home. A deputy drove your car. It's parked outside." He glanced at his watch. "It's a school day, Jack."

It was his way of pulling me up short. "Yes, I know," I said quickly. "I'll be on my way."

I turned to leave, then, driven by my own curiosity, faced the room once again. "What are all these boxes?" I asked.

"The innards of Great Oaks," my father said. "Payment receipts. Canceled checks. Invoices." He went back to work. "I wanted to look them over before I spoke again with Eddie."

"Eddie?" Nora said. "What do all those old papers from Great Oaks have to do with Eddie?"

We were having lunch on the bleachers of the athletic field, one of the few places on the school grounds where we could be alone.

"I asked him that," I said. "He said it was because Eddie was working on more than a paper about his father, or even Lakeland, which we already knew. Now he's writing about—can you believe this?—my father's actual words: 'Eddie is writing about life on the Delta.' It's some kind of history, it seems, and my father has become quite animated about it. A great project, he seems to think. He even quoted Melville before I left, that to write a mighty book, one must have a mighty theme." I shrugged. "Anyway, it seems to include Great Oaks."

"And that bothers you," Nora said. "I can see that."

"I guess it does," I admitted.

"Why?"

"Because it's . . . sacred."

She smiled. "Only to you, Jack."

Which was a sentiment my father clearly shared, given the fact that he was busily going through the vast accumulated papers of Great Oaks at what appeared to be Eddie's behest.

Nora offered me a bit of her sandwich.

I shook my head.

"Still off your feed?" she asked.

"I'm not used to drinking like that," I said. "My father can hold any amount of liquor and stand upright and walk straight and answer the question that's actually asked . . . but not me."

"I guess you're not the man you thought you were."

I looked at her sharply. "What do you mean by that?"

"Nothing," Nora said. She looked alarmed. "You okay?"

"Yes, I'm fine."

She reached for my hand. "God, you Branches are a touchy bunch," she said.

But something in me wasn't laughing, though even now, after so many years, I still don't know precisely what it was that drew me more disturbingly into myself that day. Perhaps it was the way Eddie later passed me in the corridor with little more than a nod. Or was it the fact that the tattered old army surplus sack in which he kept his notebooks now seemed oddly closed to me? Did I feel displaced? Dismissed? Tossed aside in favor of my father? The actual origin of my agitation, whether in a gesture or a word, or folded deep within the vagaries of my own darkening mind, remains and may always remain the unsolved mystery of my case. I know only that as I headed toward the parking lot at the end of that same day and saw Eddie's van as it rattled past, Eddie alone behind the wheel, a sinister charge went through me, some part of the hostility I'd always felt for Dirk now inexplicably transferred to him.

You're not the man you thought you were, I heard Nora say again, though even at that moment, with her hand on mine, she could not have guessed how right she was.

PART V

THIRTY-ONE

I range the fields with pensive tread,
And pace the hollow rooms,
And feel (companion of the dead)
I'm living in the tombs.

So wrote Abraham Lincoln, lines my father quoted as the epi-gram at the beginning of his biography. I was standing in Lake-land's small bookstore when *Sorrow's Last Full Measure* was placed upon its shelves. My father had had a stroke by then, and had thus been rendered far too frail for even that short trip. And so, when I returned from the bookstore, I made up a story about the book's reception, all the people who'd come to buy it, hoping to see him. I told him that he was famous now, the writer he'd always sought to be. By that time I'd covered his life in a soft drapery of lies, told him that he was to be published by a dynamic new publishing house, when it was, in fact, an ob-scure vanity press I'd paid to publish it, money I'd gotten by selling the very orchard that had once called to mind Lincoln's melancholy end.

"Lincoln would be proud of you," I told him as I placed a copy of the book in his wrinkled hands.

He stared at the cover for a long time, his failing eyesight no doubt unable to make out the portrait I'd chosen for the cover, the cracked portrait of the fallen president that had been taken only days before his murder. He seemed hardly to notice when I drew the book from his hands.

"Jack," he said. "I'm . . ." He stopped, lowered his head for a moment, then lifted it again. "I'm so sorry." His eyes glistened. "About Eddie."

Memory's old wall cracked a little and behind it I heard my father's voice as it had sounded in the courtroom that day, speaking of Eddie's "mighty effort" to find that "Shakespearean web" of connections that make up a region's life, connections that, as he'd gone on to say, "both darken life and illuminate us."

It was a display of that melancholy eloquence that was the gift of the Branches, at one with their gloom and their grandeur, and which I knew, as I drove my father back to Great Oaks after his brief testimony that day, I had once hoped myself also to embody, though it was clear to me by then that I never would.

And so I said, "What made you so sure about Eddie?"

His answer was direct. "Jake's that night."

Thus, as I knew then, I'd seen the shattering moment of conviction myself, because, like Iago stalking Othello through the murky streets of Venice, I had followed him.

———

Almost two weeks had passed since Nora had taken my hand, laughed about the touchiness of the Branches, but nothing had calmed within me. Nor had Eddie failed to sense my agitation. In reaction to it, he rarely approached me anymore. But this careful distancing from me only fed the flames of my disquiet. What secret was he hiding? What was he talking about in his sessions with my father? My curiosity was incontestably un-wholesome, the type that drives a man to drill a peephole or lift his eyes to a neighbor's windowsill, and in me it generated the preoccupation of a stalker, one that must surely have been at work that afternoon, when I saw Eddie's van leave the school parking lot. For why else would I have quickly pulled into the line of cars that snaked behind him, though cautiously at a dis-tance, shadowy and unseen.

It was a slow line, but it moved steadily, so that during the next minute or so I passed Sheila, head lowered, reading in the bus, and Nora at the top of the stairs, brightly exchanging pleas-antries with Mr. Rankin, and Wendell, clowning with Betty beneath the awning of the lunchroom, and at the far end of the parking lot, hatefully alone, Dirk smoking a cigarette.

I saw the whole panoply of Lakeland High, the stream of students, the moving traffic, but like a hawk high above, lethally circling in a cloudless sky, I remained focused on Eddie's battered old brown van, his head and shoulders visible through its back window, though only as a figure fixed in black silhouette.

The knot loosened a moment later, traffic moving faster now, so that Eddie passed smoothly under the traffic light and headed down Lafayette Street, the thoroughfare that led farther out of town, past North Hills, and into the plantation district.

I thought, *He's going to Great Oaks.*

And something in that thought, of yet another rendezvous between Eddie and my father, sprouted like an evil vine, so that rather than swinging right toward my house, I swung left, and from a concealing distance, once again fell in behind Eddie's van, hoping in some odd, inexplicable way that he would turn from the route, drift into some neutral territory. But he proceeded into the outskirts of town, then made a turn onto a road that could take him only to Great Oaks where—as I realized suddenly and disturbingly—I now could not go.

MR. TITUS: So what did you do at that point, Mr. Branch?

MR. BRANCH: I turned around and headed back toward town.

MR. TITUS: Where in town?

MR. BRANCH: Jake's. I decided to wait there.

MR. TITUS: What were you waiting for?

MR. BRANCH: For Eddie to leave Great Oaks. I figured I'd see his van when he came back by, then I'd go over to see my father, find out what was going on between them.

MR. TITUS: Going on?

MR. BRANCH: What the nature of their . . . discussions was.

MR. TITUS: How long did you wait at Jake's?

MR. BRANCH: Until almost nightfall. Then I decided it was getting too late to visit my father that night. That's when I headed for my car.

I had reached it by the time I saw Eddie's van pull into the lot at Jake's, then make a slow, gliding turn that presented me with the passenger side of the van, a little glimpse of gray that seemed to shine in the light from Jake's window.

MR. TITUS: Is that when you saw your father?
MR. BRANCH: Yes.

He remained in the van until Eddie came around and opened the door for him. Then he lowered himself to the ground, and as he walked toward Jake's, took Eddie's arm.

MR. TITUS: They were alone?

Like the last two people on earth, I thought.

MR. BRANCH: For a while.

They took a booth by the front window. My father ordered what appeared to be the usual fare of Jake's, food so humble I could barely imagine him being in the same room with it, though he politely made a show of satisfaction with such lowly fare.

From my place inside my car, I watched them eat and talk.

MR. TITUS: Until when?

Until another car, a rusted-out Chevy, pulled into the lot, bearing a woman in a cloud of smoke.

MR. BRANCH: Until Eddie's mother arrived.

Eddie and my father both rose as she came down the aisle toward them. Eddie gave what were clearly formal introductions. My father offered his hand and Mrs. Miller took it and waited while my father peered at her with an intensity that must have proven awkward because she finally drew her hand away.

MR. TITUS: And after that?

After that, the die was cast, I thought, though, "They sat and talked awhile," was all I said, and thus gave no indication of the changed sense of my father, how oddly brightened he seemed in Eddie's presence, as eerily radiant as Captain Vere in the light that came from Billy Budd.

True, my father did nothing overt to suggest any reason for the new mood I observed in him. Nevertheless, I sensed a lightness of being and rejuvenation of spirit, as if Eddie had taken some part of life's burden from his shoulders, a duty that should have been mine. But that was not all. For I also noticed that Eddie seemed far more at home with my father than he had ever been with me.

MR. TITUS: So it was not just your relationship with your
    father that was at issue, was it, Mr. Branch?
MR. BRANCH: No. It was also my relationship with Eddie.
MR. TITUS: Do you think that Eddie was aware of this
    change?

MR. BRANCH: Yes, I do.

MR. TITUS: How do you know?

I know because during the next week, when he nodded to me as we passed in the hallway or on those few occasions when we spoke, I felt that he was watching me from behind an invisible mask. In class he rarely spoke or raised his hand, and when I called upon him, his answers were brief and not always to the point. As to questions, he had none.

But worse than any of this to me, and feeding the tumor that was growing in my mind, was the sense that Eddie was up to something, that he had a secret agenda, his visits to Great Oaks being part of some scheme he might well have concocted long ago. For this reason, and against reason, I began to think of him as a worm in the very wood of Great Oaks, burrowing in and weakening its structure, squirming and conniving as it inched its way into the core.

And yet I could find no way to breach so sensitive a subject with my father, so that our dinners and conversations remained exactly as they'd always been.

"Lincoln's wife believed in ghosts," my father said on one such occasion. He was peering toward the open window of the great dining room, where, as he spoke, a little gust moved the gossamer curtain. "She had séances in the White House."

I forked a bit of roast duck into my mouth. "Did she?"

"Everyone gathered around a table, holding hands." He actually laughed. "Can you imagine Lincoln in such a ridiculous situation?"

I stopped chewing and faced him squarely. "Even great men are not immune to chicanery," I said pointedly. "Even great men can be . . . deceived."

This was meant to strike like a hammer, but it glanced off my father without leaving the slightest dent.

"As to our next dinner," he said, "I wonder if we might make it a bit later." He drew the napkin from his lap and neatly folded it. "Eddie's coming by. We're going over some things I found."

"Things?" I asked.

"About the family."

"His or ours?" I asked.

He smiled, but something moved behind the smile. "Both," he said.

"Both?"

My father looked like a man who'd misspoken and now had to cover his tracks. "The family of the Delta," he said.

"Isn't that a bit broad for a little high school term paper?" I said.

My father read the vaguely dismissive tone in my voice. "Nothing is too broad for a broad mind, Jack," he scolded. "And nothing is too small for a small one."

He had not spoken to me in this way since I'd been a little boy, chasing at his feet, demanding that he divulge the end of a story.

"Yes, but in this case, Eddie is simply a—"

"Enough," my father interrupted. He rose and headed out of the room.

I got to my feet and trailed after him. "I mean a mighty work requires a mighty—"

My father whirled around, and in a voice he had not used with me since childhood, uttered the very word that had so pierced me long ago.

"Forbear, Jack." He lifted his hand as if against a hostile force. "Forbear."

When I left Great Oaks a few minutes later, I left it as a scolded child, and with the feeling of having been purposely humiliated. I was, after all, a Branch, sole heir to Great Oaks, not only its splendor, which was considerable, but its history and tradition. It was I, not Eddie Miller, who understood the symbols of its heraldry and could read its Latin motto. It was I who had lived my whole life in both its sunlight and its shadow, taken on the burden of its demanding past, carried its flag into the breach. Had I not all my life upheld its honor, vigilantly guarded its prestige? Had this not been a mighty effort? And in view of that effort, was I not worthy of respect?

These questions were painful enough, but others were yet more stinging to me: *Who was Eddie Miller to be writing about the Delta, this Bridges boy? And why did my father prefer his company to mine?*

At home, I poured myself a tumbler of scotch from a bottle I'd never opened and brought the glass to my lips.

No, I thought, *not that.*

There'd be no drunkenness in my personal history, nor suicidal depressions, either. With me, I decided, the Branches would be born anew, cleansed of their ancient maladies by force of will alone.

I walked into the kitchen, emptied my glass into the sink, and returned to the room, intent on writing a new lecture that had suddenly come to mind. Until nearly dawn, I went through the books on my shelves and piled beneath my bed and which rose in stacks along the walls of the house. I flipped through indexes and tables of contents, scoured the dramatis personae of scores and scores of plays.

But for all the frenetic labor of that long night, I failed to find a genuine representative of the evil I wished to expose, and so, as morning broke, I settled upon a different strategy, and simply made one up.

THIRTY-TWO

"He was first of all a schemer," I began once the class had settled down on the following Monday morning, "and he used innocence as his tool." A dramatic pause, as always. "But his innocence was a mask, and deception was his aim."

After this suitably theatrical beginning, I identified the villain I'd created out of whole cloth only hours earlier. "His name is Emilio Corazón," I said, "and in Serrano's famous tale, he hides behind a pose of boyishness and uses his own tragic past to insinuate himself into a great family and from there create new tragedies of his own."

From here I detailed Emilio's bitter past, the son of a man hated by his village as a bringer of plague. He was orphaned as a boy, I told the class, and lived all of his early life as an outcast.

"But hardship had honed his devious skills," I said. "And like a beggar who cuts off his fingers to augment his alms, Emilio made a spectacle, however subtly, of his wounds."

The class remained attentive as I continued my tale of Emilio's deceits, how he'd first come to the attention of a young man of great means and revered family, charmed and seduced him, wiled his way into a great house, and from within, slowly eaten into its heart.

"Until the great house fell," I said at the end of my lecture. "And nothing was left but for Emilio to move on to another great house." I glanced from one student to the next as I continued.

"And on."

Stacia.

"And on."

Sheila.

I paused, now careful that at the final repetition of the phrase my eyes would settle upon him for whom my lecture had been intended all along.

"And on."

Eddie.

But my lecture failed to make any actual point, and as a result I saw only confusion in the faces before me when I ended it.

"So, what did Emilio do, exactly?" Stacia Decker asked. "He was just trying to get ahead, wasn't he?"

I allowed that this was a possible interpretation, though Emilio's crimes, flattery and subterfuge, the ploy of false innocence, manipulation by charm, hardly made him an admirable character. He was, I said, "like rotten mackerel in moonlight, a thing that shone and stank."

"But it's not like he killed somebody," Debbie Link protested. "I mean, he could have been a thief, but he never really stole anything."

"His crimes were subtle," I insisted. "He wore his misfortune as a mask, and turned a father against his son."

They stared at me unconvinced.

"He just cleared things up, really," George Frobish allowed. "I mean, the family that took him in, it already had problems."

"But he widened every gap between the father and the son," I protested. "He used the nature of their relationship to divide them."

"But they were already divided," Sheila Longstreet said.

Then Toby Olson voiced the same sentiment, and after him another and another, until even Wendell Casey released a weary sigh and Dirk Littlefield a quick, dismissive grunt.

So that I realized as the bell mercifully sounded, that alone within my classroom's puzzled throng, only Eddie Miller had said nothing at all, nor given any outward sign that he'd gotten the point of my lecture, his gaze utterly without expression, though behind the curtain of his eyes, I thought I saw a smile.

One class followed another, as always, but as the day wore on, I couldn't get Eddie off my mind, so that rather than meeting Nora at the end of the day, as I usually did, I ducked out the side door of the building and headed toward the far corner of the school grounds. Despite the open space that surrounded me, I felt strangely like a man in custody, though the exact nature of my captivity eluded me. I knew that I was still smoldering in the wake of my father's "Forbear," as well as the complete failure of the morning's lecture. But something else was at work, as well, an ironic sense that Eddie was my own creation, that I'd fallen victim to my own romantic vision of salvaging a wayward boy, and intoxicated by that dream, had chosen one among my many students and simply imagined in him possibilities that were not truly there. Moving blindly on, I'd later proposed a grand future he might lack all ability to attain. In doing both, I'd created the Coed Killer's son when, in fact, no such boy had actually existed. For who was Eddie Miller before I'd taken him in hand? A mediocre student, invisible to both his teachers and his classmates. Member of no club or team. An outsider, yes, but wasn't Toby Olson, to choose one of many, as solitary as Eddie? For that matter, wasn't half of Lakeland's lowly student body as unfortunate as he? Were they not, like Eddie, orphans in some storm? So what had made Eddie emerge from the roiling mass? Nothing, save that, more or less by accident, I'd gotten him in trouble, then, guilt-ridden at having done so, had sought to redeem myself by redeeming him. After that, everything he'd done, he'd done at my instruction, following my lead every step of the way, choosing his father as the subject of his paper, compiling information, making a list, doing interviews, and finally going to my father.

You have to charm the people you need, the people you want to get something out of, I'd told him.

And he had.

In fact, I concluded, he'd charmed me.

Surely then, my father, trusting, idealistic, prone to great swings of mood, depressive, had to be warned about the likes of Eddie Miller, a warning that would not be subtle this time, and from which, no matter what my father said, I would not forbear.

But when I arrived at Great Oaks a few minutes later, the Coed Killer's son was already there.

His father's old brown van seemed to rest comfortably before the great doors, wholly at ease, as if it belonged there. I drew up behind it, and for a moment stared through its dusty back window, half expecting to see Eddie sitting motionless behind the wheel, his eyes a ghostly recall of his father's, staring back at me through the smudgy blur of a rearview mirror.

But the van was empty, and so I got out of my car and walked to the door. My family's motto spoke of honor and truth, words that now fortified me in my mission to warn my father of deceit.

I gave a soft knock at the door, as courtesy required, then waited for my father's customary call. When no call came, I knocked again, waited, but again no summons came from inside the house.

I knocked a third time, and when there was still no response, I opened the door and stepped into the foyer where, for the first time in my life, I felt oddly like an intruder in Great Oaks.

"Father?" I called.

Still no answer.

I glanced into the library as I headed for the stairs, perhaps with the expectation of seeing Eddie there, waiting with his black notebook, head humbly lowered, hair in some concocted disarray, and with that wounded look in his big brown eyes.

But the library was empty, and so I climbed the stairs, twining slowly upward through the portrait gallery of long-departed

Branches until I reached the open door of my father's study, and silently, almost stealthily, stepped inside the room.

My lips parted in dark wonder at what I saw. For they were not aligned in the positions my father and I had always taken in his study, he grandly at rest behind his desk, I standing before it like a soldier at attention. Instead they were seated together at a small round table piled not with Eddie's notebooks or any of my father's Lincoln research but with a volume of his *Book of Days* open before them, its white pages glowing nakedly beneath a lamp, my father's hand at rest on a page he seemed to have withdrawn from the body of the manuscript, especially to show Eddie.

I drew in a quaking breath. "Father," I said.

He looked up, exchanged a quick glance with Eddie, and then, as if in collusive agreement on what they should do next, he soundly closed the volume and sat back.

"Hello, Jack," he said. "We were just finishing up." He looked at Eddie. "Perhaps we can continue tomorrow," he said.

Eddie nodded and got to his feet. "Yes, sir," he said. He looked at me and smiled his swift, indecipherable smile. "Hello, Mr. Branch."

"Eddie," I said crisply.

"I'll see you to the door," my father said to Eddie as he rose with unexpected agility from his chair. Even so, Eddie took his arm gently. Then my father pressed his hand against Eddie's back and in that formation they drifted out of the room like two small ships in the pull of identical winds. "I'll be back in a minute, Jack," my father said as they sailed by.

MR. TITUS: So your father and Eddie Miller were looking at
one of your father's manuscripts?
MR. BRANCH: Yes.
MR. TITUS: And when your father saw you at the door, he
closed that book?
MR. BRANCH: Yes, he did.
MR. TITUS: And after that?
MR. BRANCH: After that they walked down the stairs and
out of the house.

Which I knew because I strode to the window and stared
down at where they stood together on the portico. For a time
they talked, their voices too soft for me to make out what they
said. Then Eddie opened the door of the van and started to
get in.

MR. TITUS: And after that?

After that a silence fell between them and they only stared
at each other, until my father suddenly, as if overwhelmed by
an emotion he could not contain, stepped forward.
And after that?
He opened his arms.
And after that?
He drew Eddie into his embrace.
And after that?
He hugged him closely, and with all his might.

———

I felt my legs give way beneath me, and had to reach for the open door of the cabinet to hold myself upright. A wave of trembling emptiness passed through me, followed by another and another, a quaking over which I had barely gained control when my father came back into the room.

I stepped away from the window, walked around his desk and stood before it, watching silently as he swept past me and took his usual place behind it.

"There's something we need to discuss, Jack," he said. "Before I mention it to Eddie."

I waited as my father opened a drawer and shoved a few papers into it, all done quickly, with a businesslike efficiency of movement.

"There's some possibility that he's . . . well . . ." He seemed to struggle for the words before he said them, "That he's a Branch."

I could not conceal the shock of this, but neither could I find a way to express it.

"I have certain papers I need to consult," my father said. "But if it turns out to be true, I'll take the proper action regarding Eddie and his mother."

"Of course," I managed to say, though my voice was barely above a whisper. "What makes you think that Eddie could be . . . a Branch?"

"It has to do with the grandmother I mentioned," my father answered. "On his mother's side, not his father's. So there'd be no relation to Luke Miller." He let this sink in, then added, "His mother suffers from the Branch family disease, you know."

"No, I didn't."

"It comes on slowly, just like mine," my father added. "Like a steel net. That's how she describes it. A steel net that settles over her."

So they were in it together, I thought, Eddie and his mother, she providing "proof" of our shared lineage by claiming to suffer from the "bottoms," he providing, writer that he is, the telling image.

"Depression is hardly evidence that she is—"

"And when I met her," my father interrupted, "I saw a great resemblance between herself and my father. It was in her eyes."

I could find nothing to say to this that would not sound petty in my father's ears, and so I remained silent.

My father looked at me closely. "Are you all right, Jack?"

"A bit overwhelmed," I admitted. "A bit . . . disarmed."

"There's nothing you need to be armed against," my father told me firmly. "Nothing to fear by way of your inheritance."

"Nothing to fear but the 'bottoms,'" I replied, darkly hinting of our shared debility.

To which my father waved a thoroughly dismissive hand. "Pay no mind to the 'bottoms,'" he said. "You have nothing to fear from that."

In chilling silence I posed a heartfelt question:

Why not?

But it was not a question I ever asked. Instead, I indicated no further concern with the matter with which my father had so abruptly confronted me.

"I suppose we'll know in time," I said. "About Eddie."

"Yes," my father said. He drew his gold watch from his trousers and checked the time. "I left my work in the garden. A little editing, so it doesn't require my full attention. Care to join me? We could talk while I scribble about."

"Of course," I said.

With that we walked down the stairs and out into the garden, my father now focused on the manuscript pages that lay in a neat pile beside his chair.

"The Scots allow for three verdicts," he said. "Guilty. Not guilty. And not proven. I've come to believe that the charge that Mary Surratt had something to do with Lincoln's assassination is not proven."

I glanced at the veranda, its white rocking chairs forever in ghostly, languid motion, and recalled the two of us together on summer evenings, father and son listening to the Negro preachers speak of all they had, a faith that seemed no less uncertain to me now than my own long suppositions.

My father peered at me a moment, then returned to the mound of his scholarship. "Not proven," he repeated as he made another note.

I looked at my father's notations, a minute script that reminded me of Eddie's. There were scores of them on the page, and I had no doubt that in each of the hundreds of pages he'd written on Lincoln he'd made the same number of alterations and revisions, a vast labor that had continued through year after isolated year, but which now, for the first time, struck me as futile and unending, with something at its center to which I suddenly felt curiously unattached.

"Where does *The Book of Days* begin?" I asked.

My father seemed to find my question somewhat discomfiting. "When 'Our Hero' meets the love of his life," he answered quite dismissively, as if nothing in the book could possibly be of interest to me, a reaction that only deepened both my interest and my dread.

"A girl of the cotillion," I said quietly, the phrase my father had often used in referring to "the love of his life."

My father held his attention to the paper in his hand. "Eyes like amber," he said.

My mother appeared before me, insubstantial, almost translucent, staring at me from the far end of the garden, a cotillion girl who'd died only a few weeks after I was born so that all we'd shared, or so it seemed, was the vastness of the sea upon which she had perished.

My father looked up and caught the passage of this thought through my mind.

"What are you thinking about, Jack?" he asked.

"*The Book of Days.*" I smiled as if it were but a passing curiosity. "How many volumes is it now?"

"Twenty-five," my father said.

"So, you began writing it right after I was born," I said brightly, like a man discovering a pleasant surprise, his name listed among those acknowledged in a book.

Even so, my father appeared to see my remark as a snake in his path. "It's not worth being read by anyone," he said with a shrug. "And certainly not you, Jack." His pencil moved slightly, a nearly imperceptible tremble. "Yours would be the last eyes in the world I'd want cast upon those pages."

But it was the record of his days, wasn't it?

And hadn't he opened it to Eddie?

Opened it to Eddie, and yet felt that I, his only son, should be the last person in the world who should read it?

Why?

These questions were still lingering in my mind as evening began to fall, warm and oddly fetid, with a curious hint of rot in the air, I still with my father in the garden, watching silently as he made yet another note, then said, "Jack, would you mind getting something from my study? Lincoln's poems. They're in a folder on my desk."

Ever the good son, I returned to the house, mounted the stairs, and entered his office. The poems were exactly where he'd indicated, but as I drew the folder from his desk, I glanced to the right, the still-open cabinet stocked with the volumes of his *Book of Days*. The first one rested on the top shelf, the others following it in chronological order.

"Jack?"

My father's voice came loudly from the garden, alerting me that I'd been staring into the cabinet far longer than I'd thought.

"Do you see the folder?" he called.

"Yes," I called back to him. "I'm coming."

And so it was several hours before I returned to my father's study. In the meantime, I gave him the folder he'd asked for, then watched as he flipped through it, found the poem he sought, and made another note.

"All right, I think that's enough," he said. "Shall we have a drink now, Jack?"

We walked back into the house, where my father went immediately to the liquor cabinet and poured two glasses of whiskey.

During the first drink, my father and I talked as we always had, of books and authors and historical events. But with the second, he returned to Eddie, the blood connection he was pursuing. It had come to him through a chance remark, he said, the fact that Eddie's mother suffered from "black moods." This, in turn, had led to a discussion of the heritability of such things, one initiated by Eddie's fear that he might inherit his father's violence. It was then that Eddie had mentioned his grandmother, one Adela Saint James, a pretty girl in the pictures he'd seen of her, who, he said, "worked in people's kitchens." A servant by that name had worked at Great Oaks, my father had recalled, also a pretty girl with large brown eyes. Eddie had produced one of his notebooks, and there she was, a tall slender woman with, according to my father, "those same striking eyes." Could it be, he'd wondered, that his grandfather had taken advantage of this poor servant woman, sired a daughter by her? After all, such things had been done all the time, for these were the same men who, as boys, had "frequented" the brothels of New Orleans, and whose sons, carrying on the same tradition, had made Wanda Ruth a "woman of means."

Through all of this, my father appeared quite captivated, like a boy excited by some new prospect in his life.

"You seem happy about this possibility," I said finally. "That Eddie might be . . . one of us."

My father took a sip from his glass, his gaze now drifting over to the shelves of the library. "I suppose I am," he said. He looked at me. "Because I sense something in that boy," he added. "A tender heart, without which, despite all the learning in the world, a man will remain a monster to the end."

Was it this "tender heart" he'd always sought in a son, I wondered, and which he'd found lacking in me?

"But doesn't learning engender tenderness?" I asked cautiously.

"Not in everyone," my father replied crisply. "And in some, learning becomes a wall that keeps others out, rather than a gate that lets them in."

I might have risen and gone directly home in the throes of such a remark, but my fear had found a mission, and so I waited my father out, sitting almost silently as he shifted the subject to certain "American originals," as he called them, small-town boys who'd gone on to write mighty things about their regions, Maxwell Anderson, for example, and Edgar Lee Masters.

"A last one for me," he said as he rose and headed for the liquor cabinet. "But none for you." He smiled. "I know your limit, Jack."

But he didn't.

Nor did I.

It was nearly nine when he drained the last of his drink, got to his feet, and headed up the stairs to bed.

"Just let yourself out, Jack," he said.

"I will," I told him.

But I didn't.

Instead I waited until I knew he'd fallen asleep, then made my way up the stairs to his study. The door was still open as was the mahogany cabinet that contained the many volumes of *The Book of Days*, each bound in black leather and embossed in gold with the year of its composition. I took the first volume from the cabinet and began to read.

It was written in a style far different from my father's speech or the passages of the Lincoln biography he'd shown me. My father's writing style, like his speech, had always been dramatic, at times even florid, but what I read now was monstrously over-wrought, a literary exertion that went beyond eloquence or even grandiloquence, so that for a moment I thought the whole thing a caricature of literary effort. The style was exceedingly self-conscious, with ornate turns of phrase that would have em-barrassed the most inflated of amateurs. He'd also given differ-ent names to the people about whom he wrote, as well as to the ancestral estate, which he called Dark Haven, a name more suited, it seemed to me, to some cheap novel of suspense. The family name was changed to Falls, an appellation so obviously symbolic it bordered on parody. The "Falls into whose waters" my father "fell" was dominated by a tyrannical patriarch named Leander, a "strutting dynamo" who oversaw vast acreages of cotton and soybeans where untold numbers of tenant farmers and former slaves "tilled and toiled and provided the spoils by which the Falls rose in opposition to both gravity and equity and thus against the hand and eye of nature basked in a wealth that flowed upward from the bottoms." A similarly tortured prose described Leander's wife, Phillipa, an "ethereal creature of jasmine gardens" whose "long tapered fingers" were forever playing Chopin and thus "caused to undulate among the glittering glass and shining silver of Dark Haven a cherubic dance of notes and graces that themselves were as sweet and fleeting as she who released them into the inhospitable air."

It was all terrible, even laughable, but the prose by which my father had recorded the days of his life held no interest for me. And so I flipped forward until I came to a section called "The Pip of Dark Haven Enters the World."

The story of my birth unfolded in a saga of strange urges and gross deceptions borne of my father's intense need to please his father, a man who "in all the teeming, multifarious world sought nothing but that the branches of Dark Haven should bear an heir as fruit." But the "amber-eyed cotillion girl" known as Tara had turned out to be barren, and my father, referred to only as "Our Hero," had swept her away on a grand tour that was nothing but a ruse they'd both agreed upon, she because she loved and wished to please her husband, my father in order once in his life to please "the tyrant-king of Dark Haven." In that effort, they'd gone to Europe, where they'd remained long enough to write letters home with news that Tara had been "blessed" with a child, a little boy "born" in Paris, though he'd been "arranged" in "a place called Chueca, on the dark side of Madrid."

Their Pip was a foundling, the son of a fishmonger and maker of codpieces for the Plaza de Toros, a black-haired boy, delivered in faded linen, wrinkled and unclean, as the child himself, so new to the sun, this son of Dark Haven.

And so, as I coldly realized at that instant, I had begun my life as the object of a silly pun.

Three months later, bundled in "a bodacious cloud of snowy swaddling" and housed in a costly berth of a passenger ship, I'd experienced the first luxuries of what would be a long good fortune.

Pip was healthy, though not robust, and for a time he'd appeared doomed by the fever that claimed his mother on the crossing. But he had lived, a little Spanish peanut of a boy, with hair blacker than the true progeny of Dark Haven, but as Our Hero had earlier ascertained, something strikingly redolent of the dark sparkle in their eyes. He would do, Our Hero knew, and with proper training and education, become a fine young man, though since the laws of nature cannot be subverted by mere human guile, Pip would never be a true master of the Delta.

I closed the book and returned it to its place among the other volumes of *The Book of Days*, then walked to the window and stood for a long time, staring out at Great Oaks.

"Jack?"

I startled as if touched by a bony finger, then turned to find my father standing at the door, clearly surprised to see me in his study.

"What are you doing, Jack?" he asked.

I drew in a long breath and steadied myself. "Just looking out," I said. "The view here . . . in the dark."

My father glanced over to the table where a later volume of *The Book of Days* lay open. "I should put that away," he said.

"Shall I do it for you?"

"No," my father snapped. "It's my secret passion. Never to be read."

I stepped away and let him pass, then watched as he returned the volume to the cabinet, closed the doors, and locked it, careful, as I saw, to drop the key into the pocket of his robe. "Time for you to depart the kingdom, Jack," he said in a broadly dramatic tone that reminded me of the grotesquely overheated prose of *The Book of Days*.

I nodded. "Yes, it is."

Together we walked out of the room, which, as I noticed, my father locked behind us. Then we strolled to the top of the stairs, where he stood, waiting for me to leave. It was clear that he intended to remain there to make sure I was gone before he safely returned to bed, gone and not lurking around Great Oaks, eyeing the crystal and the silver, as if I were a stranger in the house.

"Well, good night, Jack," my father said.

"Good night," I said, and almost added "Father," but stopped myself in time.

THIRTY-THREE

For all my father's idle speculation on the matter, none of us will ever know whether it is preparedness or the lack of it that constitutes the real tragedy of life. I know only that when he spoke to me the next morning, I was unprepared for what he said.

"Someone has broken into Great Oaks."

He seemed both astonished and stricken, an inner sanctum violated, one he'd thought invulnerable.

"Please come right away, Jack."

He didn't tell me what he'd found missing, and I didn't ask. Nor, despite the frantic nature of my father's tone, did I feel any great urgency to rush to his aid.

Nor did any sense of urgency result when, a few minutes later, my father began to enumerate the "treasures" he believed to have been taken.

"My jewelry box is gone," he told me as he ushered me into the library. "It had the gold cuff links your mother gave me. And my father's watch."

"Where was this box?" I asked.

"In my study," my father said. "Someone invaded my study."

We were standing in the library, my father's back pressed to the wall, as if he were guarding his books from some still-lingering thief.

"Do you want a drink?" I asked him dryly.

"No," my father answered. "I want my wits about me when he gets here."

"When who gets here?" I asked.

Then, as if programmed for dramatic effect, a knock came at the door.

My father looked relieved. "Drummond," he said.

When I opened the door, Drummond quickly came to attention, a finger to his hat, a crisp nod. "Good morning, Mr. Branch," he said. "I understand there's been some trouble."

I stepped back and opened the door. "My father's in the library."

Drummond took off his hat as he walked into the house. Briefly he scanned the ancestral portraits that hung from its walls. "Such a fine family you have, Mr. Branch."

"Yes," I said coolly. "Please, this way."

My father turned as Drummond entered the library, and for a moment I saw them as fellow bondsmen, linked one to the other by an old heavy chain of the Delta, great families to lowly ones, masters to servants.

"Good morning, Mr. Branch," Drummond said.

My father nodded.

Drummond's eyes drifted over a room whose majesty dwarfed him.

"Don't worry," he assured my father. "We'll find the one responsible for your trouble." He looked as if he expected to be asked to take a seat. But no one did, and so he remained on his feet. "Do either of you have any idea who might have done this?"

My father shook his head.

"What was taken?" Drummond asked.

"Watches," my father said. "Cuff links. Assorted items. My grandfather's dueling pistols. Precious things."

"Was any cash taken?"

"I keep household funds in a special place," my father said without revealing the location. "It would not have been easy to find. My jewelry box was kept in my study. Along with the dueling pistols."

"So everything that was taken came from your study?" Drummond asked.

"Yes," my father answered.

Drummond considered this with a show of great concentration.

"Who goes into your study, Mr. Branch?" Drummond asked.

"I do, of course, and Jack, here."

"Anyone else?"

My father hesitated, and I knew why. He was protecting one of his own, one who shared his noble blood, a true son of Great Oaks. Yet some part of my soul remained intact, and so I only waited.

"Eddie," my father said finally. "Eddie Miller."

"Eddie Miller was here?" Drummond asked. "When?"

"He's been here a few times," my father admitted reluctantly. His gaze swept briefly over to "Pip" before returning to Drummond. "But I'm certain that boy is not a thief."

How could he be? I thought. No Branch could be a common felon, not even one shaped by the misfortunes of the Bridges.

"He's not that kind of boy," my father added, this time with great firmness, as if giving Drummond an order to "Forbear."

An order to which Drummond nodded in full obedience, or perhaps simply agreement. "No, I wouldn't expect so," he said. "Not from what I know of him." He stroked his chin. "Of course, no one can be ruled out."

My father's instruction was unmistakable. "I wouldn't want Eddie to be falsely accused, Sheriff," he said.

Drummond smiled amiably. "Of course not, Mr. Branch." He glanced out the door of the library, to the grand staircase beyond it. "Would you mind showing me your study?"

With that, we ascended the stairs, my father and Drummond in the lead, I following behind them like an aide-de-camp. Once in the study, my father stood near the door, watching as Drummond walked farther into the room, glancing here and there until his attention settled upon the tree outside the study's still-open window.

"The intruder could have shinnied up that tree." Drummond appeared to imagine some unknown culprit doing exactly that. "Could have been in and out in a couple of minutes," he added matter-of-factly.

My father walked into the room and slumped down in one of the chairs opposite his desk. "Terrible," he sighed. "Terrible."

Drummond walked to the window and leaned far out, his gaze on the nearby limbs, then the ground below, covered in thick clover.

"There won't be any footprints," he said. For a moment he continued to stare at the grounds as if he were imagining a figure below him, beside the great oak or approaching it from out of the darkness.

"Don't worry, Mr. Branch," he said, his assurance directed, as I noticed, solely toward my father. "I'll find the guilty party." He smiled as he slowly twirled his hat. "And whatever was taken from Great Oaks will be restored."

Eddie's mother would later make clear what Drummond did directly after leaving Great Oaks.

MRS. MILLER: I was sick to death and had been for a day, and there he was at the door, asking for Eddie.

MR. TITUS: And did Sheriff Drummond speak to Eddie?

MRS. MILLER: Yes, he did. And Eddie told him he'd been with me the whole time that robbery was going on, which was the truth.

MR. TITUS: Did Sheriff Drummond indicate that he believed Eddie?

MRS. MILLER: He said he did, and believed me, too, but it was just a mother's word.

And so Sheriff Drummond had taken the next step in what was, following my father's instructions, an obvious effort to clear Eddie of all suspicion:

MR. CARLTON: When did you learn that Mr. Branch's father had reported a robbery?

MISS LONGSTREET: Tuesday, I guess. Sheriff Drummond said it had been done the night before. He wanted to know if Eddie had ever mentioned anything about Mr. Branch and his house and what he had in it. I said he hadn't, and Mr. Drummond said it had to be a young person did it, a person that could shinny up a tree, and did I know anybody at Lakeland that might have known about Mr. Branch, the stuff he had.

MR. CARLTON: Did you know such a person, Sheila?

MISS LONGSTREET: Yes, sir.

MR. CARLTON: Did you give Sheriff Drummond that person's name?

MISS LONGSTREET: Yes, sir, I did.

MR. CARLTON: What name did you give him?

"Dirk Littlefield," she said.

It was then, she added, that Drummond had put his finger to his hat, smiled "real nice," and turned back toward his car, "whistling as he went."

And so it was Dirk Littlefield that Drummond now had in his sights, and to whose house in the Bridges, little more than a tumbledown shack, he now made his way that evening.

MR. CASEY: We was working on Dirk's old pickup when he
come up. He didn't say nothing, nor nod nor nothing.
He just come up and told Dirk to get up out from
under that car 'cause he knew what he done.

MR. TITUS: And did Dirk comply with Sheriff Drummond?

MR. CASEY: He done what he said, yes, sir.

With greased hands, his clothes covered in the red dirt from
his grassless yard, Dirk got to his feet and faced Harry Drummond in the slowly fading light that now settled over the Bridges.

"You know who I am, don't you?" Drummond asked.

"Yeah, I know."

"You think I'm dumb?"

"What?"

"You think I'm dumb?"

"I don't think nothing about—"

"No, you think I'm dumb, because if you didn't think I was
dumb you'd've known you couldn't get away with it."

MR. CASEY: And Dirk just looked at me, like he couldn't
figure nothing out that was going on.

MR. TITUS: And what did Sheriff Drummond do in the face
of this?

He stepped forward and pressed a finger into Dirk's chest.

MR. CASEY: And there wasn't no buttons on that shirt so it
was just open and flapping, and so he put his finger

right on Dirk's chest bone, and he pressed it real hard so I could see a red mark when he pulled it back.

"You see what I can do?" Drummond asked. "I can lay a hand on you and you just have to stand there, don't you?"

Dirk stared at Drummond silently, as Wendell said, "like he just couldn't figure nothing out that was going on."

Then Drummond said, "Great Oaks. You know where that is?"

Dirk nodded.

"You ever been there?"

Dirk shook his head.

Mr. Casey: By then some people had begun to hang around, just looking at what was going on, how the sheriff was there in the yard, talking real serious to Dirk, and him just standing there, taking it.

"Don't you lie to me," Drummond warned. "You don't know trouble 'til you lie to me."

"I ain't lying," Dirk said. "What's all this—"

"You don't ask me questions," Drummond barked. "You answer the questions I ask you."

Dirk glanced about, into the eyes of the crowd, "looking small and helpless," according to Wendell, "like he wasn't a man at all, but just some snot-nosed kid."

"Now I'm gonna ask you again," Drummond said coldly. "You ever been to Great Oaks?"

"I took a ride out there once," Dirk answered.

"What for?"

"Just to see it."

"Why were you wanting to see it? You don't have call to go out there, do you?"

"No . . . sir."

"You don't have any business out there at all, do you?"

"No, I don't have no business, but—"

"I don't want to hear buts," Drummond shouted. "You've got no business out there at Great Oaks, but you went riding out there anyway. Why'd you do that?"

"Just riding around," Dirk said. "Me and . . . Sheila—"

"Sheila?" Drummond interrupted. "What you doing with her? She's Eddie Miller's girl."

Dirk stiffened. "I guess she is."

"You guess?" Drummond laughed. He glanced out at the gathering crowd and gave them a broad, clownish wink. "This boy doesn't know when his girl's been stolen."

MR. CASEY: And they laughed, all the people there. They
    laughed at Dirk.

Drummond waited until the laughter died away, then stared grimly into Dirk's face.

"You get me back what you stole from Great Oaks, you hear?" he said.

"Stole?" Dirk asked. "I didn't steal nothing from—"

Drummond's hand shot up. His fingers grasped the flapping collar of Dirk's shirt and yanked him forward, so that their faces were almost touching. "You get it all back, you hear me."

"But, I didn't—"

Drummond released the shirt and stepped back. He was still glaring into Dirk's eyes. "Do you hear me?" he repeated.

"But—"

It was at that point, Wendell said, that Drummond yelled at the top of his voice.

"I said I don't want to hear buts from you," he screamed.

Then, to the grim wonder of the people gathered around, he slapped Dirk Littlefield's face.

THIRTY-FOUR

It was a story that rang through the corridors of Lakeland High the next morning, so that Nora had heard it by ten and Mr. Rankin by ten thirty. By eleven all the school knew that Great Oaks had been burglarized and that Dirk Littlefield had been slapped by Sheriff Drummond. It was a tale told many times that day, but it never reached the ears of Eddie Miller.

For his seat in my classroom was empty, Sheila looking terribly troubled in her place next to it. The others were cautiously silent, with Dirk fuming mutely in their midst, more sullen than I had ever seen him, a grimly seething cauldron of a boy.

MR. TITUS: What do you think he was feeling, Mr. Branch?
MR. BRANCH: I don't know.
MR. TITUS: Well, he'd been slapped in full view of his
    neighbors, hadn't he?
MR. BRANCH: Yes, he had.
MR. TITUS: He'd been taunted and humiliated, hadn't he?
MR. BRANCH: I suppose so.

MR. TITUS: Been made to feel that he was nothing. Just a Bridges boy.

MR. BRANCH: Yes.

MR. TITUS: Well, how would you react if you were suddenly made to feel that you weren't the man you thought you were?

It was at that moment, near the end of my testimony, that it all came rushing back to me, the last hours of the day before, my father's *Book of Days* trembling in my hand, the dreadful lie I'd been told all my life, the knowledge that it was true, what Nora had once said, *that I was not the man I thought I was.*

But who was I?

Pure artifice, and when you are nothing but what good fortune has made you, as I soon discovered, you are truly nothing at all.

And so I moved through the day in a kind of bitter trance, giving my lecture without the slightest energy, then on to the next class and the next, hoping that the waves of anger and dread and emptiness that were washing over and through me might finally subside.

But they only built as the day continued, so that as I sat in the faculty lounge, listening to the drone of conversation, I felt entirely removed both in place and time, a harborless boat, unmoored and drifting, without so much as a small-craft warning to signal the storm ahead.

Save the one raised by Nora.

"What's the matter, Jack?" she asked. "You look like a ghost."

It was the end of the day, and we were standing together at the bottom of the steps, our usual place for saying good-bye at the close of school.

"I mean, it's just stuff, in the end," she added.

"Stuff?"

"Whatever was stolen from you."

"Yes," I said. "Just . . . stuff."

"So get some new stuff," Nora said lightly.

Then she poked me in the ribs, and for what would be the last time in her life, tossed back her head and laughed.

I returned home, but the air around me seemed charged with the opposite of energy, a force that drained whatever force I raised against it. I felt like a defeated army, hopelessly demoralized and trudging down some muddy road, head lowered, with nothing left but the desolate memory of one's own lost cause.

The only energy I had was the energy of anger, of resentment, of having been the victim of a grave deception. For a long time, I sat in the gloom of my living room, sat first in the evening shade and then in the darkness, so that the only heat and light around me seemed to come from the licking flames of my own steadily building ire.

When the phone rang, I yanked it from the cradle like a pistol from its case.

"Jack?"

"Yes."

"It's your father."

Not really, I thought.

"Jack?"

"Yes."

"Have you heard anything from Drummond?"

"He would report to you, not me," I said.

"Have you heard from Eddie?"

His name shot fire through my every artery and vein.

"He wasn't at school today," I said starkly.

He heard the stiffness in my voice.

"How are you feeling, Jack?"

It was not a question I'd expected, but I saw immediately that it was one by which I could make a final test, determine once and for all if I'd made no mistake, misread nothing in his *Book of Days.*

And so I said, "Like . . . Pip."

The silence that followed was short but stark, and in it I sensed a near lethal spike of anxiety on my father's part.

"Pip?" he asked in a voice that was unmistakably edged in dread. "Why would you . . . feel . . . like—"

"No reason, I suppose," I interrupted sharply.

When my father spoke again, his tone was very grave.

"Jack," he said slowly, as if barely able to lift the weight of the words themselves, "we should have dinner tonight. I need to talk to you about . . . certain things."

So he's going to reveal the truth, at last, I thought.

"Can you come around seven?" he asked.

"Of course," I answered crisply.

"Good," he said softly. "See you then."

In a state of strange suspension, like a wooden marionette,

I returned to the living room where some book waited for me. I don't recall what the book was, neither its title nor its author, but there are times when all that followed comes flooding back over me, and I think that had I picked it up, gotten lost in a haunting scene, I might have glimpsed some little spark of light, grasped a tiny shard of what really matters in this world, and through these things found myself again.

But I merely stared at its closed covers, and so Dirk Littlefield found me first.

When I opened the door, his breath came toward me in a rancid wave of cheap whiskey, his eyes glittering in the dark.

"You put the cops on me," he said.

Over Dirk's massive shoulder, I saw Wendell staring at me helplessly, oddly fearful himself, as if we were both precariously balanced on the rim of a volcano. "Dirk didn't do it, Mr. Branch," he said meekly. "He don't know nothing about it."

Dirk glared at me with an animal rage. "I know you put the cops on me," he snarled.

In Dirk's mounting rage I saw the storied privileges of the old order go up in smoke, the great estates of France and Russia consumed in revolutionary flames as, suddenly, I wanted Great Oaks to be consumed, with my father and Eddie standing alone over its charred ruin, inheritors of nothing.

"I didn't put anybody on you," I told Dirk coldly.

The air around him smoldered with his festering ire, the sheer hatred of the children of the Bridges for those who had ground their fathers into dust and were now grinding them beneath the same unforgiving wheel. It was the hatred of the lowly for the grand, the cursed for the blessed, of those forever excluded from the fabled and unreachable ranks of those who rule over them, a hatred of Great Oaks that was at that moment no different from my own.

"So who done it then?" Dirk shouted.

He seemed actually swollen with rage, and there, in his trembling visage, I glimpsed again the frightful mob, black-toothed, simian, made low and held down, as he surely saw it, by the foppish sons of the great estates, the bow-tied and the prissy.

"Who put the law on me?" Dirk cried again.

"Not I," I told him firmly. "Nor anyone at Great Oaks."

"Who then?" Dirk shouted.

I gave no answer, and for a moment Dirk glared at me so fiercely that sparks seemed actually to fly from his body. Then, suddenly, I saw a separate weed of black conspiracy sprout fully in his head. "Sheila," he murmured. But this was too unbearable a betrayal, and so he added, "Eddie."

It was the malignant shift of an infected mind, and for a few brief seconds, I thought to clear that mind of the dark vines that choked it. But evil assumed its long-awaited mastery, and so I only closed my door.

THIRTY-FIVE

Sometimes I feel night as a gathering of ghosts. I sit in the front room, and distract myself from the lingering visions of Nora and Sheila, Wendell, and, of course, of Eddie, by writing new lectures for my old course on evil. I have hundreds of them now, the last written just two nights ago, not a bloody tale, bloated with malignancy, but a story of subtle, almost invisible corruption, the fall of Ovid, that ancient singer of love and metamorphosis, walking the bedraggled streets of poor Tomi, sentenced to lifelong exile for a "mistake" he never in his life revealed. Now alone in this old crumbling house, I wrote of Ovid's early advantages, born into the equestrian classes, favored by a high intelligence he augmented with a superior education. *Ovid was blessed by his good fortune,* I wrote, *and yet . . .*

It was then I heard a knock, and with an old man's brain thought it came from inside my chest, the product of an exploded heart.

But it was only the postman.

"Good evening, Mr. Branch," he said, when I opened the door. "Got another package from New York."

I signed for the package and drew it from his hand.

He smiled his old, dutiful smile. "Well, good evening then, Mr. Branch."

With that, he turned and began to make his way back down the road, night falling around him as it had fallen around me on that long-ago night, the scent of black earth hanging in the air as I made my way to Great Oaks, where the table of the dining room had already been set with its finest china.

"We have much to discuss," the master of Great Oaks said as we took our places. "But first, some she-crab soup."

He'd served it steaming from a porcelain bowl, the great chandelier twinkling above us, its many lights holding back the darkness through which Sheila Longstreet was at that very moment running.

MR. CARLTON: Where were you headed, Sheila?

Toward the only one to whom she could have gone in her fear and peril, that other Bridges girl.

MISS LONGSTREET: I was headed for Miss Ellis.

She ran through the Bridges, high along its splintered trestles and low into its dank ravines, across vacant lots littered with rusty nails and broken glass, stumbling once and then again, cutting her hands and piercing her feet, so that when she arrived at Nora's door, she looked bloodied and beaten, her dress torn, her hair in wild disarray, almost too exhausted to speak the four words that came from her.

"Dirk's going after Eddie," she gasped.

"For what?" Nora asked.

"He thinks he stole that stuff from Mr. Branch," Sheila said. "And put the law on him."

He'd come to her door drunk, she told Nora, sputtering confusedly about a plan Eddie had hatched, a way of paying him back for what he'd done to Sheila in the shed, robbing Great Oaks and blaming it on him. She'd told him that she'd done it herself, mentioned his name to Drummond, but Dirk had only stared at her brokenly, then glanced back disconsolately at Wendell. *See how she'll do anything for him?*

"Where is Dirk now?" Nora asked.

"On the way to Eddie's," Sheila said.

And so Nora sprang back into her house, then emerged again with the keys to her car.

MISS LONGSTREET: Because she knew Dirk was already on the way to Eddie's, and so there was no time to do anything but go after him.

By then, the she-crab soup had cooled, and our bowls were almost empty.

"Ready for the next course, Jack?"

I said I was, though outside the regimented protocol of the formal dinner, who is ever truly ready for the course that comes next?

"Honor rests in truth, Jack." His tone was oratorical, like Cicero before the Roman Senate.

And truth rests secretly in your Book of Days, I thought.

"Yes," I said softly, eyes averted so that I glimpsed a tiny chip at the rim of my glass, an effete detail I considered briefly as, some miles away, Chambers Road swam into Nora's view, faintly illuminated by the twin beams of her headlights, dusty and sharply winding, as Wendell said, "so you couldn't see what come up next."

MR. CARLTON: So you'd never been down Chambers Road?
MR. CASEY: No, sir.
MR. CARLTON: But you knew where you were going, didn't you?
MR. CASEY: Yes, sir. We was headed to Eddie Miller's house.

At Great Oaks, light from the chandelier caught the many facets of my glass and tossed little shining beads over the usual array of silver and crystal.

"I have great faith in Sheriff Drummond," the master of the house intoned.

It was another grand pronouncement, and it came just as Dirk's battered pickup skidded to a halt and Eddie, distracted by the sound, looked up from the many pages of his still-unfinished paper.

"So I have no doubt that he'll find the guilty party."

Now Eddie was on the porch, staring down to where Dirk stood in the steaming air, a length of chain dangling from his hand, determined, as he later said, "to git back what he took and get the law off me."

"A guilty party who could not be Eddie, of course, though

I think I know who it is, and intend to speak to Drummond in the morning."

But it was still many hours until morning, and at that moment, just after eight, Drummond sat in his own small living room, smoking his pipe silently, unaware that only a few miles away a blue Ford was swerving to the side of the road, a blown tire flapping loudly as it ground to a halt.

MR. CARLTON: Where were you at that time?

MISS LONGSTREET: It was after we'd gone a ways down Chambers Road when a tire blew out and Miss Ellis got out to look, and I did, too, and it was all torn up, that tire, so I figured we had to stop, but Miss Ellis said . . .

"No, we have to go on."

And so they began moving down Chambers Road, Nora in the lead, Sheila limping just behind her, both frightened of Dirk's fearsome wrath, but undeterred, because they were Bridges girls, and so they . . .

"Proceeded on," the master said. "That was the phrase Meriwether Lewis wrote repeatedly in his journal of the expedition." He seemed oddly moved by the sheer simplicity of it. "And that is what we must do now, Jack." He drew in a slow breath. "In light of what I've discovered about Eddie."

Who had come down the stairs by then, and thus faced Dirk in the darkness that enclosed them both.

"They're putting what you done on me, and I ain't gonna let 'em," Dirk said. He whirled the chain. "So you go get me what you stole from old man Branch." He slapped the chain against the battered bed of his truck. "You go get it right now."

Among those stolen things were not the papers of Great Oaks, the ledgers and accounting books, the invoices and bills of lading, the canceled checks of servant wages, all of which now lay in boxes, the story they revealed at last ready to be told.

"Eddie's grandmother worked here from the spring of 1911 to the fall of 1912."

I nodded dully, as other dates were recited, all of them as the grandson of that long-dead kitchen servant stared at Dirk Littlefield with an innocence that could only have stirred his fury, so that once again he whipped the chain into the night air, its metal links barely short of human flesh.

"As you see, we keep fine records here at Great Oaks."

My eyes were two dull metal points, barely able to reflect the twinkling light around us.

"Complete and beyond dispute in what they show."

I stared at him lifelessly.

"Which is that Eddie Miller could not possibly be a Branch."

I felt my lips part wordlessly.

"Any more than Sheriff Drummond could be a Branch. Or your own dear Nora."

The Bridges girl who had reached the sharpest curve on Chambers Road by then, Sheila breathless at her side, the two of them proceeding on as women of their kind have always forged on, through the thick and thin of things, for better and for worse, in sickness and in health, till death came roaring out of the wall of darkness that faced them, speeding on, a tower of swirling dust like a woolly tail behind them, a roaring motor, skidding tires, blasting out of heat and damp, her white arms uplifted, crying out, *Stop, Stop.*

"Stop!" Wendell cried as Dirk slammed his foot on the brake, an old truck's brakes, worn threadbare, so that the truck barreled on, skidding to the right until the hard metal of its frame hurled into the terrible softness and fleeting pliancy of mere flesh.

"Miss Ellis!" Sheila cried.

But Nora never heard a human voice again.

"And as to Pip." His voice was pointed, and so I knew the time had come. "Whose story I know you've discovered."

As he spoke, another story was being discovered along the dark reaches of Chambers Road.

"And which you should not have done, Jack. You should not have gone against my wishes and read the story of that little boy in *The Book of Days.*"

Miles away, in a world apart, a quite different little boy had noticed something in the bed of Dirk's truck, a chain coiled like a snake, bloody at the tail.

My father laughed. "But you did read about him, and so you know I've wasted days and days writing a novel." He shrugged. "A very poorly written novel, as I'm sure you judged it."

"A novel?" I asked.

"One embarrassing for anyone to read," my father said. "Least of all my son."

"But you let Eddie read it."

He looked at me puzzled.

"You had it open on your desk," I said.

"But I wasn't reading from my book," my father said. "I was reading something from Eddie's paper. A passage about two Bridges kids he saw while waiting for Drummond at the sheriff's office."

It was a single page Eddie had left behind when I'd come upon them in my father's study, a passage written in his tiny script.

"I don't know if Eddie will be a great writer," my father said as he handed it to me, "but I feel he will have a . . . tender life."

There were quite a few people in the police station when I got there. I noticed two kids from Lakeland, Bobby Drew and his girlfriend, Donna. I didn't know why they were there, but I knew they were in trouble. It was a different kind of trouble than I had, but it was trouble all the same. I could see it in the way their arms hung, like people already dead. They were young, but they looked like life had passed them by. I saw Donna reach up from behind Bobby's back and tug his hair. She meant it as a joke, just playing with him, but when he didn't react, her hand fell away, and I thought, okay, that's the way it'll always be with her. Like that hand, she'll just drop away from husbands and jobs and maybe even her own kids. Like that hand, she'll drop away from anything that asks much of her or doesn't go exactly like she expects it to. The only energy she'll ever have will be the little bit it takes to drop away. And I thought of Linda Gracie, how young she was, all the things she'd wanted in life, and was working hard to get, things I wanted, too, simple things, just to grow up, have a job and a family, live a life that didn't have to be anything great, because even small, it would be so much.

Drummond found him gathered in his mother's arms, the swing his father had built for him floating softly in the wind, his legs shattered and oddly askew, a trail of blood running from the great open wound on the right side of his head, trailing down and down to puddle at his side.

"Eddie," Drummond whispered, then looked at the woman who seemed unable to release or even loosen the grip in which she held all that remained to her on earth. "I'm sorry," was all he found to say.

THIRTY-SIX

The next weeks passed in a blur of trials, Dirk and Wendell first, both found guilty and sentenced to Willard's Bluff, though Wendell, only seventeen, and clearly the least culpable of the two, received far less time than Dirk.

Then came he whom my father had suspected, a cross-eyed delivery boy named Sandy, who, as it turned out, had had no idea where to sell a pair of antique dueling pistols, and thus had merely tucked them under the rumpled bed where Drummond later found them.

And after that?

After that, one by one, as the years passed, they fell like trees in a steadily dying orchard.

The first to go was Morrell.

Snow is rare on the Delta, but it came the night he left us, a little miracle of white that blossomed first on the coldest stones, then unrolled in a pale transparent carpet over the grass-less lawn, and gathered in small, delicately balanced mounds to outline the great, but leafless, oaks.

Through this snow, Wendell came, driving the hearse I'd

called from Gillette's Funeral Parlor. He wore a suit and tie, as is still the Southern custom when a loved one's body is received, and pushed before him a stainless-steel gurney covered with purple velvet.

"Good morning, Mr. Branch," he said.

I nodded. "He's in the library."

"Yes, sir."

I stepped back and waited until he'd wheeled the gurney into the library and lifted Morrell from the chair in which he'd been sleeping when it hit him.

"It's a mighty fine thing you done, Mr. Branch," Wendell said as he rolled the gurney back out onto the portico. "Taking care of Miss Ellis's brother all this time." He glanced toward the front room of Great Oaks, where my father sat in a gray light, sunk in the "bottoms" that had settled over him at the news of Morrell's death.

"We owe what we owe," I told Wendell dryly.

He looked puzzled by the remark, but was careful not to pursue it. Instead he looked down at the mound of lifeless flesh that lay beneath the velvet curtain.

"Sometimes I think it's better living like Morrell," he said. "Like a child all his life."

"No," I said, "we're meant to grow."

He smiled. "Maybe we could talk sometime."

"Yes, I'd like that."

"I have a trailer now," he added. "At the end of Lawton Street. You could visit. I'm off on Tuesdays."

"I'll come the very next one," I assured him. I offered my hand. "Thank you, Wendell."

Next Mr. Rankin, and after that Mrs. Miller, and after that Wendell himself, and after him, Dirk Littlefield.

And after that?

My father.

His death came at the end of a long ordeal, two years after the stroke that had taken him to the same hospital, where, during one of my long vigils, I'd glimpsed Mrs. Miller in her room.

The next day found him back at Great Oaks, where he sat hour upon hour in the shadowy air of the library, scanning books he could no longer read, so that in the final days he'd had nothing to occupy himself but the television I'd by then set at the foot of the hospital bed in which he lay.

It was there we watched *The Civil War* together, my father's eyes focused with a terrible intensity on the photographic history of our region's ruin: Charleston, Atlanta, the swath of sheer destruction Sherman's army had carried out. In the final episode, a strange and splendid mercy falls over the land, as if, as my father wrote, "those better angels of our nature upon which Lincoln had rested his last best hope had gained ascendancy at last."

The sad refrain of "Ashokan Farewell" filtered through the library as the documentary's last images flicked over the stainless-steel foot of my father's bed.

"Well," I said. "That was quite a fine thing, wasn't it?"

He lifted a shaky hand, formed it into the shape of a pistol and put it to his head. "Useless," he said. "Useless."

The last words, as I'm sure he knew, of John Wilkes Booth.

At his grave site I read "My Childhood Home I See Again," a poem written by Abraham Lincoln:

Air held his breath; trees, with the spell,
Seemed sorrowing angels round,
Whose swelling tears in dew-drops fell
Upon the listening ground.

When it was over, and he was lowered into the earth, I saw Sheila Longstreet standing alone not far away. I walked over to her and drew her beneath my arm, and together we made our way among the stones, past those of Wendell and Dirk and Nora and Morrell and Drummond and now, at last, my father's.

"I have a present for you," I told her. "My books. I'll have them sent to you when I'm gone."

She saw that this would be soon.

"I know you're the one who'd most appreciate them," I added.

She warmed in the radiance of my unexpectedly high regard, and for a moment seemed to regain her youth, return to my class on evil. "You were a great teacher, Mr. Branch," she said.

I thought of all that gathered round us in this life, the passion of our striving, the sting of our regret, how mighty it is and huge with feeling, our little book of days, even when, especially when, it is touched by darkness. And facing Sheila, I felt a great wave of mercy sweep over all the humble stones that broke the earth around us, a wave that was vast and deep, and finally inexpressible.

So that "Thank you" was all I could find to say.

———

And so at last, I lived alone at Great Oaks, an old man waiting for the postman.

"Mighty nice day we had," he said. His gray hair peeped from beneath his cap, his coat a little ragged and unkempt, as it always was. "Don't like to see it go dark on a day so fine." He drew a package from beneath his arm and handed it to me. "It came all the way from New York."

"Yes, I see."

"You sure do get lots of packages." This clearly amused him, though he made the same observation nearly every evening.

"It's only books," I said.

"So a book, you read it just once?"

"Some books require more."

This appeared to strike him as new information, though not the sort that mattered.

"Well, see you tomorrow, Mr. Branch."

He turned to leave, but I drew him back, and for the last time offered my services.

"Eddie?" I said.

He turned around slowly, dragging his right foot behind him like a sack with a brick inside.

"I could read to you," I told him.

It was an offer I'd made many times, so I expected the same answer. "Well, that's nice of you, Mr. Branch." He looked at the book in my hand, but seemed more interested in its heft and shape than what might lie within its covers. "But I ain't much for books." He regarded me with his still oddly piercing eyes. "Was once though." He laughed. "Least that's what my mama told me." He peered over my shoulder, into the vastness of Great Oaks, the terrible emptiness over which I now presided in my fallen mastery. "All cleared out."

I nodded softly. "'Forever honour'd, and forever mourn'd.'"

A wide, boyish smile lit his face, and I saw the delight he still took in the lilt and flow of words. "That sounds nice, what you just said."

"It's from a poem," I told him. "The first poet. The poet's name was Homer."

"Homer?" He chuckled. "That sounds like a poor boy's name, like a boy from the Bridges."

I smiled. "There are poets among the poor."

He took this into brief consideration, then set it free in the easy way his damaged brain released everything, quickly and with nothing left behind, like a bird from the hand.

"Well," he said, "I best be going. Dark's coming in."

I could see that he was anxious to be on his way. Dark was falling over us, as it ever is, and before it fell he wanted to be back in the little house on Chambers Road that he had long ago inherited from his mother, the modest gift of all her worldly goods.

"Well, see you tomorrow, Mr. Branch," he said, then softly hobbling, made his way back down the road and into the descending darkness, though there yet remained enough light to drag his shadow just behind him, deformed and misshapen, as it would always be, by the evil fortune that had come to him through the good one that was mine.